HEART OF MIDNIGHT

Cinders In Midnight Glass 3

J. DARLENE EVERLY

WISHING WELL BOOKS

To request use of the copyrighted material, please contact the author at jdarleneeverly.com
Hardcover: ISBN 978-1-954719-33-0
Paperback: ISBN 978-1-954719-34-7
Ebook: ISBN 978-1-954719-35-4
First paperback edition March 2022.
Edited by Jupiter Alley.
Cover art by Miblart.
Interior Hardcover by Jupiter Alley.
Layout by Wishing Well Books.

J. DARLENE EVERLY

HEART OF MIDNIGHT

INTRODUCTION

Heart of Midnight is just the third book of the Cinders in Midnight Glass series, the first book, Heart of Cinders, and the second book, Heart of Shattered Glass, are out now. And the fourth book, After Midnight Strikes is coming soon! If you would like to be the first to hear about the next book in the series, get an exclusive prequel to this story and more free books, as well as see what else the author has written, please go to jdarleneeverly.com and sign up for her newsletter.

CHAPTER 1

FRESH WOUNDS

The wounds on Gus' leg were getting worse. Not better.

Even though her arm, so gruesomely broken, looked at first as if it would be the hardest to mend, the physick had done a good job of setting the breaks and casting it.

But her leg and my cheek lost more flesh every day to the poison. It left behind black stains on our skin long after it had been washed off, and that darkness ate away at us every minute.

When she was awake, she writhed for a moment, then held as still as possible while grinding her teeth and squeezing her eyes shut.

I didn't return to my bed. Instead, I stayed next to hers, cocooned in a blanket, holding her hand, and sleeping when I could with my good cheek on the edge of her mattress.

Nothing the physick did seemed to help. Not with the pain, or the wound itself.

The arcing torment in my face made me want to move until I could get away from it. My only relief came when Tristan was at my side, his warmth acting like an analgesic, chasing the pain away.

Gus didn't have anything that could whisk away her pain, and it hurt my heart to think of her never finding any respite.

Our King checked on us frequently, and refused to sleep anywhere but in a chair next to mine. But another day-and-a-half came and went before Jacquetta arrived in a flurry of frenetic energy and panicked breaths that made me ache just trying to imagine accomplishing them myself.

She unceremoniously dropped the many things she carried in a heap by the foot of the bed, and rushed to stand right next to me.

"Gus," she said, her voice coming out like she was holding back a sob. "Oh, Cinder, thank you for getting her back."

"Jacquetta," Gus moaned from the bed. I whipped my head her way, closing my eyes on the wave of agony that washed over my face at the movement.

"You're awake," Jacquetta said, leaning down to press a tender kiss to Gus' forehead.

But she wasn't. Gus was back to sleep as fast as she had awoken.

Jacquetta looked at me, terrified eyes wide.

"She can't stay awake very long," I said, through barely moving lips. The more still I held my mouth when I spoke, the better.

"That is because she is in too much pain," Madam Valentin said, gliding through the door, weighed down by satchels and a large case.

It was everything I could do to hold my face as still as possible while tears collected in my eyes.

Exhaustion washed through me. Too much hurt, not enough sleep, and less and less relief somehow immediately began to ebb away now that I knew Madam was here.

Madam would make it better.

Somehow, I knew she would. Even though the physick had been unable to help, and even though I wasn't sure if she had any experience with the poison eating away at my cheek and Gus' leg, I was so positive she would help us that it was like a physical weight lifted from the room. We were already starting to improve.

"Here, Jacquetta," she said, starting to place containers on the dresser across from the bed.

Jacquetta touched my shoulder as she passed me and joined her mother in her efforts.

The dresser was soon crowded with items, and I had to fight to keep my eyes open. No wonder Gus was fast asleep again.

I simply laid my head back down and watched them work, looking up at them with what I hoped was clear gratitude while they checked on both our wounds.

"Thank you for coming," I whispered, when Madam "tsked" at me as she tilted my head one way and then the other before letting me set it back down on the bed.

Madam's rich, dark skin warmed and shone as she gave me a soft smile, the kind I never would have guessed her face could form when I first met her.

"Lady Cinder," she said, with a shake of her head like I didn't understand anything, "thank you for taking care of them, my darling girl."

Her darling girl. She didn't say I took care of her darling girls, she included me as though I was her daughter, too.

There was no holding back the tears that streamed down my face, dripping sideways across my nose, down my good cheek, and into the blanket, slowly soaking it with all my feelings from the last week.

Finally, Jacquetta and Madam put some kind of thick paste on both our wounds.

Covering mine only took a moment. The second the mixture touched my face, the relief was so complete I almost fell asleep again.

But I shook my head as soon as she was done with me,

forcing my eyes to remain open, and watching as they administered to Gus' more numerous, more extensive, and more serious wounds.

Some of the black wounds on Gus' leg seemed to have grown to twice their size and depth.

"We will need to do the suction on these," Madam muttered to Jacquetta, looking even closer at the terrible tunnels of destroyed flesh on Gus' thigh.

"How about on Cinder's face?" Jacquetta asked, nodding as she darted back to the dresser, and collected small jars, a vile of hellfire water and another pot of one of their mixtures.

After knowing Jacquetta and her mother only a little while, I stopped trying to make sense of their amazing skills with herbs and flowers. But this was new, so I paid closer attention.

Madam stared across the bed at me, studying the wound on my face, smeared with paste.

"We might need to do the vacuum on her, too," Madam said, still looking at me. "I am not yet sure what exactly we will need to do there. The flesh of the face is so thin."

Then she went back to Gus, her focus singular and complete as they finished applying the mixture, and started on the next step.

Once every one of her wounds were covered in the thick medicine, Gus' whole body sunk further into the bed as if even in sleep she held herself rigid, and finally relaxed with the softening of her pain.

But Jacquetta and Madam were nowhere near done.

First, they tackled the worst of Gus' wounds, the ones that were originally circles of black-tinged, chewed-up thigh, but now looked more like the kind of tunneled wound left behind after removing a spear…if someone then filled it with black paint.

Jacquetta smeared the inside of one of the jars with the other mixture, this one a yellow color, and handed it to Madam.

Madam took the jar, placing it upside down so the opening was over the wound, and dropped a single drop of hellfire water on the center of the bottom of the jar.

The bottom of the jar, which faced up at her, had a curve to it creating a divot that held the bright green hellfire water perfectly.

Next, they lit the hellfire water on fire.

Hellfire flame—green at the very center instead of white like burning wood and the usual orange and reds at the edges—flickered and steadied.

I raised my brows, not allowing my jaw to drop like it wanted to.

Since when did anyone use hellfire water to heal?

Part of me thought I should have known they were going to use it, but I assumed it was to power something. Not this... whatever this was.

They kept moving, repeating the steps, until Gus' leg looked like she was a shelf for a bunch of jars while the interiors of the jars themselves went from clear with yellow smeared on them to purple, then finally to black.

Once the jars were completely black, Madam used a tiny wooden spoon to lift the edge of the jar. It made a popping sound, and she carefully tipped the jar over.

Underneath, the skin of Gus' leg was raised in a circle that matched the opening of the jar, but all the black seemed to be gone from the flesh for the first time.

Even after it was cleaned, poulticed, and cleaned again by the physick, the black still remained. But now it looked like her body could actually start to heal instead of just trying to fight off the continued desecration of her flesh.

The process, though, revealed the extent of the damage.

Jacquetta sucked down a shuddering breath, and had to blink rapidly while staring at the ceiling before she could focus again on what she was doing.

Madam's face settled into grim determination as she, too, kept going.

I didn't know exactly how long that stuff was left to chew through Gus before I got there, but it had remained on her, continuing to hurt her, for days more now.

And in the process, it had tunneled through her leg. In some places, I could see bone.

"Do that to my cheek," I said, the medicine already on me making it much easier to speak.

DEATH MASK

Madam and Jacquetta snapped their eyes up to look at me.

"I know why you don't want to," I said. And I did. I wasn't sure I was ready to see exactly how ruined that side of my face was either. "But we need to do it."

"Cinder," Jacquetta said, her voice fragile.

"Do it."

They stared at me for a moment longer, Jacquetta swallowing hard.

But Madam finally took a deep breath and nodded. "Do her cheek, Jacquetta."

Jacquetta looked at her mother. Even though her hands shook, she came to my side of the bed with her supplies.

I laid my head down on the blanket and shut my eyes.

Placing the jar on my face, right on my wound, should have hurt. But because of the mixture they slathered on me first, I barely felt it.

What I did feel was the moment the hellfire water was lit where it sat on the bottom of the jar.

Madam wasn't wrong when she called it a vacuum. After the

last war, Ash had some scientist bring in a machine that he called a vacuum to try and suck the flames out of the hellfire mine that dropped ashes on Lehar. It didn't work.

The jar, though, sucked on my cheek like that machine tried to suck on the mine. Hopefully this was more successful for me.

There was no other way to describe this than as a vacuum—the strange feeling of my skin being sucked into the jar, lightly at first, then stronger.

In the beginning of the process there was no pain. The mixture they put on beforehand was still doing its job.

Eventually, though, it forced me to lock my jaw tight and grip the blanket on the bed, squeezing my eyes shut to keep from crying out and toppling the jar off me.

Finally, just when I didn't think I could take it anymore, Jacquetta popped the seal on the edge, just as Madam had.

The noise coincided with a whistling sound and cold flooded into my mouth.

I snapped my eyes open and watched as Jacquetta and Madam saw what was left of my wound when the jar had done its work.

"My cheek is gone, isn't it?" I asked, and Jacquetta's eyes widened as I spoke until the whites showed all the way around her dark irises.

"We are going to fix it as soon as we think the wound is ready for the next step," Madam said, nodding to Jacquetta with one brow high.

Jacquetta grabbed another mixture and reached for my cheek like she was going to cover it up.

But I surged from the bed and stepped back from her.

"Let me see it first," I said, sidestepping her as her mouth worked around unsaid words.

There was a vanity near the bathroom door, but I didn't look in the mirror until I was directly in front of it, staring at my feet instead.

Once I stood right in front of my reflection, I raised my eyes, my heart hammering at me from inside my chest like it wanted to break my ribs from the inside out.

I could see my teeth through a hole in my cheek about the size of the first part of my pointer finger.

Even though it wouldn't have made any sense to the others in the room, I wanted to laugh.

After all this time, I no longer just delivered death. I looked like it.

"Soon we will work on repairing that hole," Madam said, continuing her work on Gus, waving Jacquetta over to her.

When I first met Madam, she said I was pretty enough, but far too muscular. Now, I was still too muscular, but I doubted she would describe me as pretty.

It was impossible to suppress the huff of a laugh that bubbled out of me.

Here I was thinking that as soon as Tristan questioned Brix, my time with him would be over. The reality was that he would have to set me aside now.

At the edge of the hole, there was still an area of black beneath the smeared mixture they put on me at the start.

"Do it again," I said, turning back to them.

"No," Jacquetta said, refusing to look at me longer than a glance.

"There's still black on my skin. We need to do it again, or I'll lose even more of my face." They knew I was right. But Jacquetta wouldn't look at me, and Madam's mouth was set in hard lines.

"Cinder," Jacquetta said, my name a careful note on her tongue as if she were trying to decide what to say next.

"Just do it. While you have everything already out." Nothing I said seemed to move them to finish this. But I wanted it done. I needed to know.

"If we finish it, you can do what you need to for me to heal sooner."

At that, Madam looked up at me, and Jacquetta looked to her mother.

For a long minute, I stood in front of the vanity, my back to the new tear in my reflection, and waited for them to do what they needed to while a sick feeling built up from my stomach and lodged in my throat.

Madam finally nodded, and Jacquetta deflated.

I went back to my place at the edge of the bed, and held onto Gus' hand.

"When this is done," I said, looking at Gus' sleeping face, "we'll find a way to heal your leg, too."

Looking as if half my face wore the death I dealt to so many was one thing, but leaving Gus scarred in such a way that she might be left with ongoing pain and unable able to walk…

Would something like Inara's wooden leg work for Gus? Would they want to amputate? I hoped for her sake that they could heal her.

All I could do was believe until they proved me right or wrong. Until then, I laid my head down and closed my eyes while Jacquetta repeated the process with my cheek. This time she shoved something into the existing hole that sent sharp, stabbing pain lancing across my head.

But I didn't move. Moving wouldn't help. I kept breathing.

As the pressure and the searing shards of pain built, I clawed at the blanket so I didn't squeeze Gus' hand too hard.

Once Jacquetta popped off the jar and pried the stuff she'd shoved in the hole from my cheek, I returned to the mirror.

It was even worse than before. The hole was the same width but longer, exposing more teeth.

"Forgive me for intruding, I want to apologize for not greeting you when you arrived," Tristan said, coming into the room.

Watching him in the mirror, he looked down at Gus, wringing his hands together as if he wanted to have them around Brix's neck for hurting her.

"You have a war to attend to. Think nothing if it," Madam said, dipping her head even as she continued to administer to Gus.

Finally, Tristan swallowed and looked my way.

His face went ashen, and his mouth dropped open while those wringing hands turned white-knuckled and his nails bit into his own skin. His eyes went from a dark golden hazel to the bright green of hellfire water, and tightened at the corners.

I stood up straighter and turned toward him in the direction that showed him the full extent of the damage to my cheek without the mirror to blunt the impact of it.

We needed to get this over with. My face was already causing me pain. Did I really need my soul intact?

Deep within me, I tried to erect a dark layer of steel over my heart and prepare for him to run from me, from this mask of death over the face he thought to crown a queen.

But instead of running, he came to me and turned my head with a gentle hand as hot as a flame so he could study the wound closer.

"As soon as that bastard is healed," he said, his voice low and rough, "I will make him pay for doing this to all of you."

"For making me ugly?" I whispered.

It wasn't quiet enough to stop Jacquetta and Madam from freezing with their hands suspended in the air while they looked our way, eyes wide.

"No one could ever make you ugly," he said, that grating tone still there as he looked into my eyes and wrapped me up in the heat of his arms. "Your scars just show your strength on your skin."

"Tristan," I breathed as the hard shell around my heart disintegrated, allowing him to become even more firmly entrenched.

He bent down and kissed me, the heat of him streaming through me in a tidal wave that made me hold him closer, feel his entire body mold to mine.

Madam made a throat clearing noise, and I pulled back from his lips, hoping that whatever else they needed to do to my face wouldn't stop me from breaking into his room for long.

Keeping me tucked into his side, he turned to the rest of the room.

"If you need anything," he said, tipping his head to Madam, "everyone in the castle knows to provide whatever you request."

"Do you have to go back so soon?" I asked, looking up at him and trying not to beg him to stay. Even though I knew how important it was for him to work, it was an act of will.

"Yes." He kissed me on the forehead, his arm tightening around me, his voice low and just for me. "I know you're in good hands. And I'll be back as soon and as often as I can."

He left me, trailing his hand down my arm until our fingertips lingered as he walked away.

Even though he had to go back, he had kissed me, looked at me. Even this version of me, he loved.

I took a deep, shuddering breath and returned to my place at Gus' bedside, holding her hand, and keeping any further comments to myself as Jacquetta finished the packing, smearing, and covering of my wound.

On the inside of my mouth, the packing she put in the hole felt like I had food stuck, but at least it didn't dry out my mouth like leaving it open to the air would.

"King Tristan seems to have found our queen," Madam said after a time, once she moved on to doing the same to Gus' wounds as they had to mine, packing and bandaging them.

Maybe I was a coward, but after watching them pack one of her wounds, I lowered my eyes to where our hands were intertwined so I didn't have to imagine the pain involved.

And maybe it was cowardly not to answer Madam, to let her believe I would be queen one day.

What I would be was a casualty, whether they could fix my face or not. No matter how much he loved me, or I loved him.

This death mask I now wore wasn't an outward representation of my strength. It was a prediction.

CHAPTER 3

RIGHT NOW

Tristan visited more over the next day as Jacquetta and Madam continued to work on both Gus and me. I only woke up occasionally, making up for all the rest I missed, but he didn't sleep in the chair next to mine.

Not that I blamed him for that. I wasn't brave enough to risk the wrath of Madam Valentin either.

Although...I did want to find out from Jacquetta what her mother would think if I invited him to stay. She was the one who had all the little scraps of fabric made for me that she called nightgowns. Some of them were so small it made more sense just to sleep naked.

Besides, they all had to know Tristan wouldn't be my first. I wasn't a teenager.

My brother had his own ways to prepare me—ones he said prepared him—but I still thought it was Ash's way of avoiding having the conversation with me.

Part of me wanted to find out for sure if I needed to sneak around Madam, and all of me never wanted to explain my experience to her.

Gus and Jacquetta, though…Maybe I could have the discussion with them first.

Besides, the very first thing I needed to do when I felt well enough, wasn't break into Tristan's bed. It was kill Brix.

"Unfortunately," Madam said, looking at my cheek closely by staring down her nose at it, "we cannot stitch this up yet."

"You can't?" I asked, wondering exactly how long I would have to wait. I was already more awake today than yesterday, and I felt much better.

What were the chances Tristan would tell me anything about the war while I had stitches in my face? What were the chances that he would let me know how best I could fight? What were the chances I would be able to sneak to the cells and kill Brix when my death mask would make me too recognizable?

Madam began the process of putting the stopper back in the hole in my face, and smeared everything with another mixture that allowed a level of immediate relief before she bandaged me up.

"No," Jacquetta said, brushing Gus' hair along the pillow while Gus slept. "We have to see if there will be any more death to the tissue, and then debride it before we stitch it up."

"Debride?" Stitches weren't new to me, but I had never heard of debriding. Maybe it was something like the vacuum jar process. That wasn't so bad.

The medicine was a cool wash over my raging cheek, and I could focus more fully now that Madam was finishing up.

"It is an unpleasant process," Madam said, shooting a look at Jacquetta.

Jacquetta raised her eyes to me from Gus, her mouth opening and closing.

"Okay," I said, sitting up straighter, "I don't like that look."

"Lady Cinder," Madam said, "it will not be too bad for you. I will make sure it is not. And by doing this, we can ensure a better, cleaner scar."

"A scar won't bother me." I was going to die soon. A scar was nothing, and Tristan didn't care, either.

"No, but if I can help it be a better one, I will." Madam's tight eyes allowed no room to argue.

Really, it didn't matter. But if it made Madam and Jacquetta feel better, I was fine with that.

"What about Gus?" I asked, looking at the packed wounds on her leg. I didn't think there was any way around her having terrible scars.

"If I can keep my leg, I'll be happy," Gus said, her voice a raspy whisper.

"Gus," Jacquetta yelped, tears falling down her cheeks as she bent over Gus' face, with a huge, watery smile.

"Hi," I said, leaning over her other side, and smiling at her as though she didn't look like she had never been outside before. Even her freckles were the wrong color—washed out—and her eyes still didn't look like she was entirely present with us.

"Can someone get me something to drink?" Her voice was barely a croak by the time she finished the sentence.

In the last few days, she drank so little, and ate even less, that she had yet to need to relieve herself.

None of us were eating well or drinking nearly enough.

Madam went to the corner and the pitcher of water there for us, but I made eye contact with Jacquetta.

Panic raced across her face. I didn't want to let Gus see it, so I shoved my own back.

"We need to sit you up," I said, voice low in the hopes she didn't hear the quaver in it. How much were we going to hurt her in the process?

She nodded and I took a deep breath.

"Jacquetta, we'll slip our hands under her shoulders. As soon as we get her up to sitting, I'll keep her in position, and you prop her up with pillows."

"I need more pillows," Jacquetta said, and darted out of the room.

Moments later, she came back, her face barely peeking from the stack of them in her hands.

She dumped them next to her spot near Gus' head, and looked to me with a tiny nod.

We slipped our hands into position, and I counted down from three out loud.

Even doing that, Gus squeezed her eyes shut, and sucked in a hissing breath as we moved her.

Jacquetta and I did as we planned, and a moment later, Gus relaxed back into the giant pile of pillows and drank greedily from the cup Madam held out to her.

I stepped back and gave her some room.

Her leg was still full of holes under her bandages, and they were all stuffed full of

what looked like fabric that was soaked in something Madam said would help.

Yes, Madam Valentin and Jacquetta were brilliant at healing, but Gus had to be in so much pain.

Brix was going to die.

Right now.

"I…" I said, and when three sets of eyes turned my way, I realized I didn't have a good plan to even leave their presence. "Everyone needs to eat, and I have something to ask Tristan that might help Gus. I'll be right back."

At least my brain was still working. They bought my excuse and went back to helping Gus while I walked out the door, made my way to my room, grabbed one of my knives from the cloak sitting in one of my trunks, and prepared to go down to the cells.

Death mask or not. Recognizable or not.

He was a fucking dead man.

CHAPTER 4

ARRIVAL

I made my way through our parlor, tucking the blade in the cuff of the shirt I wore. Somehow, Madam didn't ask me even once to change, although I was wearing pants for training and one of Tristan's long, loose shirts.

Now, though, making my way through the castle felt in a way like I was breaking the law more than a kill ever did.

My face wasn't the face of a lady or a queen anymore, and neither was my outfit.

Voices carried through the first door to the right of the hallway after ours.

One of them sounded like…

I paused and tilted my head toward the room.

It was Tristan. The minute he spoke, I recognized him.

Although he wasn't exactly speaking. He was tearing someone apart. They kept trying to interrupt him, which only made him louder and harder to understand.

Queen, or not, I needed to know who would talk to him like that.

Maybe I could make double use of my knife.

But when I flung open the door, it took me a minute to realize what I was looking at.

Tristan stood in the middle of the room, his hands in fists at his sides, looking down and sneering at General Pace as she stood in front of him, facing him, while a red-faced Chamberlain panted behind her.

What in the hellfire source was happening in here?

"Is…" I said, my voice trailing off as Tristan snapped his head toward me, but his face remained full of rage.

"Sorry, but I heard shouting, and wanted to make sure everyone was alright." The urge to stammer apologies and walk backward out of the door, closing it behind me, and hoping they ignored me was strong.

But what was happening here?

I couldn't leave until I understood why General Pace seemed to be standing on the Chamberlain's side against Tristan.

"Lady Cinder," Tristan said, turning from them and making his way to me, the tension in his body held solely in his stiff back and a tightness in his mouth, "are you feeling better?"

"Starting to." I looked past him and raised a brow when I met his eyes again, asking the silent question.

He let out a long breath as if he was partially holding it since I opened the door.

"Can I come and check on you and Augustina later?" he asked, his brow furrowing in a silent apology.

"Of course. And you have no further need of me right now? Nothing I can help you with?"

All he had to do was say the word. No one got to disrespect Tristan when I was around.

"No, that is alright," he said, his words as formal as my own for the Chamberlain's benefit, "but I do have something I need to speak with you about later."

"You do not need to ask," I said and smiled with half of my face.

His spine relaxed, his face turned soft, and his eyes were on my lips as he squeezed one of my hands.

I squeezed back and let him go.

What I wanted was to drag him away from there, but I shut the door and reminded myself I had work to do. I didn't want to make him think I was disrespecting him, too.

Making my way through the castle, I again darted through the spaces that had openings with no glass, and took my time wandering through the rooms with enclosed windows.

As soon as I saw Inara again, I was going to ask about the ridiculous lack of glass between those of us inside and any murderous Corvid outside. It was fine normally, but this was war. Precautions needed to be taken and changes made.

Rounding the corner before the stairs down to the cells, I encountered my first real problem.

Unlike last time, I didn't have a free pass to head down to confront Brix.

Two guards were posted at the top of the stairs, with far more blades on them than the small one in my cuff. And these were Onyx citizens, not the free-to-be-killed-at-will Corvids. And they weren't my target.

Damn it.

Stepping in front of them as if I were just going to walk right past them and they should take no notice of me, went against everything I was taught and my natural instincts. But it was my only option.

One of the guards reached out a hand and blocked me.

"I am sorry, Fighter Cinder, but I can't let anyone pass. Even you." The guard swallowed hard. His lower lip shook, and he fumbled with the formalities, but he held his ground.

"There is a prisoner down there I would like to question," I said. "My understanding is that he is to be questioned soon anyway."

"King Tristan ordered that no one other than the physick

and certain guards are supposed to go down there without the King himself. Not even General Pace. He is going to do the questioning himself once the prisoner is healed."

"Himself?" Why would he insist on that? Didn't he have plenty of guards to do the interrogation?

"Yes," the other guard said, stepping closer and staring openly at the bandage on my face, "he said it was personal."

Personal.

It was that.

"Thank you," I said, resisting the urge to touch my bandage, and unsure what to say now. "I...I will ask him about questioning the prisoner then."

What I was going to do was be with him every single time he questioned Brix, and try to stop the piece of human-shaped vomit from telling Tristan anything until I could find a way to kill him.

If Brix told Tristan who I really was, I would never see that look he gave me only moments before again.

Brix already took far too much from the world and me. He was going to die before I allowed him to take Tristan from me, too.

On my way back to my rooms, servants went from strolling by to darting all over the place, running from one room to another, with whispered comments to each other.

I picked up my pace.

Something was going on.

My hands started to shake, and it didn't matter that it would be painful for my face. I ran.

Dodging all the people I came across, I finally skidded to a stop in front of the open door of the room that Tristan was in, but he wasn't there now.

"Fuck," I muttered, turning around and continuing on because I only had one place I knew to go to protect my people.

The first time I scrabbled at the doorknob to my rooms, my

hand couldn't get purchase. But the second time, I flung the door back and barreled through the rooms to Gus'.

Leaning against the door frame, breathing hard, I forced my stomach to settle because they were all sitting around and eating. Even Gus was eating from her place on the bed, piled with pillows.

"Cinder?" Jacquetta asked, a piece of food in her hand dropping back to her plate instead of being delivered to her mouth.

"Something is going on," I said, shaking my head, not sure how to explain without sounding paranoid. "I was just worried."

Jacquetta stiffened, looking to Gus.

Gus just put another bite in her mouth, and closed her eyes as she chewed.

Madam stared at me and stood up, setting her plate to the side.

"You can stay here," Madam said, "and I will go find out what the details are."

"No," I said, taking a step to block the entire doorway and using my full formal voice. "I am sorry, Madam, but I will not have you at further risk if it is something to worry about. You are safest here. With me."

"And I am sorry that I do not think this is a threat of any kind or we would have been warned."

"Cinder?" Tristan yelled from the other room and all my internal alarms clanged at once. He looked harried as he came around the corner.

I wanted all my weapons.

The pain in my face didn't matter.

If the castle was under attack, healing time was over. My new face and I needed to send these Corvids a message.

Death had arrived.

CHAPTER 5

THIN LINES

"**I**s there a way that you can be ready for a formal meeting by tonight?" Tristan asked.

My brain emptied of every thought.

"What?" I asked, sure that something must have gone wrong with the healing because that had to be an hallucination. We had to be under attack.

"They weren't supposed to be here for another week." He ran a hand through his hair, leaving it sticking out in all directions, intensifying that frantic look about him.

Something about this formal meeting made it very different from anything we had done together before. That much was obvious now that I was thinking again, my brain back to functioning.

"Who wasn't supposed to be here yet?" I asked, taking his hand because he had to stop acting like this was the worst possible thing when we were in the middle of a very real war. Just thinking about the worst made my mouth go dry.

"A group from Amethyst is almost here to discuss a possible alliance during this conflict." He looked at me as if his bland statement included an apology, as if any minute he would beg my forgiveness.

"She is with them, is she not?" Jacquetta asked from behind me.

"The snake is here?" I asked, standing up straighter, understanding finally dawning as he nodded, sorry still written all over his face.

"King Tristan," Madam said, and I turned toward her, as did everyone else, "are you sure that Lady Cinder should be there? Perhaps it would be better if she remained out of sight until after the potential from Amethyst is gone."

I balled my hand into a fist at my side and set my teeth, but Tristan rubbed a thumb over the back of the hand he was holding. I didn't yell about what I thought would perhaps be a better plan: that we tossed Marquessa Ziya out of one of the windows and let her get smashed by the waves.

"No, Madam Valentin," Tristan said, looking at me, "I do not want her to think it would be a good time to try for an engagement during the negotiations."

"Does that mean Lady Cinder will be there in her capacity as a potential, or representing her position as Fighter?" Madam asked, and I wondered if there was a difference.

Tristan looked back and forth from Madam and me.

But I saw it on his face.

He didn't want to say what he knew would be best.

I reached out with my other hand, loosening the fist, and ran my fingers along his jaw.

"You told them all that the potential search was on hold, and nothing would happen. I need to be Fighter Cinder for this."

"Good," Madam said, walking past us toward my trunks.

Good? What did that mean?

Tristan wrapped me up, his lips finding my neck, his heat sending shivers through my body. It relieved the last of the pain in my face, and all the concern over Madam's cryptic words ran far away.

"Soon," he said into my skin, "I will be able to tell all of them that this is my Hellfire Queen, and no one will make me separate from her again."

Hellfire Queen.

The words set my heart aflame. I wanted to drag him with me to my bed and forget about the world.

"I love you," I whispered instead, my body thrilling to the way he held me tighter, one hand running through my hair where it hung down my back, and his kisses on my neck included the occasional flick of his hot tongue.

"You have no idea…" He pulled back enough to look me in the eye, his eyes a golden hazel. "I love you, Cinder."

"Will I be able to see you at all outside of these formal meetings while she's here?"

"Not much, no. I'm sorry. This isn't what I want."

"I know. You have to play the game while we're at risk of attack from them, too."

He lifted my hand to his mouth, the kiss he gave me on the back of it a promise that it would be different once she was gone. And the look in his eyes enough to make me press myself tighter against him.

"Somehow," I whispered, "I will find a way through these stone walls."

"Madam," Tristan called, "I need to show Lady Cinder how to get to the meeting. We will be right back."

He didn't wait for her reply, just tugged me by the hand down the hallway.

Almost on the first floor, he finally opened a door and pulled me inside.

"Can I kiss you?" he asked the second he shut the door behind us, looking at my bandage for a moment, a line between his brows.

Instead of answering, I grabbed the back of his neck and pulled his mouth roughly to mine.

Opening his mouth and allowing my tongue inside, all the heat of him set a fire burning through me that centered first in my heart and moved lower.

His hands pressed me against him while my fingers tightened on his shoulders, the jacket he wore too fitted to give me purchase.

I pulled back my head, breaking the kiss, and he followed me, his eyes full of hunger like he wanted to devour me whole.

"Tristan," I said, and he closed his eyes, taking a deep breath.

"Cinder," he said, his voice low rumble which only made my temperature rise even higher.

"Do we have time?" I asked, wishing I didn't give a damn. But we needed to be ready for this meeting. And if all I could think about while we were there was this, and how we cut it short, it was already a disaster.

He growled, low in his throat, touching his forehead to mine, while his fingers bunched in the loose fabric of the shirt I wore.

"No, we don't have time." He loosened his grip, pulling back and running a hand up to play with the small hairs at the nape of my neck. "I don't want to be rushed when I'm with you. I want to take my time. Savor you."

It was everything I could do not to say fuck the meeting and destroy more of his buttons.

"And I already want them gone," I said, my voice raw.

His eyes widened for a second. A wicked grin bloomed on his face before he leaned in to kiss me again.

But I stepped back, and he let me.

Taking a deep breath, he let go of me and wrapped one arm around my back, turning me to see his rooms.

We were in a parlor, but all the furniture that looked like it was normally in place in this room was shoved unceremoniously against the walls, and it was now dominated by a massive table full of maps just like the one from the training grounds.

I bit my lip and looked at him with one brow high.

"You know," I said, "I like that table."

"Cinder," he said, turning his head away from me like he was hiding his face.

Laughing, I grabbed his hand and pulled him forward, continuing to look at the space.

But a second later, the laughter died in my throat.

"Tristan," I said, whirling on him and shoving him back toward the door. "Get in the hall. Let me deal with this."

"What's wrong?" he asked, taking me by the arms and standing firm.

"Go," I yelled, wrenching out of his hands, and running to the other end of the room. I scrambled for the large glass doors, swinging them shut, my breathing frantic.

"Cinder?" Tristan asked from right behind me.

"No," I said, turning and shoving at him. "You have to get out of this room. One of them could be behind that door, waiting. They could have gotten in when you weren't here."

"One of who?" He looked from side to side.

"A Corvid." Did he drop his brain? "In their bird form, they could have flown in through the open doors. You shouldn't be in a room with a balcony. It isn't safe."

"It's fine."

"No, it's not." I shoved at him again, but he was an immovable wall.

"Yes. Please, let me explain. Duchess Inara has taken precautions." He raised his brows, his eyes soft, and zero concern showing on his face.

I stopped pushing, although I wanted him far away from here, somewhere safe.

"Tristan," I said. I didn't have the patience for this.

"Listen to me. I'm fine. I wouldn't allow you to be in this

castle without precautions." He put a hand to my good cheek, and the look in his eyes sent me tumbling through space again, lost in my love of him for a moment.

Swallowing, I flattened my fists, and placed them on his chest as I nodded.

But he had at most five minutes before I pulled him out of this room.

He took one of my hands, and stepped around me, pulling open the glass door I had just shut.

Gripping his hand with both of mine, I touched a finger to the knife still in my cuff. It wasn't enough. One blade wouldn't be enough.

What if a Corvid swooped in and grabbed him, carrying him off like they had Angeline, Gus, and Layton?

How could I stop it?

Panic raced through me as he walked us through the open door and out onto the balcony, but I held back, fighting with the part of me that said I needed to trust Tristan.

A few steps later, Tristan reached out with his other hand as if he were going to wave to the sea foam beyond the railing of the balcony. Instead, he plucked a filament in the air I hadn't even seen before.

I stepped closer, peering at the thin line in front of us, and noticed the spiderweb of them crossing the entire open space of the balcony.

"What is this?" I asked, touching it.

Taught, but with a certain flexibility, it was wholly different from a rope, and yet that was the only thing I could compare it to. A rope so thin and fine it was almost invisible if you didn't know to look for it.

"Duchess Inara and her people have affixed this to all the open spaces without windows, and to the other side of all the windows that open in the castle to keep everyone safe. This is fishing line. Strong enough to bring in some of the massive fish they catch. They say it's strong enough to block Corvids, and slice them up pretty thoroughly should they try."

"How do we get this for the rest of the country, too? We could do things with this to protect more people."

"She has ramped up production so it can be sent out. They already use it in their towns, running it from one roof to another, over the town squares, and they have it protecting portions of their boats."

Across the squares of the towns…I must not have seen it because I was at the back of one of the houses. But still, I felt like I should have known this.

"How bad have I been while recovering? How out of it?" I asked, looking at Tristan and biting my lip.

"Nothing you could do while you started to heal from what that human stain did to you could ever be described as bad." He pulled me into his arms. They were strong around me, yet his hands were gentle.

The cold spray of the sea splashing up and misting into the air from below the castle tickled along my eyelashes. I held him back, knowing I needed to get up to speed on everything I missed while I could barely think.

Especially if I was going to start being part of these meetings.

CHAPTER 6

GODDESS

Tristan gave me a perfunctory kiss and left, shutting the door to my rooms behind him.

I turned around to Madam and Jacquetta standing ready to prepare me for the meeting.

They would make sure I was perfectly dressed. But no matter how thoroughly they made sure I looked the part, I didn't completely trust that I would be able to give much in the way of actual value to the rest of the meeting.

What were the chances that I would even be able to keep myself from stabbing the Marquessa?

"You need to put on that stone face you adopted while I was trying to teach you to dance," Madam said, leading me into my bathroom to the tub already prepared for me.

"Stone face?" I asked, trying to think back to that time.

"Cinder," Jacquetta said, taking my clothes from me as I pulled them off, "most of the time I had no idea what you were thinking until we were talking in your room."

"Oh." I swallowed and climbed into the bath while they spoke of what kind of negotiations might be involved, how long the Amethyst group might stay, and what members of their court might come.

All those years I tried to hide what I was thinking from Ash, all that time I thought that he always saw through me, he might have been the only one.

For this meeting, I needed to put that to use, to think of the Amethyst people as Ash.

But even doing it for a second nauseated me.

He couldn't have known.

No matter what Ash had done, he couldn't have known the extent of Brix's evil. I couldn't believe that.

Ash might have seen through me no matter how hard I tried, but he couldn't have seen that darkness in his best friend. He probably thought Brix was like he was, had the same level of rage and cruelty within him, but was still a decent person.

Maybe it was just because I was his sister, and he had known me from the moment I was born. Maybe that was why I couldn't hide anything from him.

But these supposed negotiators, they didn't know me at all.

I smiled and dunked my head in the water.

Jacquetta and Madam helped dress me in my new favorite outfit.

"When did you have this made?" I asked, admiring the shine on the metal bustier with its black, painted dragons and the pauldron on the shoulder that reached down that bicep. As much as I disliked pauldrons—or anything limiting on my shoulders—for this meeting it was perfect. The bustier ended at my navel. A crimson panel of leather hung down in the front, and another one in the back, acting almost as if they were a skirt with huge slits for my legs. Under the leather panels was a strap of red fabric that acted like panties, but was also connected to the bustier.

"This was part of the collection I had made for your time at the training grounds," Madam said, a hint of a smile playing with the corner of her mouth.

I missed the training grounds. Being able to train, being healthy enough, surrounded by it every minute of the day made me feel at home, like I actually belonged in this fight.

These meetings and fancy affairs, whether with the other potentials or with foreign nobles, made me itch for a chance to spar with someone.

"Now," Jacquetta said, lifting her chin high, "sit down, because I have one last thing to add."

I followed her instructions, strapping both of my spikes onto my thighs once I sat down, and she started tugging on my hair.

Finally, she yanked on my shoulder, and I smiled, giving up on the last strap on my last spike. I would finish once she was done with whatever she was adding to my hair.

They had already braided it, but it felt like they were pinning it.

"Done," Jacquetta said, stepping back, and I finished my strap before turning around to look.

She pinned my hair, alright. The braid was wrapped like a crown on my head. Imbedded in it were silver gems that looked like dragon scales, as well as red and black gems scattered throughout.

"You gave me a crown," I said, my voice hushed, a weight settling on my shoulders.

"We gave you a style," Madam said, a grin with an edge on her face. "That it will be a discreet way to stake your claim that they cannot afford to inquire about, is just a bonus."

"Subtle," I whispered, looking at Jacquetta and Madam wearing matching expressions of pride.

They believed in me. In this. The future they saw.

"Lady Cinder," the General said from behind us.

I turned around and her eyes widened as she stood up even

straighter than she always did, which I would have said was impossible until that second.

"Are they arriving?" I asked.

"Yes. They have arrived. It is time to go."

Nodding to Madam and Jacquetta, unsure what else there was to say, I took a step past them and paused.

Turning around, I looked at my reflection again, and pulled off my bandage, tugging out the packing in my cheek, and wiping off the medicine.

"Please, Lady Cinder," Madam said, holding out a hand like she was going to reach for me and replace the bandage.

"Let them see what King Tristan's Fighter really looks like," I said, that weight on my shoulders settling into a more manageable place, as if it were a sword now strapped to my back.

I turned around and stalked out with General Pace.

Once we were in the hallway, the General said under her breath, "None of them will know what to make of you."

"Good." Anything I could do to help, including keeping them confused, was a good thing.

We made our way to a large room with the largest single piece of driftwood I had ever seen turned into a table sitting in the middle of it.

The wall facing the sea was one giant opening, with massive pieces of coral acting like pillars holding up arches. While most of the room was in various shades of cream and brown, the sea was a vibrant blue, the spray being sent up at regular intervals the purest white, and the coral was a bright orange with a pink cast to it. It was beautiful.

Amethysts, festooned in shades of purple from their hair to their shoes, were easy to spot.

Standing among them, Inara was in a flowing, teal gown with dark blue straps that cinched it tight to her waist and wrapped over her shoulders and down her arms. It made her a unique flower in the brightly-colored garden.

Of course, I was here to ruin the illusion in my stark black-and-red and metal.

Making my way to her side, the Amethysts stopped talking and turned their focus to me one by one.

Ziya stood between the Chamberlain and a man Tristan's age with dark purple hair, lilac eyes, and golden skin like Inara's.

While Ziya's hair turned lighter as I approached, all the color leeching out of it, the man's grew a touch more vibrant. A smirk formed on his face as he looked me up and down.

"Marquessa," I said into the silence while Inara pinched her mouth on the smile that played there as she took in my hair, "how nice to see you again."

"Your…" her voice was a squeak, and she couldn't get out the rest as she stared at my torn cheek, her focus only changing when she looked up at my hair.

"Fighter Cinder finished training the guard," Inara broke in, her smile successfully buried at the moment. "Now she is here to help protect Breakwater as a personal favor to me."

Well done, Inara, I cheered in my head.

General Pace was right. There would be no way for them to make sense out of me.

"The Lady Hero," the man drawled, that smirk turning into a grin, "everyone is talking about you."

"I am surprised that in Amethyst anyone would talk about a Fighter from Onyx," I said, my voice cold.

This guy was clearly used to getting what he wanted. He was going to be disappointed here. None of them were going to get anything they wanted out of this trip. Unless what they wanted was a waste of time.

"People are talking about you in every kingdom. But nothing they're saying comes close to the reality."

I lifted my chin and tightened my mouth so I wouldn't

speak, not just because the lack of formality in his speech was shocking for a meeting like this.

Whatever he meant by his statement, it had to be an insult.

But if he came right out and said the words, just looking at his manicured hands, wiry build, and the sheer height of his heeled shoes told me I wouldn't even break a sweat making him pay for it.

"Terrifying and beautiful," he said, a light in his eyes as if he was enjoying this, "like a goddess of death."

"King Tristan," the Marquessa said, brighter purple returning to her hair as she looked over my shoulder at him.

I turned around and almost fell over.

CHAPTER 7

SECOND PRINCE

Now I knew why he usually didn't wear the formal court clothes.

So many times in the past I thought he was attractive, or even beautiful, but he had never looked like this.

While the crown on his head was a simple circle of silver with a dragon head in the center, the rest of his attire was so intricate it was almost impossible to take it all in at once.

A soft ruffle of lace framed the neckline of his jacket, as if sea foam had been turned into silver, flame-patterned lace fabric. The exquisite softness against the hard lines of his jaw...he was a work of art.

His jacket was black leather, cut tight to his body, allowing me to see the strength of the muscles in his chest and arms. At the end of his sleeves, the lace draped over his strong hands that were festooned in dragon head rings.

But if I thought the jacket made me want to kiss him and never stop, the pants...

They may as well have been painted on his body. Gray and fitted to the knee, they gave me an even better idea of what to expect when we could finally be alone than rubbing myself against him the night of the attack in Bridgeton had.

The hem of the pants ended past the knee and silver hose, with the same flame pattern as the lace, covered well-muscled calves, showcased to perfection by his heeled black shoes.

If I was a goddess of death, he was a god of beauty. And I was his devoted supplicant.

His eyes were on me, bright green as he looked at my face, but when they tracked down my body, his pupils dilated, blocking some of the green.

Oh. I was going to pass out.

Tristan looked…hungry by the time his eyes returned to mine.

"Welcome everyone to Onyx," he said, his eyes still not torn from mine.

General Pace stepped in front of me and went to Tristan's side, breaking whatever spell I was under long enough for me to turn away, stand next to Inara, and not look directly at him again.

He came to my side and made idle conversation with the Amethysts, Ziya trying in vain to catch his eye for more than a moment.

Meanwhile, every single time I looked at the man with Ziya, whose name I still didn't know, he was smiling at me with eyes like a predator.

"Duchess Inara," I finally whispered to her, "who is the man next to Marquessa Ziya?"

"Her cousin," Inara said, her voice as quiet as mine, but seething in tone, "Second Prince of Amethyst, Nevan ."

Nevan could have stayed home.

"They sent the second born Prince?" I asked, managing to contain the snort of laughter that bubbled up in me.

"Apparently he does a lot of their international meetings."

Of course he did. They kept the heir at home, and this gawking, disrespectful asshole was the spare.

Well, it was nice of his parents to make it so obvious that they didn't love him, and he was expendable.

A servant stood behind us, and leaned down to whisper in Inara's ear.

She nodded and said, "Everyone, dinner is ready."

When Tristan turned around, I swallowed and averted my eyes. His ass in those pants, flexing with each step...my mind imagined it flexing as he did other things, and I had to refocus, trailing behind everyone else.

They all made their way to the table, Tristan claiming the one end, and Inara the other. General Pace sat to Tristan's right, while the Second Prince sat to his left, and the Marquessa next to him.

Her look my way, smug and sure, told me she still underestimated me.

I walked around to stand directly behind Tristan, placing my hands flat on my exposed hips as if I was ready to grab my spikes at any moment, and turned slightly to show off my open cheek while I smiled and looked back at Ziya.

"King Tristan," Nevan said, shaking his head and openly appraising me again, "I don't know where you got her, but I want one."

"We do not trade in people," Tristan said, and I wanted to cheer while some of the Amethysts sucked in breaths. "Fighter Cinder is a noble Lady in this country. Show some respect." His voice was hard with a gravelly quality to it that was as if his growling sounds when we were alone had turned violent instead of loving.

If he kept talking like that, using that voice so close to the one that made my skin heat, I was going to have a hard time paying any attention to what was happening.

"No disrespect meant," Nevan said, raising his hands, palm

out, and shaking his head. "I only meant that to end this war, all you should have to do is show her to the Corvid monarchs. She looks like a Goddess that would have no problem killing us all."

"Why do you think she trained the guard, and everyone is calling her a hero?" General Pace said, surprising me so that I snapped my attention her way.

"So, it's true," he said, leaning forward on the table, every bit of his focus now on the General and Tristan.

He baited us all into that. I wasn't sure how, but I felt we lost ground and now he believed he had some kind of upper hand here.

Fuck.

My blood sang in the chill that came through the open wall, and made me slide my hands a fraction closer to my spikes.

"That she trained the guard and fought for us, killing a host of those damn birds?" General Pace asked, raising a brow, her tone as if she was bored. "Yes."

"No, General. I mean, is it true that the Corvids would have won that battle without her?" His eyes remained riveted on General Pace while Tristan's hand clenched into a fist on the arm of the chair he sat in.

"I just made it end faster. They were nowhere near successful," I said, my voice with as much threat in it as I could give. "Onyx was never at risk of falling, and our King has always been well defended. I am just more...efficient."

Nevan smiled up at me, his eyes shining.

Tristan turned my way enough that I could see the smile playing on the corner of his mouth although his eyes were still tense.

Servants laden with plates, platters, bowls and all manner of other things, entered and placed food in front of everyone.

I remained standing in the same position, watching the occupants of the table go back to what seemed like small talk.

Who cared about the intricacies of trade?

This was supposed to be a war meeting. We needed to get back to talking about the war and what they thought they could bring to the table. Because, so far, I didn't see anything worth partnering with Amethyst.

Once everyone at the table ate most of the courses and dessert was placed in front of each of them, they finally mentioned something that made me pay attention.

Hellfire water.

"You see, King Tristan," Nevan said, playing with his dessert spoon, not touching his food, "the kind of Hellfire water in Amethyst can't be used for fuel. We have to rely on secondhand hellfire stores that some countries are willing to trade, stone lights, and wood burning. None of those are wonderful options."

"No, I am aware," Tristan said, taking a bite of his food, that fist forming on the arm of his chair again.

The Second Prince needed to tread lightly now. Tristan was already unhappy with the way he spoke about me, and now he brought up the poison that had hurt me and Gus, and killed little Angeline?

He didn't know that we had such recent terrible history with it, but he was walking through a maze of blades with a blindfold on at this point.

"We all still hope that an alliance can be formed that would be more permanent between our two countries," Nevan said, patting the Marquessa's hand, causing her to brighten and look from under her lashes at Tristan, streaks of color returning to her hair.

It only took a moment for her to look past him and make eye contact with me.

Ziya's face fell, and her hair drained to palest lilac while she went back to looking at her dessert.

That's right, coward.

She might have been genuinely fearful of the wound on the

side of my face, or my weapons on clear display. But, whatever the reason, I didn't think I had to worry about her trying to weasel her way into Tristan's room while she was here.

Not as long as I was in the castle, too. Especially not if she wanted to avoid my death mask being the view she woke up to in the middle of the night.

"For now," Tristan said, "my sole focus needs to be this war."

As far as any of them knew. Meanwhile, I intended to make my King forget anything else existed soon, and as often as we could.

It would be hard to stop myself from wanting to spend all my time forgetting the world with him if he kept wearing his formal clothes.

"Of course," Nevan said, grinning at me, "with that in mind, you know that Amethyst has long had a trading relationship with Corvid."

Tristan nodded. I wanted to roll my eyes.

Yes, we knew. Which was exactly why Ziya should never be queen.

Fucking slave trading snakes.

"Possibly turning our backs on that relationship remains a difficult proposition for my kingdom. Queen Phailin is part Corvid."

CHAPTER 8

WANT

Ziya snapped her gaze to Nevan, her eyes widening, and a streak of darkest purple, almost black, shot through her hair.

A muscle jumped in Tristan's jaw, and I clamped mine tight together, too.

I didn't know that about their Queen. I was willing to bet Tristan didn't either. And the look on Ziya's face said she didn't expect Nevan to reveal that little bit of information.

Queen Phailin was his mother. He was part Corvid.

So…why did he say it that way? Why admit it at all?

"Understood," Tristan said, his voice sounding thoughtful instead of disgusted like me.

Nevan gave a slow nod, still playing with his food while everyone else was done with theirs.

What was remarkable about Nevan was that even as his voice, his face, his demeanor shifted with the conversation, his hair never did. It remained the same since that first barely-there change.

Could it be possible for him to have so little emotion? Or did he have greater control over his hair somehow?

I still didn't understand how the Marquessa's hair changed color, and whether that was the magic everyone said Amethyst possessed. So I didn't want to read too much into Nevan's hair.

That didn't stop me from paying closer and closer attention to what he said, what we said, and his reaction to it all.

"But since we do not have our own stores of hellfire water," Nevan said, "and we know how useful it is, we have to look at how much that might help our kingdom."

"When you say 'that,' what exactly are you hoping to gain from our hellfire water trade?" Tristan's voice was careful, a study in neutrality, although there was no way he could be middle-of-the-road about this.

"Queen Phailan has come to believe that half ownership over the stores of hellfire that reside in Lehar, which is conveniently near the border of Onyx and Amethyst, would be worth cutting all ties to her family."

Fuck this smarmy bastard snake asshole. He really thought their 'help' would be worth half the value of my duchy?

Near the border my ass. Thirteen Rivers Valley sat between Lehar and Amethyst. Was that why they came to Lehar in the last war?

"Do you know who the Duke of Lehar is?" Tristan asked Nevan, with a hand gesture to me down by his leg.

"No," Nevan said, "unfortunately I do not."

"My brother," I said.

For the first time since he sat down, that smile Nevan had whenever he looked at me dropped from his face. Still, his hair didn't change.

I narrowed my eyes, searching for even a strand that was different.

The Marquessa on his other side stared at her plate and pursed her lips, some bright violet appearing in her hair.

So he didn't bother to ask her opinion before this little meeting, and she wasn't happy with him.

Interesting.

"Well," Nevan said, putting down his spoon and leaning back as if preparing to stand up, "I think we have more to discuss tomorrow. But after this lovely meal, and the travel of the day, I believe we need to retire to our rooms.

"Of course," Inara said.

Tristan stood, then all the others.

"I look forward to talking to you again," Tristan said, although the tight set of his jaw told me that was a lie.

All the Amethyst nobles left the room, and Inara with them to show them where they would be staying. Tristan took a deep breath as the Chamberlain ran to his side.

"That request is ridiculous," the Chamberlain said, voice almost vibrating with rage.

"Of course it is," Tristan said, running a hand through his hair, mussing its perfection.

"What else did we expect from a slave trading snake?" I asked, drawing all their eyes. But it shouldn't have been a surprise that I thought any partnership with Amethyst was a terrible idea from the start, and I wasn't sad that it wasn't going well.

"Don't worry," Tristan said, "I will never let them take the hellfire water. General, do we have reports to go over?"

"Yes, we do," she said.

"Then I will leave you for the night," the Chamberlain said, brow furrowed. Muttering, the Chamberlain left the room.

"I'll see you tomorrow, then," I said, trying to file away how breathtaking Tristan was.

"Let me walk you to your rooms," he said, and fell into step beside me.

Once we were down the hallway far enough from the General, I said, "Just so you know, you could wear that more often."

"You like this?" he asked, grinning at me.

"Why *don't* you wear the formals more often?" I would have thought that he would have at least worn them at the first ball.

"A long time ago a horse stepped on my foot, breaking bones. These heels have killed me ever since. And the lace itches." He tugged at the collar, and I bit my lip to stop from giggling.

He sounded like a sullen teenager, and for some reason it made me want to kiss him.

"Try it without the heels," I said as we neared my rooms, "and I bet Madam could find you lace that wouldn't itch."

"You really do like this, don't you?" he asked, his smile turning into a leer.

My heart sped up. I didn't want to let him have another meeting with General Pace. I wanted him to stay, but I nodded.

We got to my door, and he opened it for me, looking around before ushering me inside.

The second the door was shut, he whirled me around, pressed my back into the door behind me, and braced himself with one arm above my head.

"Nothing," he whispered, that growl that started a fire in my body changing back from violence to promise, "nothing will compare to how much I like seeing you in the dresses you wear."

He put a hand to my hip, but with no fabric there, he wrapped his hand around to the back, his fingers clamping down on my ass.

I sucked in a breath and grabbed his neck, pulling his mouth to mine.

Every bit of the want running through me poured into that kiss, and he poured his desire back to me in response, pressing the length of his body against mine.

Oh, Gods and Goddesses.

The pants that concealed nothing allowed him to press

against me more, but now my stupid leather panel for a skirt blocked me from feeling him.

Reaching down a hand, sliding it between our bodies, I grabbed ahold of his cock through his pants. It jumped in my hand, and he groaned into my mouth.

It was bigger than I thought through all our clothes before, but I wanted to see him, I wanted to feel him with nothing between us.

His hand grasped my ass harder, and I wrapped that leg around his waist.

"Cinder," he said, nipping at my bottom lip.

"Lady Cinder," Madam's voice came from the other room. Tristan stepped back, his breathing as heavy as mine, and I wondered if he would fall over just as I felt like doing.

"Yes," I said, my voice a croak. I cleared my throat and tried again, "Yes, Madam."

"King Tristan needs to go back to his rooms now," she said.

Checking over his shoulder, I knew she wasn't in the room. She didn't watch. But she knew and gave us a moment.

I stepped to him and wrapped my arms around his neck, keeping my body back from his, and giving him a sweet kiss without the heat coursing through my veins.

The warmth of him that was always there was scorching hot, and made me even more molten in response, making it harder to keep back from him. But he just wrapped me in his arms, and leaned his forehead to mine.

"Give me just a minute," he whispered, eyes closed.

"Mmmm…" I mumbled, running a hand along that jawline where it met the lace and made me want to never stop kissing him.

"I love you," he said after a time.

"I love you, too."

Watching him go, it was an effort not to snatch him back to me and drag him to my room. Even if it upset Madam Valentin.

Because that beautiful man was mine. Torn apart face and all, he loved me.

And after I got something to eat, I was going to be the Goddess of Death for Brix, and find my way to Tristan's room to be just his goddess for the night.

CHAPTER 9

THE FIRST

"**L**ady Cinder," Madam Valentin said after late dinner to make up for the one I didn't eat at the meeting.

We sat around the small table I dragged into Gus' room. Madam folded her hands in her lap and sat back in her chair across from me.

Moving my tongue inside my mouth to touch the packing in the hole in my cheek covered by a bandage again that allowed me to eat with no problem, I tried not to be unnerved by her.

The way she said it...For some reason it reminded me of when I was scolded by my mother as a child.

Looking at Gus and Jacquetta made me think they felt the same way.

Especially Jacquetta who looked like she wanted to hide under her own chair by Gus' bed.

"Yes, Madam?" I asked, my voice small before I popped the last bite of my dinner into my mouth in the hopes it would delay responding to whatever she was going to say. Because if she tried to tell me not to be so close to Tristan, I was going to refuse. And I didn't want to upset Madam, to let her down. But I might have to.

"If you are going to spend your nights with the King, there is a medicine I insist you take first. Even though I already gave the King his own."

She gave Tristan his own...Oh.

Gus tried to hide her grin.

Jacquetta popped her eyes wide, and looked down at the plate in her hands.

"No need, Madam," I said, sending a silent prayer up to my parents that she would stop now.

"He has the medicine, but I do not know if he has taken it. You need to think about that before you refuse to take some of your own."

Madam took a deep breath and leaned forward again as if she were just getting started on her lesson in contraceptives.

"Really," I said, trying to be forceful enough that she would stop.

Gus and Jacquetta wouldn't look at me. They focused on each other, each of them trying in vain to hide their need to giggle while their shoulders shook in tight little movements.

"Lady Cinder, I must insist that you listen. I know your parents passed away when you were young. Someone needs to explain this to you." She shook her head, and I wanted to scream.

"Please, Madam Valentin, I am no longer a child. My brother did...explain it to me. And I took the root a long time ago. Should I ever want to have a child, I will need to take it again. Until then, I have no need of anything else." She needed to stop asking, but I said the wrong thing.

I could tell by the way all of them went too still. A moment later, Jacquetta set down her plate, every eye in the room intent on me, and no hint of laughter among them.

"Cinder," Jacquetta asked, low and careful, "what do you mean that your brother explained?"

Shit.

Of all the things I didn't want to talk about, with them or anyone else, my first time was high on the list.

Later partners were random people I met on the road for a one-night moment to forget. But that first time was…different.

"Ash explained how it all works, and brought me to someone who showed me how it works after he gave me the root." That part was fine. That much I could handle speaking about. Although I had come to learn it was weird over the years from overheard roadside tavern conversations, but it didn't bother me.

Please, I prayed to Mom and Dad, don't let them ask about the details or what came after.

"He took you to someone who showed you," Madam said, each word fully enunciated and separate as if she couldn't believe they were coming out of her mouth.

"Yes. It was fine." Sort of.

"So," Gus said, her voice still rough from so long not using it, "you've seen a cock?"

Madam squeezed her eyes shut like she was pained by hearing the word, and I saw an opening to get as far from this conversation as possible.

"I know what to do with a cock, yes. Ash said I needed to know, that it was a good investment to take me to a professional."

There. Was that shocking enough to make them stop asking me about it?

"Did that so-called professional only show you what to do to him, or did he return the favor?" Jacquetta asked, disgust clear in her tone.

"What does it matter? I know what I'm doing in the bedroom, and I've already taken care of protecting myself." Please, I begged in my head. They needed to stop.

Madam sat back in her seat again and studied me. Jacquetta and Gus stared at me, too.

All it did was remind me that even though my friends knew some of me, they had no idea about most of it.

No one did.

I wasn't sure I would ever be able to explain to them that my first sexual partner was also the first person Ash told me to kill. The order came right after I confessed that I developed feelings for the man after spending so much time with him in bed.

The Duke's sister couldn't be known to have gone to a prostitute, let alone stayed for a week to learn, and started to care for him, believed she was in love with him.

We had no future.

Ash said killing him was the only way to protect me. To protect my secret. One of many secrets Ash gave me.

Grabbing my glass of wine from the table, I downed it in a rush, trying to signal to them that I didn't want to talk anymore about this. I definitely didn't want to think about that first time when I wanted to be with Tristan soon.

Bad memories running through my head might destroy my time with him.

"Cinder," Jacquetta asked, her voice full of a sadness that made my heart ache, "how did you meet anyone when you didn't have any friends?"

"It's very easy to proposition a man in a bar who is a few drinks in, and never tell them your name." Or bother to learn theirs.

All of them stared at me, and I didn't want to explain this anymore. How many times did they have to be reminded that I was a murderer? Not fit for society? Not fit for their friendship?

Not fit to be close to Tristan?

My brother made it pretty clear that first time that if I tried to make any connection beyond just a temporary, one time, physical one, they wouldn't survive.

He had to protect his investment.

"No one is in charge of me anymore," I said, standing up and taking all my dishes. "I am going to be with Tristan while I can, and I know how to protect myself. Thank you for your concern, but it is misplaced."

I walked out the door, taking my dishes with me to drop on the tray, and then continued straight to my room.

"Lady Cinder," Madam called as I was shutting my door.

Fuck.

"Yes, Madam?" I asked, through a tight jaw.

"We need to do your debriding tonight and sew up your cheek," she said.

"The Amethyst Prince seemed to think it was terrifying. Maybe I should leave it until they are gone and the meetings are done." And I didn't want to answer any more damned questions.

"If we do not do it soon, with the way it is healing so fast, I am afraid we will not be able to close the wound without damaging other parts of your face."

Closing my eyes for a second, I took a deep breath, wondering if it was worth it to risk never easily drinking or eating again just to fuck with the Princeling's mind some more.

But he had seen me. He already labeled me Death.

"Fine. Let's get this over with."

Going back into Gus' room was like going back in time to when none of us knew each other well enough to be comfortable. Only now they knew too much.

I swallowed and lifted my chin.

Madam led me back to the table and made me sit while she and Jacquetta cleared it of all the remnants of dinner, then laid a white sheet over it.

Jacquetta put a hand to my good cheek, and lowered my head down to the table.

"I'm not going to lie to you, Cinder," Jacquetta said, biting on her upper lip, "this is going to hurt."

"Do you want someone to get King Tristan?" Gus asked from the bed.

I tilted my head to look her way.

Ensconced in pillows, her bad leg covered in bandages and her arm tightly wrapped, she looked so much more like herself that I smiled.

"No, but thank you, Gus. I have all of you. I'll be okay," I said, and she smiled back.

Gus didn't have any of us with her through so much of her pain. No hand to hold, no one's love to lean on when her own strength waned. So many times in the past when Ash taught me lessons, he was the only one I had.

I was better off already, no matter how bad this was going to be.

"Lady Cinder," Madam said, standing over me while Jacquetta undid my bandage and the packing of my wound, leaving me opening and closing my mouth for a moment, "the most important thing you need to do is to hold still."

She wiped my wound down with a liquid that smelled minty and stung, while it cleared my sinuses and made my nose want to run.

Then she took what looked like a tiny porcupine and scraped at my wound while Jacquetta grabbed my head and pushed my skin into a strange position that put pressure on my cheek bone.

My eyes opened wide, the feeling of tearing in my face made every muscle in my body want to recoil from it.

I had to hold still.

I needed to move. Everything in me screamed to move.

But I had to hold still.

Just at the edge of my vision, past Madam's hip, I could see the end of Gus' bed. Staring at it while I pressed my toes down into the floor and my fingers into the table, I focused on Gus, on what she went through, on the rage that built even contemplating Brix still living while Gus still hurt. At the hideous pain he put poor Angeline through. So much so that she was already gone.

Grinding my teeth as they tore apart my face again, as my eyes watered and I could feel the exact outline of the hole in a way not even the packing made so clear, I curled my hands into fists and pressed my knuckles into the sheet so hard I felt the grain of the wood under it.

Adjusting my feet wider, I shoved down into the floor, my ass beginning to lift from the chair even as I kept my legs bent and my head tight to the table.

"Ngggg," I growled, low in my throat through my clenched teeth.

"You're almost done," Jacquetta said.

Desperate for a way out of my body, away from this room, away from the tearing, searing sensation, I tried to find the ashes of Lehar in my mind.

Instead, flashes of so many times Ash punished me went through my memories.

Everything in me wanted to lash out, to make the person hurting me stop. To make Ash stop.

My shoulders shook and curled in while I managed to keep my face still, but I opened my eyes wide, my breathing ragged.

Ash wasn't here. Those times were over.

This was temporary, this was the only way for my friends to help me.

"Good," Madam finally said, taking a step back. I breathed in great gulps of air as I shook out my hands and collapsed back onto the chair. "Now we can stitch it back up."

The pain was still there, but by comparison, it was so much less that I almost wanted to fall asleep. But we weren't done.

She stitched me with little tugs and the occasional searing zing that made me squeeze my eyes shut, the eye on that side of my face feeling suddenly tight.

Finally, Jacquetta put a paste of some kind on the wound that eased the ache, and covered it in a fresh bandage.

I kept my head down for another minute while they packed up their supplies and patted me on the shoulder.

One of my wounds was closed, but when I lifted my head and made eye contact with Gus, the one that still laid bare and bleeding on her and Angeline's behalf screamed for Brix's death.

CHAPTER 10

BLEND

Alone in my room, I surveyed my nightgown options.

Most of them were white, black, or red. Why Madam thought those were the only colors for nightgowns, I didn't know and wasn't going to ask. None of them managed to cover much, let alone warm me.

But I needed something specific if I was going to do this without worrying about being spotted by a Corvid or one of Inara's people on a ship, if there was one close enough.

I had a scarf that had been a wrap for some of my new shoes that would cover my dark hair.

My skin would blend well, but I didn't really want to go naked.

Not a single pair of panties I owned would work for this, and the stone was rough. Some kind of protection, no matter how thin, would be better than nothing.

Taking a deep breath, I dug into my last trunk, my last chance to find something— anything— that would work.

With one of the dresses, there was a silky piece of beige fabric.

I tried not to get too excited as I pulled it out.

But it was perfect.

Not a nightgown, and not a dress, it was a thin-strapped, simple slip.

The likelihood that I would be able to wear the dress it was designed for without it was slim, but I didn't bother to check before I started to shove my clothes back into trunks and pulled the slip on over my head.

It was thin, and I could make out a little too much through the fabric. But I didn't intend on anyone seeing me in it besides Brix, who wouldn't be alive to remember.

Strapping my spike on my leg—my old one because it felt like the right weapon to use—I wrapped my hair up in the scarf and checked in the mirror.

My skin, the beige slip that fell to my knees and covered the spike, and the scarf made me almost monochromatic.

The only thing that didn't blend was the bright white bandage on my face.

Going against what Madam and Jacquetta wanted me to do for my wound made me question myself, made me wonder if I should just wait.

Patience was a good quality to develop.

How many times had I used patience for a kill?

But...

Looking at the pile of beautiful nightgowns, thinking about Tristan in his formals and what he would think seeing me in those nightgowns, and all I had to look forward to...

No, I wasn't going to wait and risk this life.

I pulled the bandage off my face and saw a jagged line that curled up toward my cheekbone at one end while it pointed down toward the corner of my mouth at the other.

This wasn't the death mask it had been, but a scar like this, out in the open, and impossible to hide, still marked me for what I was.

Leaving my reflection behind, I went to my window and opened the glass pane.

On the other side, I plucked the strings of fishing line, finding the widest opening between them, and climbed onto the window ledge.

While the temperature here on the coast never got quite as cold as it did inland, the breeze was still icy as it touched my exposed skin. I maneuvered myself into place on the outside of the castle wall.

Using the pocks and divots in the stone itself, I found more than enough handholds and footholds to move at a steady clip down the wall.

Steady until the first spray of water hit me.

The constant waves crashing against the bottom of the castle and the shoreline just beyond it, sent tiny particles of frigid water splashing against me with increasing frequency as I got closer and closer to the sea.

At first, with every new drop, I shivered and sucked in a breath, but kept moving.

Just a little further down the wall, I clung to the now slick surface of the stone, the holes in it no longer helping much because they were so sodden.

My beige slip was soaked through as if I had gone swimming. Every part of my skin dripping and beginning to feel like ice.

Finally, I got to the round openings in the wall of the room of cells.

But trying to shove a hand through and dive inside, I slammed into fishing line.

Here? In these small openings that would even be hard for me to slip through, and were far too close to the raging water for a Corvid to even try to use on the tiny chance any of them were small enough?

Fuck.

My arms and my legs started to weaken as my shivering intensified and my teeth chattered.

Hand over hand, adjusting my fingers until I got a decent hold on the slick holes in the stone, I made my way back toward my room.

The cold seeped into my bones, and every part of me shook as my fingers and toes started to grow numb.

I didn't know if I could make it to my room. Another room, one with a balcony, was closer, and I headed that way instead.

So much for showing up looking decent to a night with Tristan. I would be lucky if I got there at all.

Another hold, and another. I was careful to test my weight as I went while water sluiced down my soaked body like I was a stone in a waterfall.

This human-shaped stone was about to go tumbling down if I didn't get to the balcony faster.

I shook out my hand before I made my next grab, opening and closing my fist and blowing on the ends of my fingers.

None of it seemed to help bring the feeling back to my fingertips.

Fuck.

Going faster sounded like a good idea in my head, but my next grab ended in my hand slipping off. I was happy I didn't rush too much.

But there it was, Tristan's balcony.

All I had to do was…

I stretched, reaching with a partially numb hand and hoping I didn't hit the stupid fishing line.

This time I didn't. I found a gap large enough to wrap my hand around the top of the balcony railing.

Pawing around, plucking the fishing line, I found an opening big enough to worm my body through, and dropped, unceremoniously, to the floor of the balcony.

On the other side of the glass, Tristan had his back to me,

standing next to a desk shoved against one wall with a small stack of papers on it.

No one else seemed to be around.

Shivers overtook my body completely once it knew it could quake without sending me plunging to my death. I flung myself at the glass door.

Opening it, I stepped inside and slumped to the floor.

Just in time for a knife to go flying inches over my head and slam into the stone next to the glass door, sending bits of the wall flying against my skin that was too numb to care.

CHAPTER 11

WALLS

I looked at Tristan, standing ready with another knife in hand, and pulled the scarf from my hair.

"Cinder?" he asked, dropping his hand and standing up straight, his mouth falling open.

Of course, he recognized me the second the blade was past his fingers. But showing up like this, I couldn't blame him for the knife.

Getting my feet under me, I stood up in front of the open door. The cold wind at my back sent a fresh wave of shivers down my body.

His eyes went wide, and I knew what he saw.

Me, standing in front of him in a now see-through slip, my entire body on display, my nipples hard, and every inch of me soaking wet.

"I told you," I said, my breathing labored and my teeth still clattering together. "Walls don't usually stop me." Although this was not my plan.

"Shit, Cinder." He dropped the knife in his hand and darted through a door to another room, emerging with three bath sheets and a basin of water, and running to me with them.

Tristan threw one of the bath sheets around my shoulders and slammed the glass door to the balcony.

While I pulled the bath sheet tight around me, a shiver racked my body at the warmth it was now so unaccustomed to feeling.

He came back to me, shaking his head, a smile on his face, and the other bath sheet in his hands.

"You need to stop this." He took that bath sheet to my hair first, gently running the lengths of my hair through it, soaking up as much of the excess water as he could.

"Stop what? I thought you liked the idea of me coming here and spending nights with you?" He didn't need to know exactly what order my priorities had been in.

"Cinder." He looked at me with a stern face, his eyes shining green, and kissed my forehead, the intense heat of him thawing me, ending my shivering. "The last thing I want you to do is risk yourself in the process. We could have found another way."

"This way worked. I'm here now."

"And what about the Corvids? They could have picked you off that wall."

I stuck my leg out and lifted the hem of the slip to show off my spike.

"Every way I could try to make it safer, I did."

He looked down at the spike strapped to my leg and a muscle in his jaw jumped.

"Cinder, you have to stop doing this." His voice was hard, all the pleasure at having me here replaced by a simmering fury that shone in those bright green eyes. "Think about it, if I died trying to get to you, how would you feel for the rest of your life?"

"I..." I opened my mouth and closed it again as my soul put myself in that place, the one where he tried to save me, or just tried to do something for me, and died in the attempt.

Tears collected at the backs of my eyes and my throat grew thick.

Somehow, I couldn't let him know about the risks I took for him anymore.

Not that I could stop taking the risks. It was all I was good at, all I could bring to this war effort and to Onyx.

But he didn't need to know about it anymore.

I nodded, and he took a corner of the bath sheet, dampened it in the basin in he set on the floor, then slowly, tenderly, one tiny area at a time, wiped away the sea water from my face. He followed it with the dry bath sheet, being just as careful.

When he got to my freshly-stitched wound, he slowed down further so he didn't get too close to the new stitches.

"You are beautiful. And now your scar will look like a flame is licking up the side of your face. And the whole world will think they know why I call you my beautiful flame."

He leaned down and touched a feather light, hellfire-source-hot, kiss to the skin right above the wound.

All that heat poured through me, filling my veins with him the way I wanted my body filled with him tonight.

He kept kissing along my face until he touched his lips to mine at last.

"Tristan," I said, dropping the bath sheet from around my shoulders to the ground, standing in front of him in my still-soaked, see-through slip, with my nipples still hard even though I was no longer cold.

Not hiding it at all, he looked my body up, then down, and smiled.

"Beautiful," he said.

He bent to my feet, wiping and drying them off and kneading his fingers into all the points of most tension in them, eliciting a small groan from me as the pain from my climb fled from his touch.

He looked up at me and focused on my calves, repeating the

process, although his fingers spent more time massaging into me than they had on my feet.

And when he started on my thighs, taking off the strap holding my spike, he spent even more time drying me off, and rubbing those clever fingers into my muscles.

Tracing the lines of the well-defined cords of my muscles with his fingers in a touch so light it felt like the wind blowing on my skin, he looked up at me again, and it grew difficult to breathe.

Kneading all the knots and aches in my legs until they were left free from pain for the first time in so long made me feel not entirely connected to the floor.

Running the wet towel against my sex, slow and torturous, had me sucking in a breath and standing on my toes. When he repeated the process with the dry one, I groaned.

He grinned at me, that perfect face I loved framed by the soft lace. I throbbed in response.

Oh, Gods and Goddesses, I wanted him. Right now.

I grabbed for him, to pull his mouth to mine and his body to me, but he took hold of my hands and pushed them from his face, with a slow shake of his head.

"Cinder," he said, his voice thicker in a way that thrummed through me, "I need to…"

He bit the side of his lower lip as he looked up and down my body again, "I need to keep going."

Unsure what he meant, I sighed, letting my hands fall back from him like he wished.

"Good girl," he said, sending a fresh wave of buzzing through me.

Then he grabbed me roughly by the hips, making me yelp, and flipped me around so he could dry and massage my ass, too.

What was he doing to me?

My entire body turned into a molten, semi-solid hellfire

source as the scorching heat of his hands kneaded and rubbed and trailed along my skin.

A tug on my slip had me lifting my arms over my head so he could peel the sodden piece of fabric off me.

He flung it aside. It hit the wall and slumped down into a wadded pile. Before I could draw my attention back to him, he was running the wet towel up my back, over my shoulders to tickle the tops of my breasts, and down my arms. Repeating the process with the dry one.

But he didn't stop with drying me. No. He went back to rubbing, deep into the muscles of my ass, my breath coming faster.

Those hands. What could he do with those hands on me in the way I most wanted them to be?

But even as I luxuriated in his touch, his fingers, and his ministrations, they drove my need to new heights. I wanted him to stop so he could be with me. Inside me. Moving in me.

Grabbing my ass with his thumbs almost to my sex, he rubbed upward so that it stretched me right where I wanted him to be, and I moaned.

"Tristan," I said.

"Are you warm, Cinder?" he asked, coming just shy of doing it again, teasing me.

"Yes. But I want you to come here."

"Not yet."

"Please."

"I need to make you burn for me first."

"But I already am."

"Not yet. But you will."

Continuing up my back, he rubbed and loosened every muscle, setting fire to the blood in my veins until I thought I was as hot inside as he always was. That heat traveled through me, converging in the throbbing of my need for him.

When he got to my shoulders, and those hands began to rub down my arms I said, "Tristan, now."

"Not yet, my flame. Soon."

"Oh," I moaned, because I was already there, growing wetter by the second, an inferno building within me.

He turned me slowly to face him, his eyes, dilated and smoldering, brightened as he took in the look on my face.

I leaned toward him, but he tilted his head to the side and ran his fingers along my throat, "tsking" at me.

"What did I say?" he asked, that voice rumbling through me as I curled my toes against the floor and grew even wetter. "You need to wait, my Lady."

He untucked the bath sheet from his arm and finished drying off the front of me. The feel of the soft sheet against my raised nipples made me moan again, and he rewarded me with a languid smile.

Once I was finally dry, he continued his work on my muscles, rubbing and releasing all the tensions in my stomach muscles and my shoulders, saving my breasts for last.

While he turned me into a being of pure need and desire, I got to look at him, still breathtaking in his formals although he wasn't wearing shoes or hose now.

And when my perusal found his cock, so clear, and so restrained by those skintight pants, I knew he wanted me as much as I wanted him.

Looking me in the eye, he cupped one of my breasts, sending my breath into an uneven rhythm, and rubbing it roughly, kneading into the muscle underneath, repeating the process with the other breast.

I bit my lower lip and groaned when he flicked my nipple with his thumb while rubbing my breast.

"Now are you warm?" he asked. His voice was so quiet, just loud enough to make me want him inside me so desperately that wetness pooled at my sex. My body responded more to him than I ever had to anyone before.

"Yes."

He moved those hands down my abdomen to hold me by the hips, and I met his mouth in a crash of heat and tongue. It made me even wetter, so ready for him some of that wetness trickled down my leg in a thin line of need, marking the way.

Tristan broke the kiss, and I opened my eyes.

"Come here," I said, my voice rough, and his answering smile with his bottom lip between his teeth made me almost slam him to the floor so I could finally get my way.

"But I have something to do first," he said, turning us both around like we were one body, my ass coming up against the end of the large table. "Tonight, my Queen, I bow to you."

Taking both my hands, he brought his mouth to mine and guided me to grasp the table behind me.

When he pulled away from me again, I whimpered, and he grinned.

He got down on his knees, but what he was preparing to do, I didn't know. This wasn't part of any of the things I was taught.

Running those clever hands down from my hips, he tilted my legs apart, opening my wet sex to him.

Looking up at me, his grin grew even more wicked, and he licked that trail of wetness up my thigh.

CHAPTER 12

QUEEN

I gripped the table behind me like I wanted to break it in two as his wet, hot tongue made its way up the top of my thigh, stopping at the edge of my sex. I shuddered.

He closed his mouth and made the sound of someone consuming their favorite dessert, his eyes closed as he hummed.

"Tristan," I said, breathless and aching.

One hand on each thigh, he pushed them open further, exposing me more fully, and looked up at me.

"You have no idea how good you taste." He dipped his head and licked up the length of my sex, drawing a moan from me as my heat met his, and replaced my blood with hellfire water.

When he reached my clit, he tugged it into his mouth, grazing it against his teeth, and the muscles in my legs spasmed.

He grabbed me, taking my weight on his arms so my legs dangled over his shoulders and his grip tightened on my ass. And he devoured me, licking and sucking and stroking that spot of pure sensation.

Pressure built in every part of my body, my hands clenching on the table, my breathing frantic, every exhale turning into a moan, while my legs shook where they hung down his back.

Tilting my hips with his hands kneading my ass, stretching me that fraction that felt so good, he dove deeper, using his tongue to enter me, and I cried out.

"Oh, Tristan."

In and out of me, he used his tongue to drive me close to the edge, to leave me needing his cock inside me, and to make me wetter than I had ever been.

But just as I was at the verge of that exquisite shattering, he pulled his tongue out of me, licked up to my clit again, and surrounded it with his mouth, using his tongue to keep massaging it.

And I broke.

"Yes. Oh, Tristan, yes."

He didn't stop, sending me over that cliff, again and again, my cries growing louder and louder each time he drove me into pieces and my body pulled back together again. It left me wanting more and more.

"Tristan," I said, my voice plaintive.

Laying his cheek along my thigh, his lips still brushing against me as he looked up at me, in a voice so deep and rough it thrummed through me, he said, "What do you want, Cinder? Tell me what you want."

"You."

Closing his eyes like he was basking in the word, he hummed low in his throat and said, "I'm not done yet," before he returned his mouth to me, the rough humming vibrating against me.

Explosions went off in my body in wave after wave of pleasure. They ricocheted down my limbs, leaving me quaking.

Finally, he pulled his face away and dropped me down his chest as he stood up, so I had to wrap my hands around his neck alongside my knees while he grinned up at me and carried me across the room through an open door to a bed.

Putting me down slowly on the soft bed, I pulled his face to mine, our mouths crashing together, my legs wrapped around his back.

The taste of me was still on his lips and I wanted him inside me.

He was right.

I did taste good. Mixed with the taste of him in his kiss, it was divine.

Moving my legs from around his back, I pulled his pelvis to mine, his hard cock pressing against his tight pants and directly against the wet, waiting center of my need.

He groaned into my mouth and pulled away as I tried to grab him back.

Staring down at me, he unbuttoned his shirt with one hand, reaching down to rub my clit with his thumb and send me writhing as I neared the edge again.

"Come here, Tristan." He just grinned.

"You're beautiful. Maybe I should just stare at you for a while."

His words, the way he said them, his voice low and playing along my skin like I was a bow he strung himself, made me burn for him.

"But I want you. Now."

"And I want you forever," he said, pulling off his jacket and his shirt, exposing his archer's arms, shoulders, and chest.

Sleek along his stomach, the outline of abdominal muscles hinted under his skin and a vee of muscle disappeared into his pants. But it was his chest, the defined shoulders, and strong arms that I ran my hands along.

Leaning over me, holding himself up, he closed his mouth on mine, and my hands roamed across his body, taking in the canvas of his smooth, soft skin stretched over the strength of him. Until I dipped my hands low to his waist.

"Take them off," I said into his mouth, tugging at the waistband and the ties.

He smiled against my lips and pulled away, climbing off the bed to peel off his pants.

I propped myself up on my elbows, one knee bent and the other leg stretching to run my toes along his hip as he shoved the pants off the rest of the way.

When he stood, so did his cock, exactly as I fantasized when it was confined in those amazing pants.

Scrambling to my hands and knees as the first drops of his pleasure dripped down the head of him, I returned the favor, licking them up and staring up at him as I did.

He growled low in his throat, the sound sending me throbbing again as I took his cock into my mouth.

But he picked me up and laid me down on the bed, leaning over me and staring into my eyes, his shining bright gold with lines of hellfire green around dilated pupils.

"Cinder, were you listening?" he asked, and I grabbed for his shoulder, to pull him to me again. "Tonight, I bow to you."

"Tristan," I whined, "Please. I want you."

He kissed me, his tongue doing to my mouth what I wanted his cock to do to my sex. I pulled at him.

Situating himself between my legs, he rubbed his cock along my sex, the wetness letting it slide easily, spreading me open, ready for him. Rubbing against me, bringing me to the edge again, he kissed me, deep and hungry.

Finally, he pulled back from my lips when his cock was just at my entrance.

"I love you," he said.

"And I love you."

Sliding the tip in, finally, he kept his eyes locked on mine as my breath sped up, and I grasped at his shoulders.

Careful and slow, he moved into me as I stretched around him and moaned. The pressure of him against the walls inside me fed my need, but left me wanting more. All of him. Now.

"Yes," I said, "keep going."

"I don't want to hurt you."

"Please." He wouldn't hurt me, but even if he did, a small pain for a much greater pleasure was a better trade than pain ever was for me.

He didn't rush, but his mouth came down hard on mine, a shudder running through him that transferred to me when his tongue touched mine.

Everywhere I shook, unsure if it was my need or his driving us both to tremors.

Opening my legs further, I pressed my hips up, but he moved with me, denying me.

"We have time," he said into my mouth.

"But I want all of you."

"And I want to savor every second." His words danced along my lips, and I tried to hold myself back while he moved in small, exquisite increments.

Deliberate and careful, he made his way into me with small pushes that made me moan and grab his shoulders, digging my nails into him.

But before he got all the way in, while my body begged for more, he paused above me.

My eyes met his, met the desperate need I found there, mirroring my own.

"You are my Queen," he said, closing his eyes for a moment as I throbbed around him.

"And you are my King."

He slammed himself in the rest of the way, his hips pressing against my open thighs, and I broke around him again, screaming his name.

I rode the waves of my orgasm as he thrust into me, finally filling me the way I wanted him to. Needed him to.

When I died of pleasure and was born again as a being of pure, ceaseless need and want, he bent down and claimed my mouth with his.

My hands dug into his back, my legs wrapped around him, my feet pressed into his ass, urging him on.

Thrusting into me, again, and again, moaning into my cries, he drove me toward that edge again.

Every part of me quaked as he moved his mouth to my neck, matching the rhythm of our bodies with his tongue.

When he moaned into my skin as I throbbed around him, the sound alone made me arch my pelvis hard into his, and tangle my fingers in his hair.

He pulled back, pulling almost out of me. I whimpered, tugging at his shoulders to bring him back to me. But he stared at me until I stopped writhing and managed to focus on his eyes.

"Tell me what you want," he said.

"You. Now."

Thrusting himself deep inside me at the same time his mouth met mine, the tremors in my body turned into a buzzing in every part of me.

Kissing and driving me, he moved a hand to knead my breast and clamped his mouth down on my neck.

I shattered, spasming around him.

"Tristan," I yelled.

"Cinder," he moaned into my neck, meeting my orgasm with his own this time.

After he spilled the last drop of his pleasure, his cock pumping inside me along with the last waves of my undoing, he bent his head down again and closed his mouth on mine.

Our kiss was just as hungry, with so much desire it became reverence.

As if we were making the promise to worship at the temple of the other for the rest of our lives.

"My King," I whispered, because that was exactly my plan.

CHAPTER 13

WORSHIP

He curled around me after we climbed under the covers, his hands running languid circles on my stomach, and his mouth trailing kisses along the back of my neck.

"You've done that before," I whispered, running my fingers along the back of his hands as his kisses roused my need of him again.

"Does that bother you?" he asked, pausing in his affections.

"No. I'm glad of it. How else would you have learned?"

His laugh was a low rumbling in his chest. But then his laughter died in his throat, and he went too still.

"Cinder, I want you to know, none of them meant what you do. None of them even knew who I was, and I…It wasn't always a good choice."

"Are there any baby Tristans out there I should know about?" I asked, threading my fingers through his so he would know, no matter the answer, I was still here. If the answer was yes, then we should make sure that was known. An heir to the throne was a good thing. If the answer was no, nothing was changed from our first kiss.

"No. I've been drinking the tea every morning for years, and was before I ever thought to hide my identity and go to random taverns as far as I could ride in a day from the palace."

I rolled over in his arms, looking into his eyes in the now dim room, lit only by a light through the door.

"Do you mind that I can say the same thing?" I asked, rushing on to explain. "That I've made choices, too, at taverns. And a long time ago I took the root." I put a hand to his cheek and held my breath while I waited for his answer, not knowing what he expected of me. Did he expect the sexual equivalent of the eighteen-year-old noble girls presented at court?

"How else would you have learned?" He gave my words back to me, and lowered his mouth to mine.

Tristan's kiss held every bit of the love and adoration I felt for him, and I tangled my fingers into the hair at the nape of his neck as I slipped a leg up over his hip, finding his body as ready as mine was.

"It doesn't matter what we've done to get here," he whispered, running his hand along my back, "I never want to be anywhere but with you from here on out."

"You have all of me, for the rest of my life," I answered truthfully.

He buried his face in my neck before he opened his mouth and began to kiss and suck at the sensitive skin there.

Pushing my sex against his hard cock, he rumbled a groan into my skin and grabbed my ass, making me draw in a sharp breath.

But his hands softened on me, even as he kept me pressed against him, and he looked into my eyes as if he was searching for something.

Staring back at him, one hand tangled in his hair, I put my other hand to his cheek and tried to let him see into my heart, see himself there, as clear as a sigil and as beautiful as his eyes.

He sucked in a breath and kissed me, soft, and tender.

"I love you, Cinder."

"I love you, Tristan."

Then he grinned and tossed me onto my back to loom above me, kneeling between my legs.

"Come here," I begged, reaching for him.

"No, I told you. Not tonight." His grin had that wicked edge to it again, and it made me throb for him, my need growing.

"More bowing?" A giggle broke through my lips as I smiled back, just thinking about it making me writhe.

He shook his head, slow, as he gazed along my body and returned his eyes to mine.

"Now I worship."

Waking up after making love to him again, I was greeted by the hot touch of his fingers dancing along my back, and the weight and warmth of his body lying alongside mine.

"Mmm," I mumbled, a smile blooming on my face.

"Cinder," he said, his voice tender, sounding as if he found me in the cellar with a wound again.

Popping my eyes open, the first thing I saw was his hair mussed up in a way that made the night before flash through my mind, and a shiver run down my spine.

But the second was his face, his jaw clenched tight, his eyes brightest green, and his brow low.

I lifted my head from the pillow, dread pooling in my gut.

"Tristan, what's wrong?" Did he regret last night? Regret me?

"Who did this?" He turned those raging eyes on mine. "And don't tell me they were all from training accidents."

Looking down my side as he traced a barely-there touch from my back, down my ribs, I saw the first morning sun had lit up my faded scars. They shined as if they were made of some iridescent magic instead of skin.

Training accidents. He didn't believe my story about Ash's last beating, but he didn't push me to explain that. Just these.

Easy in theory, but...

"Madam makes me a bath that fades all my old scars. They're from a long time ago." Before Ash learned not to scar up his 'investment' and began to use his fists.

His eyes found mine and his hand found my face, brushing the hair back from my new stitches with a touch as soft as a rose petal.

"Are they from the last war?" His voice was hushed but held some kind of threat in it that I couldn't place.

I nodded, not bothering to explain how they were connected, and yet not from the war itself. Most of them occurred near the same time anyway.

Squeezing his eyes shut, a tremor ran through him, and he bent his head to kiss along the scars on my back. As light as the dawn, his lips trailed along my skin where the scars wrapped around my ribs.

"Fucking Amethyst bastards started that war for fucking hellfire water, and did this to you, and I can't kill them." His voice was heavy, each word clipped short like he was cutting them off instead of the heads he wanted to, his breath on my skin sending a shiver down my body. "They're right here in the damn castle and deserve to die."

The hand he braced himself with was near my face, and he gripped the sheets with white knuckles.

Amethyst monarchs started that war for hellfire water, not Tristan's parents. Ash…had to know that. He had to because he would have been briefed about the possibility of a remaining direct threat to Lehar once he became the Duke. It wasn't a misunderstanding. Ash…lied to me.

Rolling over, I stared at him, pain and fury all over his face.

Mine probably looked the same, but watching him hurt on my behalf chased my own ghosts of the past to a corner of my brain I could deal with later. I needed to comfort him first.

I grabbed him and pulled his lips to mine.

Gentle and tender, his kiss made me never want to leave him. Not in life, and not in the death I planned either.

"One day you won't have to think about Amethyst at all except as just another country bordering ours," I said, knowing there was only one way to make that true now.

"What really happened when you were hurt so badly in Lehar?"

There it was. Apparently, he was going to ask me about it after all.

My body went rigid.

"I…" Oh, Gods and Goddesses, how was I going to talk to him about this and not ruin everything? "I don't want to lie to you."

"You can tell me anything."

Smiling, I put a hand to his face and swallowed, knowing that wasn't true.

"But you can't kill everyone," I said.

His eyes grew even brighter, and he squeezed them shut, touching his blazing hot forehead to mine.

"Gods help the person that hurt you, because they won't find it in this life. Please tell me," he said, his voice barely more than a low growl now.

"No, Tristan," I pulled my head back, but kept my hand on his cheek as he leaned into it, "look at me."

Opening his eyes, I would have sworn the green in them moved as his pupils turned into pinpricks.

"If I can't kill the people who hurt you, what kind of king am I? I can't even punish the people who attack the one I love the most."

"You're the kind of king who does the smart thing and knows the one who loves him can look out for herself when she has to." I could look out for him, too. He already knew that. But I couldn't be mad that he wanted to protect me. Not when I wanted the same. "*And* you're the kind of king who knows that at some point you're going to have to talk me out of killing someone because they say the wrong thing to you."

At that, he finally smiled, shutting his eyes and sighing. His whole body relaxed against me, and a shudder ran through him.

"How did you do that?" he asked, opening his now hazel eyes and kissing me.

"Do what?" But I smiled back and played with his hair.

Tristan sat up, scooping me up along with him and wrapping his arms around me. He placed me on the bed facing him, and reached behind himself to pull a box from the bedside table.

"My council wants me to wait until after the war is over, until after we can stop worrying about attack from two countries at once, but I want you to know…"

He opened the little box. Inside was a Dragon King sigil ring, but this one had Lehar's flames on the sides.

I sucked in a breath, and my heart hammered in my chest. Pressure built at the back of my eyes, and I couldn't stop a tear from escaping down my cheek.

"Please be my Queen." His voice, raw and thin, matched the feeling ricocheting through me, leaving me undone in its wake.

Looking up into those eyes I loved no matter what color they were, my plan for my future melted as I realized I didn't want to let him go.

His face softened, and, instead of the rage I woke up to, love poured from him.

I couldn't tell him no.

"Will you be my wife, my Fighter, my flame? My Hellfire Dragon Queen?"

"Yes, Tristan."

His smile outshone the sun rising above the sea behind him, and turned the cold waters into a mirror of pure and perfect light.

Slipping the ring on my finger, he claimed my mouth with his, and I claimed his heart for my own.

Maybe, if there wasn't any Dragon power in the crown anymore, there could at least be a warrior Queen and her archer King. And maybe, just maybe, together we could be what was best to protect Onyx.

Our kiss deepened and his hands started touching me with purpose, my body thrilling with every brush of his fingers.

But a knock interrupted any repeats we might have had of the night before.

"King Tristan," General Pace said from the other side of the door.

He put his face to my neck, and growled his frustration.

"Go," I whispered, "I'm always yours."

Smiling wide, he said, "Yes, you are—as I'm yours," kissed me on the forehead, and climbed from the bed, throwing a robe on as he left the room.

I flopped back onto the covers and grinned at the ceiling even as my brain argued with itself.

Agreeing to be Queen wasn't in my plan. It didn't even make sense.

But to spend a lifetime with him, loving him, having him love me...it was a dream I never thought to have.

He opened the door and brought me a bundle of clothes, biting his lip on a smile.

"What is this?" I asked as he handed me the little pile.

"Madam Valentin sent the General to lead you back to your room and pretend as if we all had an early morning meeting about the guard." His brows rose while he explained until he couldn't hold it in anymore, and he broke into loud laughter.

I covered my face with my hands, and looked at him through my fingers.

"Good to know you think it's funny that she's going to kill me," I said, but I laughed with him, and he kissed me as he pulled me from the bed.

The first thing I picked up was another bustier, this one

black leather with the dragon sigil embossed on it. A little packet fell out when I held it up in front of me.

I picked it up and bent over laughing.

"What?" Tristan asked, plucking it out of my outstretched fingers. "Is this what I think it is?"

"Yes."

Madam sent us a packet of the tea men drank every morning to stop pregnancies.

"Subtle," he said, and I gave up trying to stand at all, collapsing entirely into a puddle of laughter on the bed.

CHAPTER 14
QUESTION

Running my hand through my sea salt stiffened hair again, hoping I had managed to make it even remotely less mussed, General Pace cut her eyes to mine while we walked down the hall.

"I see your portion of the meeting went well," she said.

"Yes, very," I said, and had to bite my lip to tamp down my grin.

"Well, when we see anyone else, you need to try to be just as murderous as before, okay? None of them need to know about you losing your edge."

"Losing my…" My feet stuttered a step, and I had to focus to answer her. "Anyone who thinks that I would now be *less* likely to kill to protect my King would understand their mistake as they bled out on the floor."

"Good," she said, and I peeked at her out of the corner of my eye. Was that a test?

"Do you doubt me?" I whispered.

"No. But I have protected him most of his life. Protecting his heart is no different."

"I'm in love with him."

"That's not the issue." She raised a brow, still staring straight ahead.

Pulling the sigil ring from where it was nestled against my breast in my bustier, I showed it to the General.

Her eyes widened, and she lost a step.

I tucked it away again where it remained a secret from all the people who weren't yet ready to know.

"So, you said yes?"

Unable to help myself, I smiled and thought about Tristan's face as he asked me.

"General, have you ever been able to say no to him?"

At that, she grinned and slapped a hand on my shoulder, shaking her head.

"Damn, I'm happy about that. You had me worried."

"Why were you worried I would say no after all that's happened? You know I love him."

"Yes." She dropped her hand, and the smile lost a part of its shine. "But I know what it is to be a warrior, and think you need to distance yourself for their protection."

My heart ached.

All that time I tortured myself over whether I would be a good queen, whether I would be good *for* him while negating how good I would be *to* him…she felt it all, too.

I didn't know who she was talking about. But it was someone.

Someone she was clearly still in love with.

"Have you told them you regret that decision?" I asked, my voice a strangled hush.

A quick glance was the only answer I got. And the only one I needed.

"You should. If I can be queen for the one I love, anything can happen."

General Pace swallowed and raised her chin, but she didn't speak again as we made our way to my rooms.

When we got to the door, she swung it opened and stepped to the side, allowing me to walk into range of my friends and Madam Valentin first.

"Thanks for that," I muttered as I passed her, and one corner of her mouth twitched like she was thinking about smiling.

On the other side of the door, Madam stood at the window, her arms crossed, staring at me.

Did she wait there the entire time General Pace was getting me?

"General, please come in and shut the door," Madam said, her voice impossible to read.

I couldn't even tell if there was a threat in it, and that was usually my specialty.

The door clicked shut. Madam opened her mouth, but Jacquetta stepped into the room and said, "Gus and I would like to speak with Cinder."

"Lady Cinder and I need to have a discussion first," Madam said, still staring at me.

"No, Mom. We all need to have this discussion. Together. But Gus and I need to talk to her first." Jacquetta stood her ground, and out Madamed her mother.

Part of me wanted to cheer for Jacquetta, for the steel in her spine. But the rest of me wanted to turn around and run back to Tristan, so I could pretend that I wasn't about to get in a lot of trouble with other people I loved.

With the bright sun of the morning shining on half of the dark skin of Madam's face, highlighting her facial structure in a way that made me fully understand the idea of sun-kissed, Madam finally nodded.

But I wanted to stay in this place, where the whole of the world was just a little more beautiful and no one tried to make me sad about finding something so good.

They all headed into Gus' room, leaving me to trail after them, my shoulders folding in a fraction and my eyes finding the floor.

Madam and the General stood by the table, silent sentries to watch over whatever was about to happen.

Jacquetta went to Gus' bed and sat down beside the careful pile of pillows propping Gus up, threading their fingers together.

"So…" Gus said, the word prolonged, and her voice leading like I would know what to say to that.

"How was he?" Jacquetta asked, breaking into a grin while the rest of them cracked up laughing.

I whirled back and forth, looking between them all.

Gus and Jacquetta I had seen laugh a thousand times, but I didn't know Madam and General Pace knew how to laugh as hard as they were.

Both of them looked so different, I couldn't process it, and the General's laugh was a loud bursting, barking of air that made me look at her twice.

"Wait…" I said, holding up a hand, replaying what Gus and Jacquetta said. "What in the hellfire?"

This wasn't real. It couldn't be real.

"Cinder, we saw you in the bed in the tent, the way you were snuggled up to him," Gus said, shaking her head. Even some of her weariness lessened, and she looked like she felt better than she had since her injuries.

"It was only a matter of time," Jacquetta said, sharing a private look with Gus that made them both softer, sweeter, and blunted the edges on their teasing.

"Honestly," Madam said, taking a seat at the table, her back as straight as ever, even as she smiled and dabbed away tears from the corners of her eyes, "if you two did not figure yourselves out soon, the General and I were going to set something up."

"What she thought we could set up," General Pace said, shaking her head and leaning her elbows on the back of a chair, "I still don't know."

Collapsing onto a chair myself, I laughed and shook my head, still wondering that these people, these strangers not that long ago, were people I could even have this conversation with.

"So," Gus said, wiggling her eyebrows, "how was it?"

"Uh…" Was she serious? Was I supposed to regale them with all the details?

"Just tell us whether he made your pleasure a focus or not," Madam said, shaking her head and smiling at Gus.

Thinking about how much he did just that made heat rush to my cheeks, and I couldn't make eye contact with any of them anymore.

"Oh no," Jacquetta said, "he didn't, did he? Well, I'll just have to have a chat with our King."

"No, no," I said, waving my hands and grinning so much my cheek hurt, "he did. Um…"

"Cinder," Gus said, "just because you liked the same parts that he did doesn't mean he made you a focus."

"He did, though." I had no idea how to explain. "Fine, okay? He, um, well, there was this thing he did with his mouth and…"

"Well, well," Gus said, those eyebrows wiggling again and a huge smile on her face. "Good for him."

Jacquetta leaned over and whispered something in Gus' ear that made Gus blush from her neck to her hairline. Gus whispered back to Jacquetta, her lips brushing along Jacquetta's earlobe softly, and Jacquetta squirmed, pointing her toes and rubbing one leg along the other.

My mouth started to fall open as I slowly realized how much I needed to have a private conversation with my friends.

How long had that been going on? And where was I while it was happening?

"I'm proud of him," General Pace said, smiling with a far-off look in her eyes before she turned her focus to me and raised a brow.

"There's more," I said.

"Really?" Jacquetta asked, leering.

"Yes," I said, shaking my head and rolling my eyes, "but not about that. I mean, there is more about that, but you don't need those details right now."

"We absolutely do need those details right now," Gus said.

"No," Madam said, eyes wide, "no, we do not."

"But this…" I said, pulling the ring from my bustier.

Screams.

Jacquetta and Gus screamed. Jacquetta leapt off the bed and ran to me, wrapping me in a hug.

Madam clapped her hands, laughing and shaking her head at us, while the General just smiled.

"Queen Cinder," Jacquetta yelled.

"Shhh," I waved my hands in the air, and tried to think if there was anyone staying in the rooms right next to ours. "We can't tell anyone. Not until the threat is over."

"Right," Gus said from the bed, and Jacquetta sighed.

"But I want everyone to know you're the Queen," Jacquetta said. "So many people would feel better knowing that he's chosen you and not the Marquessa."

She crinkled her nose up at "Marquessa." Even though I wasn't sure people would feel better, I knew I was thrilled no snake would sit on an Onyx throne.

"Not yet," I said.

The room turned into discussions of weddings, war, and wishes for one day.

While I was stuck in what Jacquetta said.

Some people would feel better, yes.

Probably the people who spoke of me as if my fighting was anything more than what the guard did. The guard were the ones who really protected us.

But…how would Ash feel? What would Ash *do*?

He already attacked the Obsidian Palace, killed Fiachra, and started a war. I wasn't sure if he sent Brix or not. My brother was still a massive problem.

And before any of that happened, before the dreams came true and Tristan and I could say we were safe, I had at least one more person to kill. While I was at it, I might be able to get some information.

"General Pace," I asked, while everyone else was talking of other things.

"Yes?" she asked, turning away from listening to them to focus on me.

"The prisoner that hurt us, I would like to be there for his interrogation."

Her eyes narrowed on me, "Only if you can keep from killing him before it's his time. We need some answers from him."

I nodded, not trusting myself to speak the lie out loud.

Brix and I would see each other up close again soon. This time I would be armed, and allowed to torture him.

My smile grew.

Accidents during torture were understandable. And from the beginning, my kills almost always looked like accidents.

"She destroyed it," Jacquetta said, her nose scrunched up like she smelled something bad.

"A few extra conditioning treatments and it will be fine," Gus said from the bed, braiding something out of fine strands of thread, trying to keep her hand working even as her arm was immobilized while it healed.

"I'm right here," I said, sitting at the vanity while Jacquetta worked on getting my hair recovered from the saltwater disaster I made of it. Even a bath and her treatments didn't entirely help.

"Yes, you are," she said, leaning around my shoulder to give me a look like her mother would. "And you're not going to go on the outside walls again. If you want time with him, walk down a hall like a normal person."

I grinned and shook my head, unable to keep a smile from my face every time Tristan came up.

"So…" I said, holding out the word, thinking of smiles and love, "is there something you two want to tell me now that Madam is out of the room?"

Jacquetta's eyes got big, and she bit her lip on her smile.

"Wait," Gus said, her hands going still on the thread and her gaze jumping from Jacquetta to me and back, "you know?"

"Did you think I wouldn't eventually figure it out? We're together all the time." I still couldn't understand how I didn't see it until now. Thinking back on it, there were little things along the way that I didn't even question. I should have been aware that my best friends were falling in love. It made me feel like I was a self-absorbed, bad friend.

"Yeah, but," Jacquetta said, smiling at Gus and ducking her head, "you've been a little distracted."

"Not too distracted for this. I'm happy for you. You've helped me, celebrated things with me, been upset for me. I want to be there for you, too." Although how I was supposed to do that for both of them, I wasn't sure. I wanted the chance to figure it out.

"I was going to tell you before we became real Ladies," Gus said, laughing when I pulled back my head and my mouth dropped open.

"That could take a long time. We don't know how long this war will go on for." What was she thinking? I needed to know long before then.

"Well, I didn't want to draw your focus away. And when we're made real Ladies, you need to know we'll share a title and estates." Gus said it as if they had discussed it many times, but Jacquetta sucked in a breath and held a shaking hand to her mouth.

"Gus?" Jacquetta whispered.

Oh, Gods and Goddesses, was this happening right now?

I hugged my arms around myself, and the world started to swim as my eyes grew thick with tears.

"Jacquetta," Gus said, "Star, can you look in that box your mother brought in right over there?" She pointed to a large box on the table as she set aside the threads in her hands, never taking her eyes off Jacquetta as she walked on stiff legs to do as Gus asked.

Part of me didn't think I should be there, witnessing one of the most intimate things they could do, something they would remember forever. But the rest of me was so thankful I got to see them this happy.

When she opened the box, Jacquetta laughed, that beautiful ringing laugh, and I understood exactly why Gus called her a star.

Gus closed her eyes, everything about her softening and glowing as she smiled and basked in her star's heavenly laugh.

Jacquetta pulled a smaller box shaped like a shooting star out of the larger plain one, its paint a shining, opalescent white.

"Bring it over here," Gus said, her voice soft with a tiny tremor in it that made the tears in my eyes impossible to hold back.

On shaking legs, with her breath hitching even as she smiled wide, Jacquetta brought it over to Gus.

"A star?" Jacquetta asked, her voice soft. "Gus."

"You're my star. You're what I thought about while I was down there. You're what I wished on. You kept me alive." Gus took one of Jacquetta's hands with her good one and brought it to where she could wrap both of hers around it.

Kept her alive. I almost choked on my own tears, and had to take deep breaths so I didn't interrupt them.

"Gus," Jacquetta said, "I love you. You saved me. I'm sorry I hid. I should have saved you before they took you. Fought for you." Jacquetta leaned forward and put her forehead to Gus' good shoulder.

"Shhh. You did save me. Please believe me, you did." Gus kissed Jacquetta's cheek, and pain for them rocketed through my heart.

In all the time since we got out of that cellar, I had not asked Gus and Jacquetta for the details of how she was taken. I didn't think they mattered. I was so wrong.

They struggled with this the whole time, and I had no idea.

"Jacquetta," Gus said, pulling her face back and smiling at her, "open it."

Gus bit her lip and swallowed hard as Jacquetta pulled back, nodded, and opened the shooting star box.

She let out a sob through her smile and Gus beamed.

"Will you be my star forever?" Gus asked.

"Forever." Jacquetta leaned forward and kissed Gus, putting the box down on the bed between them, and tangling her hands in Gus' hair, raising one knee up onto the bed.

Gus put her hand to Jacquetta's face and kissed her back in a way that told me what was in the box, even though I didn't see it.

A few moments later, they broke apart, but whispered to each other's lips things meant to stay between only them.

I dropped my gaze down to my lap, wiping the tears from my cheeks, giving them at least some privacy for this, for whatever things they said that were only for each other.

"Oh, they're beautiful," Jacquetta said, loud enough I knew it was safe to go see inside the box and congratulate them.

Jumping up from my seat and running to them, I careened into Jacquetta, almost knocking her over since she only had one leg down on the floor.

They both laughed with me as I hugged them and cried some more, unable to form words.

"See, Cinder? One estate, one title," Gus said, beaming at Jacquetta.

"No," I said, shaking my head as they both furrowed their brows at me.

"You can get married tomorrow, and I will still give you two estates and two titles. You more than earned them putting up with me, and you can do whatever you want with them, have your families live in one and you in the other. Whatever you want."

Jacquetta had tears flowing down her face again, too, and Gus nodded as she swiped away her own.

"Let me see the ring," I said, more than a little curious what kind of ring they would have when there weren't sigils to consider. At home, most people didn't have rings at all. Those that did kept them simple bands.

"Oh," Jacquetta said, wiping her cheeks and handing me the box, "there is more than one ring."

I looked inside to find two sigil rings nestled within. One in the star side, and the other in the shooting side.

The sigils on them matched, but they weren't anything I had ever seen before.

"What am I looking at? A shooting star over a flower?" I looked up at them as they grinned at each other, complete devotion on their faces.

"Yes," Jacquetta said.

"It's us," Gus said.

And they were one of the most beautiful things I had ever seen.

CHAPTER 16

SIGIL

"Madam has made some…interesting choices lately," I said, looking at myself in the mirror, turning from side to side to inspect the whole of my outfit, still shocked by the back.

"She is making a statement with each one," Gus said, her face quirked up like she was trying to avoid looking and failing. "But damned if I know what this is saying besides everyone wants to have sex with me."

"Everyone, Gus?" Jacquetta asked, one brow high.

"Oh, Star, please," Gus said, shaking her head and gesturing wildly, "I'm madly in love with you, and think you're the most beautiful woman to ever live. But look at her ass! You would take a bite if given the chance."

"And that's my cue to change these pants," I said, looking at the line of skin showing between the laces that held the pants together up the backs of both legs.

"No," Jacquetta said, laughing, and pointing me back to my seat, "you will keep those pants on, and all of us will only hope your presence at this meeting makes Prince Nevan screw up while not distract King Tristan too much."

I groaned and slumped back into the chair so she could put the finishing touches on my hair.

"Prince Nevan will be awful, and if Tristan or I have to kill him, we'll be at war with two countries. Why didn't she just have the pants lace up my legs? Why did they have to lace all the way up my ass?" This was a very bad plan.

"King Tristan won't kill him," Jacquetta said, tucking a dragon-shaped silver clasp into the braid at the side of my head. "If anything, the two of them can bond over their joint marveling that the ties don't cut into you because your ass is so hard."

"Can we all stop talking about my ass?" I put my hands over my eyes as they both laughed again.

"I really don't think we can right now," Gus said.

Every single dress I wore in the palace seemed designed to soften my muscles and the look of my body, to make me seem more like my mother had been, more like many of the other noblewomen I knew. Many were strong, trained and accomplished in something related to warfare like my mother was, but most of them had a life outside of that pursuit. And they didn't tend to climb things.

Now, though, it seemed like every outfit Madam had commissioned for me to wear as Fighter Cinder at the front of the war was designed to make my body more intimidating, enhance my musculature, and make me look even deadlier.

Prince Nevan said I looked like a Goddess of Death. This would do nothing to make him think otherwise.

"At least the armored chest piece finally covers my heart," I said, admiring the shining silver panel of metal that was once again formed to my breasts, but this time went up in a sweeping arch to just under my collarbones.

"She probably thought it would be too much for everyone to ask you to turn around constantly so they could get both views," Gus said, wiggling her brows.

Jacquetta lost it laughing and bent forward, bracing herself on the vanity while I growled.

"This is not funny," I said, shaking my head.

"You have been wrong before, Cinder," Jacquetta said, through her giggles, "but never more wrong than right now. This is hilarious."

Shoving myself to a standing position and glaring at both of them while I tried to fight my smile, I left the room, putting my hands over the exposed parts of my ass, their laughter trailing after me.

Leave it to my friends to make me walk out toward my duties even though I didn't want to, simply by making fun of the clothes I had to wear.

But all these clothes kept coming, and I needed to make sure Madam stopped. She couldn't keep spending her money on me. Not for stupid clothes. Her trade business had to have taken a hit from the war. I didn't know when I would be made queen and be allowed to pay her back.

There was no way Ash was still paying for everything…was he? Did he really think I would still kill Tristan?

Making my way to the meeting room, voices floating out to me in murmured tones, I knocked and shoved open the door.

General Pace and Tristan both straightened from where they bent over another table, inspecting a piece of parchment. He was dressed in his formals again, except he had flat shoes on this time, and the lace was in a dragon pattern.

Looking at him in those impeccable clothes took my breath away.

"Cinder," Tristan said, his face softening and a smile blooming, "come in and look at this. Shut the door please."

I did as he asked, looking past him to the parchment, my mind going blank as I took in the purple sigil stamped on it. It was the same sigil I found in Lord Fall's desk drawer, the one I didn't recognize.

"This sigil," General Pace said, pointing at it as Tristan slipped his arm around me and kissed me on the temple, "have you seen it before? Neither of us recognize it."

How could I explain where I found it without letting them know why I was there in the first place?

"Once," I said, deciding they needed to know. No matter how thin my excuses would be if they checked into my story.

Tristan turned to look more closely at me while General Pace just raised a brow.

"My cousin, Solaria, was married to Lord Fall of Thirteen Rivers Valley." They both nodded, and I tried to make my voice sound neutral. "Visiting once, I saw a stamp for wax with that sigil sitting next to the stamp of the Valley. I didn't think anything of it at the time. I didn't know it was purple."

"Could it be something that Amethyst just left during the last war?" Tristan asked, shaking his head and chewing on his lip as he studied it further.

"No," General Pace said, "this isn't a sigil from any lands I know of in the Amethyst kingdom."

"But it's purple, so it would likely be connected to them," I said, looking closer at the letter, trying to read between the lines of mundane reports about the weather and the wind patterns.

"And that's my concern," Tristan said, his fingers running along the lines at the back of my top in idle patterns as if he did it to avoid drumming his fingers on the table.

"Where did you find it?" I asked, leaning forward a bit more.

"It was in that house," Tristan said, his voice soft as if he was trying to make mention of the situation less of a blow.

But it wasn't what happened there that made my body freeze and the blood slow in my veins.

What happened there made my heart ache, yes. Every day, a thousand times, the thought of little Angeline came to me, and tore open the wound deep inside my soul that formed when I knew I couldn't save her.

This, though, the sigil in front of me, on paper found there, made every alarm in my body go off because there was a connection, a direct line, from that place to the last time I saw the sigil.

My brother.

I gave Ash the stamp with the unknown sigil on it.

Did he give it to Brix?

Did he endorse what Brix did there? Was he working with the Corvids even though Brix said he wasn't?

Looking at the words of the letter again, it wasn't addressed to anyone, and there was no signature on it, just the stamp. But there was something…

Sucking in a breath, my hand shaking, I pointed to the message.

"This isn't right," I said, my voice thin.

"What isn't?" General Pace leaned in further, her eyes narrowed.

"Dark clouds collect on the sea," I read the line from the letter out loud, "but winds also blow from Thirteen Rivers Valley toward the coast. They may cause a storm converging in Bridgeton."

Tristan made a sound, deep and angry in his throat and the General's eyes narrowed.

"Winds don't flow from Thirteen Rivers Valley toward the coast," he said.

"No," the General said, although with her breathless voice and the way her face crumpled, she may as well have agreed with him.

It looked like a letter about nothing more than the weather. The beginning of it included actual reports of recent flooding in one of the southernmost duchies of Onyx. And then, when we just glossed over the words because they seemed meaningless, they hid the real message.

My brother and I used the same kind of tricks to hide things in our messages to each other when we needed to write. I swallowed, and even Tristan's warmth next to me couldn't chase away the ice that flowed through my veins.

"The dark clouds are the Corvids," Tristan said, his hand on my hip curling in to press me more firmly against his side.

"And who are the winds coming the other direction?" the General asked.

"It doesn't matter," I said, wrapping my arm around Tristan and holding on tight. "Whoever they are, we need to handle it, and send a regimen of the guard out there to coordinate with Solaria. She needs to know that there could be forces hidden in her lands that want to do Onyx harm."

They nodded and started to make plans.

But I lied.

It did matter.

Especially if those forces were somehow connected to Ash, and my brother was more traitor than even I knew.

No matter how much I loved Tristan and how much he believed in me, what were the chances he would ever crown a traitor's sister Queen?

CHAPTER 17

ENTICING

By the time the Chamberlain arrived with the Amethyst group in tow, we had decided on a course of action we hoped would stave off whatever threat was amassing in the Valley. And I was trying to find a way to convince them to send me there, too, after I killed Brix.

If my brother was involved in this, I needed to know. I needed the chance to talk him out of it. The last time he got involved, it landed us in this war. He had to see that anything else would be bad for the country, for Lehar, too.

I stood just to the side of Tristan, the General to the other, and the entire room was lined with guards, some of whom I trained. The ones I knew did a double take when they saw me, their eyes going to the stitches in my face before anything else.

The Amethysts filed into the room, the Second Prince coming in last.

His look at Tristan was dismissive at best, his glance at the General barely there, and he avoided looking at the Chamberlain who was staring daggers at the Marquessa.

But when Nevan's eyes landed on me, it was like a physical

weight. A slimy, full body, recoil-inducing thing that reached beyond my clothes to dirty my skin.

I kept myself still and straight under the pressure, but my hands inched closer to the spikes strapped to my thighs.

He grinned and I glowered, only making his grin widen.

"My apologies on being tardy," Nevan said, looking back to Tristan who was as taught as a bow ready to fire under his finery as he watched Nevan's response to me, "we received reports from one of our merchant ships that more Corvid ships left dock in the last week. Of course, it took a while for that information to find us. I hope it isn't coming too late."

"No, thank you for the intelligence," Tristan said, waving a hand to a guard who stepped forward and took his whispered order before darting out the door.

"I like the scar, Fighter Cinder," Nevan said, one corner of his mouth turning up. "Although, it is a pity you didn't just leave it."

Tristan's hands, folded together at the small of his back, curled into fists.

"Second Prince Nevan," I said, trying to be as dismissive as humanly possible, "if you are going to focus on my looks for this entire meeting, I am sure my King can find something more important for me to do. Someone to kill, maybe."

He gave me a wry grin and dipped his head, holding his hands up as if he were giving up commenting. Not for one second did I trust him, but I held my tongue for now.

"Yesterday you made a request that I think it fair to say is out of the question," Tristan said, gesturing for everyone to take a seat at the chairs around the table.

They all sat, although I remained standing again, just behind and to the side of Tristan.

"If it is out of the question," Prince Nevan said, that carefully crafted facade pointed at Tristan with an almost lazy expression, "perhaps we should return to Amethyst, and declare our backing of Corvid."

"So, you have no other requests?" General Pace asked in her most reserved way, which didn't even give *me* any hints as to what she was thinking. To the Amethysts, she probably seemed like talking to a brick wall. "That seems like an exceptionally bad negotiating strategy."

"Not bad, just clear." Nevan looked at me as he leaned back in his chair, that calculation behind his eyes clear even as he tried to hide it by leering. "You must know that the most enticing thing Onyx has to offer comes from Lehar."

Tristan's hands tightened on the arms of his chair.

Nevan didn't mean me. That was obvious. He was an Amethyst snake who was baiting my King, waiting for Tristan to make a move and his chance to strike.

Leaning forward, a muscle in his jaw jumping and his hands gripping the chair even tighter, Tristan was going to let this snake win if he reacted, damn it.

I couldn't let him.

Stepping forward in one swift move, I slammed my hands onto the table and leaned right into Nevan's face.

His purple eyes widened, and his leer turned into actual fear for a moment, one lock of his hair, right in front, turned pale.

"During the last war," I whispered, my voice as sharp as my spikes, "my parents died protecting Lehar from Amethyst scum."

The flash of fear came again in those violet eyes, but he looked down at the table and avoided my gaze.

I leaned in further, across the corner of the table, "Their bodies were turned to ashes along with everything else, and if you think for one minute I wouldn't gladly feed anyone who tried to take those lands from my family to the fires still burning, you're a fool."

"Fighter Cinder," the General finally snapped like she was

giving me an order, although what she was really doing was telling me I no longer needed to rub Nevan's face in his own miscalculation.

Shoving myself off the table, standing straight, I took two steps back to my previous position, and stared down my nose at the Prince.

Tristan turned in his seat, but the look on his face wasn't anger, or even frustration at what I did. Printed in his eyes was a smoldering flame of desire before he turned around again.

He saw my pants.

"My condolences, Fighter Cinder," Nevan said with a swallow and a glance up at me that I almost took to be sincerity, even as that pale lock of hair turned back to match the rest. "Please understand, I was instructed to make that request because the power of hellfire water along with the wealth it generates is attractive to many outside your country."

There it was again. The suggestion that Lehar should be a wealthy duchy. So many people made that assumption, and I didn't understand it. Since the explosion, since Ash became Duke, he said the trade of hellfire water didn't generate enough funds to keep everyone well provided for.

Every bit of the funds I made from my hired-out kills went to Ash for him to use for our people. But all the people outside our lands thought we were wealthy…how?

"Pick something else," Tristan said. "Fighter Cinder's people have suffered far too much in the last war with your country for them to ever accept what you are suggesting."

"And that is ignoring the fact that while a member of your family is hoping to become a ruler of this country," the Chamberlain said, "to be its Queen, it would not be a good way to start off that rule to ransom a portion of the country."

Marquessa Ziya let out a whoosh of a breath as if the Chamberlain's words hit her in the chest, and stared down at the table in front of her while her hair grew even more blanched of color.

Good. She could blame herself for her eventual dismissal.

"Ransom is too strong a word." Nevan shook his head, swallowing again and slowly regaining his posturing. "It was simply a starting point for negotiations."

"Then we should discuss something else," Tristan said.

"Understood." Prince Nevan pursed his lips and looked down at the table for a moment. "Do you mind if Fighter Cinder and Marquessa Ziya leave us?"

Ziya pulled her head back, her mouth falling open, and I had never understood her more.

Tristan turned toward me. Before he could tell me to go, I stepped around the side of the table and made my way toward the door.

As I walked to the door, Nevan coughed, the Chamberlain made a long hissing intake of breath, and some of the Amethyst nobles whispered to each other.

"Ladies," Tristan called as I swung open the door.

I turned halfway around, some of the faces around the table were red, others averted their eyes.

"Do not go far, please," Tristan said, making eye contact with me.

Nodding, I turned the rest of the way and left, Marquessa Ziya right behind me.

He would tell me later what the Second Prince said, maybe when we were alone again, and he could act on the burning need I saw in his eyes.

Everyone else in that room could just keep wishing to kiss or kick the exposed parts of my ass because they wouldn't get a chance to come anywhere near it.

CHAPTER 18

CROWN'S WEIGHT

In the hallway, I leaned back against the wall and stared straight ahead, inviting no conversation from the Marquessa.

"Lady Cinder," she said, trying to talk to me anyway.

Fighting the urge to roll my eyes at her, I turned her way and wiped any emotion from my face as I stared at her.

"My Prince is going to ask for your hand," she said, her voice flat, but rage played in her eyes and the tight set of her jaw.

"No, he will not." That was the stupidest thing he could do. He had to see that. Not only had I given him zero reason to think I would say yes, but he couldn't possibly think that after what I said I would accept Amethyst as anything other than the enemy in the war my parents died in.

"Yes. That is what he will do while we stand out here."

"He does not want me." No matter how much he enjoyed toying with me and Tristan, using the taunts and teasing in a way he thought was to his advantage, it was obvious he didn't actually want me.

"No, he probably does not."

"Then, why?"

"Second Prince Nevan has many reasons. Another opportunity to gain trade in hellfire water just one of them."

"Why would he ask my King instead of asking me or my brother? That is not how this works."

"In Amethyst, it is usually how it works. Especially if the man wanting a wife is a prince." Her face grew even harder, and her words clipped at the end.

"This is not Amethyst." And I would never set foot inside her damned country if I could help it.

"No, but I would not be surprised if he asks your brother the same thing."

"I am not my brother's property. And your Prince is not my type, nor does the Prince have anything that would entice my brother to even try and talk me into it." I still had a say. And Ash would be more likely to ask me to kill Nevan than marry him.

"Are you sure about that?" she asked, a cruel, sneering smile blooming on her face while the bright purple returned her hair.

She didn't know my brother...did she?

Narrowing my eyes as I looked at her, I tried to understand what exactly she was doing, why she was saying all this. But I didn't find any answers.

The only thing I could think to make sense out of anything she told me was that she was deliberately trying to confuse me, trying to get me to respond somehow.

Well, she wasn't important enough for me to do that. Neither were her Prince or her theories.

I went back to staring straight ahead, and ignoring her existence.

Ziya made a huffing noise, like what she wanted to do was tell me to go the fuck away. But that was fine. The feeling was mutual.

Every second in the hallway, my muscles tightened, my back stiffened, and my hands itched to throw open the door to find out what was happening inside.

But finally, the door opened, and Second Prince Nevan stalked out.

He looked me up and down, smiled, and kept going, followed by the rest of his retinue, the Marquessa falling in line as they passed.

After they were all gone, I turned to go back inside, but Tristan came out and grabbed my arm, twirling me the other way, letting go of me the second I was walking alongside him.

We walked to my rooms without a word, his jaw clenching and unclenching, and the hairs raising along my arms in response.

It didn't go well. Not that I had any idea *how* it went wrong as we walked, locked in silence. But he was clearly livid, and it made me want to stab someone.

He slammed my door open when we got to my rooms, the driftwood crashing against the wall, and his fist holding it in place.

The second I was past the door, he dropped it, letting it swing shut, and he grabbed me, turning me around to face him.

Fingers digging into my hips, his gaze was golden and shot straight through me. Tristan took a shuddering breath.

"You belong with me," he said, his voice rough.

"I am with you," I said, not sure what made him so irate, but sure enough of this.

He crashed his mouth into mine.

Our kiss wasn't sweet, wasn't calm. It was frantic and bruising as he pulled me in tight to his body, and held me there with hands balled into fists.

I scrabbled at his shoulders, my need to have him right that second climbing up through my whole body.

There wasn't space between us, my body and his fitted and pushed together as tight as we could make them.

A weapon and its sheath forged at the same time.

He pulled back from me, breathing heavy and looking into my eyes, his as deep as the sea beyond the windows.

"You are not a bargaining chip," Tristan said, his voice still thick and rough, "and he can't have you. You're mine."

He actually did it. The Second Prince actually had the audacity to suggest I marry him as part of the negotiations.

"I don't want him. And I am already yours."

"Forever."

"All my life."

Tristan shuddered and closed his eyes, his mouth finding mine again, with just as much force and barely contained need. His hands loosened their grip, his fingers exploring the strips of my exposed skin in the back.

My body responded with the same intensity, his name ringing through me as if he replaced my heartbeat, and my hands tangled in the hair at the nape of his neck.

But the pounding of his name again and again morphed and grew to a sound outside my body, outside the moment, outside the power of his mouth on mine and his body molded to me.

He pulled back again, putting his forehead on mine and said, "Fuck."

"King Tristan," the General pounded on the other side of the door, "you must pack and get to the dock first."

"Pack?" I asked, kissing his neck, and refusing to pull my body from his.

"Yes. You need to pack, too. We'll have three days aboard a ship to visit the Lighthouse. Duchess Inara thinks there's something there that the Amethysts will want instead of Lehar. And we'll have three days back." His fingers dipped beneath the edge of the laces at the back of my pants, slipping inside to press me more firmly against him.

"Are we all going to be on the same ship?" I asked, breathless, into the skin of his neck.

He made a low noise in his throat, and leaned me against the wall while he pressed a kiss to my mouth, his tongue caressing mine.

On the other side of the door, the General knocked again.

With a frustrated, low groan, he stepped back from me, gasping.

"Everyone will be on the same ship. I'll send Madam up here. Please hurry." He leaned in and kissed me again. This time there was a sadness to the kiss. Then he left.

My mind reeled, stuck in the moment I wanted to have, but was walking away with him down the hall.

"Lady Cinder?" Madam asked, a few moments later, opening the door, Jacquetta right behind her.

"I'm sorry, Madam," I shook my head and tried to focus on what Tristan asked me to do, "but I need your help to pack."

"Yeah," Jacquetta said, giving me an understanding smile, "we were told you're leaving for a while out to sea. Are you sure it's safe? Do you really want to go?"

Safe…I looked toward the window and the water beyond. No, it wasn't going to be as safe as being here in the castle. But that was all the more reason for me to be there.

"Tristan will be on that ship," I said, turning back to them. "I need to go."

Madam nodded and led me into my room.

It didn't take long for my only trunk to be packed, given to the servants, and for me to be at the door to the castle, waiting on everyone else to ride in the carriages to the dock.

Duchess Inara was already there, directing everyone. She glanced my way and gave me a smile before she finished with the person she was talking to, and made her way to me.

"How are you?" I asked, looking at the more pronounced limp she had today.

"Doing too much. But these times don't care if we get to sit down or not. Our King is already headed to the dock." She cocked her head to the side, and a smile bloomed on her face as she tucked her arm through mine.

"And how are you?" she asked, her voice hushed, but heavy with innuendo.

"You know, too?" I shook my head, biting my lip and looking down at my feet.

"Cinder, this is my castle. I know most things that happen here. And how to keep others from knowing."

Looking at her, with her brows high and her smile more of a smirk, I narrowed my eyes. My mind went faster, trying to understand exactly what she was getting at.

There were only two things I needed to hide from anyone, and she wasn't talking about helping me get down to the cells to kill Brix.

"Is…Are you saying the same is true about this trip and you can make things…easier?" My blood flowed faster in my veins, riding the wave of need that crashed over me just thinking about days of him without anyone knowing.

"When we get to the ship, let me show you which cabin you will be in." Her grin spread from cheek to cheek now, and I couldn't help laughing as I squeezed her arm in silent thanks.

"Someday, I will repay your friendship," I said, with all the same ring of a vow to it as when I told Tristan I loved him.

"Just be so very you that wars like this stop happening," she said, her smile taking on a melancholy shadow.

"You might be giving me too much credit." I shook my head and swallowed, her arm in mine morphing into a weight as large as Onyx itself and all the lives within it.

"No, Lady Cinder, you do not give yourself enough."

Amethyst nobles arrived. She squeezed my arm before walking away to look after them while I tried to adjust to the weight of expectation that I was somehow more than an assassin, more than just a killer. More than a warrior even. That I could be a protector. Of the entire country.

CHAPTER 19

CAPTAIN'S QUARTERS

The ride to the dock was both longer and shorter than I expected. Part of me thought there would be a dock directly underneath the castle itself, the rest assumed the stone and cliffs around the castle extended along the shore further than they did.

My carriage—shared with Inara and two members of the Amethyst party—was a silent and uncomfortable affair.

We didn't want to speak in front of them, and they must have felt the same about us.

Purple was such a pretty color. It looked good no matter how dark or how pale the skin tone of the Amethyst citizen, but I was starting to hate it.

Second Prince Nevan and the Marquessa just needed to go home. It was too much to expect me to be kind to slave traders. Even as Queen, I didn't think I could ever be diplomatic.

I dropped my head against the seat behind me as we crested the rise of a sand dune, and the dock, with the ship alongside it, came into view.

The homes in Breakwater were simple, with clean lines and driftwood used in all kinds of ways, but this ship…

"Wow," I whispered, leaning closer to the window in the carriage to see it better.

One of the Amethyst nobles with us leaned to get a better view, too, but the other tapped them on the knee and they averted their eyes.

Apparently, even a great and striking ship was too lowly for them.

Grand, sweeping and sinuous lines of dark wood made the ship almost as large as the Lord's house in Thirteen Rivers Valley.

"Beautiful, isn't she?" Inara said, her face beamed like she looked on her own child.

"She?" I asked, smiling. She was so awed she forgot to keep her perfect formal pronunciation up.

"Everything with the water is female. The sea itself, the ships that ride her waves, and even the storms that sometimes batter us."

But she didn't sound upset that the storms were considered female. She seemed...proud. There was a level of joy there that made me look at the sea again, look at the entire way of life in Breakwater in a new way.

A twinge in my heart with Lehar stamped on it reminded me of what it was like to really feel at home.

Watching Inara, though, there was more than the sense of home.

Here, it was as if the female energy of the sea, and the way the entire duchy relied on it, gave Inara some connection to the power of the water itself.

She was right. It was beautiful.

The carriage stopped, and a footman opened the door.

We alighted onto the wide dock of worn wooden planks to look up at the side of the ship with porthole windows staring back at us.

Being this close to the ship, I was less sure how big it was because it seemed even more immense than it had from a distance.

"Lady Cinder," Inara said, grinning up at the ship, "meet Ravensbane."

"Subtle," I said, smiling at her.

Her gaze snapping to me, Inara took a second and then laughed, the sound riding the wind coming off the water, as light as sea foam.

"Fine. It is a little obvious, but the name is not wrong."

We made our way up a rope gangway with wood planks so far apart, I was thankful I was wearing pants and that I was taller than my mother had been.

A hand reached out to me to help me step down off the gangway, and the second the heat of the fingers touched mine, I knew Tristan was here.

"I was hoping to see you," I said, trying to keep the uptick in my heart rate and the want out of my voice.

"Of course. I needed to be here first so that everyone got aboard well." He smiled at me, a perfunctory moving of his lips, and stepped back, holding his hand out to help the next person get onboard.

"Lady Cinder," Inara said, taking my arm, "let me show you to your stateroom."

"Do they need you to stay here and escort anyone else?" I asked, my voice low as I tried to get my body back under my control.

Tristan was doing a much better job than I was pretending we were no more than a Fighter and her King.

"The Captain and the crew will do that. They have all the assignments for rooms, and I have a special treat to show you." She grinned and stepped under the sweeping awning of a low roof, opening the door in the center of it.

We descended a narrow stairwell into the belly of the ship and turned to the right.

"Down the other hallway where most of the Amethysts are staying," Inara said, and I looked behind us to where the hall split in the opposite direction before she turned another corner and we headed to the back of the ship. "King Tristan's quarters are at the stern, the rear, of the ship. He has the most spacious room with the best views, of course."

So, not only was I going to have to be in a different room, but it was down an entirely different hall?

How she thought this would help me, I didn't know. Unless she expected me to climb along the back of the ship. Maybe if I had not already almost lost my grip and nearly fallen to my death trying to traverse the soaked wall of the castle, I would have tried it. But I knew better.

Even when I planned on dying in this war, it wasn't going to be while wasting my life at the back of a ship, leaving my King unprotected.

"Why are so many of the Amethysts coming with us? They would be safer if they stayed behind in the castle, right?" I asked.

"Safer for them at the castle, yes. But for the castle and my people? I insisted they all come with us. Amethyst safety is not my priority."

Duchess Inara was young, and still finding her way as a leader, but she was so much better than I would ever be. Brilliant and right.

The hall was still narrow, with rooms on either side. One door opened as we passed, someone hurrying back toward the stairs as sounds of a bustling kitchen leaked out of the door before it fell closed behind them.

"Right here," Inara said, getting to the end of the hall, and standing in front of two doors.

She reached for the one on the left, and swung it open.

"It is…" I stepped inside and turned in a slow circle, taking in the entire space in one turn. "…tiny."

After so many cavernous rooms at the castle, and the palace, and even the large tents of the training grounds, I smiled at my cubby hole of a room.

"Yes, but," Inara said, squeezing inside and shutting the door behind her, "this room is special."

Running a hand along the little desk next to the only real open space in the room, I took it in and agreed with her. The space next to the desk I assumed would be filled with my trunk soon since the only other space was the narrow walking area alongside the bed. The wood in this ship gleamed in the low light through the portholes. The gentle rocking of the sea made it soothing. Maybe I would just spend the next few days sleeping.

But Inara climbed across the small bed, and I froze, my mouth falling open.

What was she doing?

A second later, she shifted a panel of the wall, and it swung open to reveal a hole big enough for me to sit up in.

"Inara," I said, climbing onto the bed to look through the hole alongside her, "what is this?"

"This is a door into King Tristan's room." Her voice was low and conspiratorial, one brow high, a grin on her face.

Laughing, I shook my head.

"You are amazing." I sat back as she closed the panel, showing me how to do it—a simple act of twisting a piece of molding in and out of place. "Unbelievable."

"Captains often have more than one way out of their quarters, which is what that room is usually, just in case. King Tristan does not even know about it." She laughed as I choked on air.

"He does not know?" What if he didn't want me to distract him on this trip?

"Not unless the Captain told him. And I doubt she did. So, what are you going to do?" Her grin was wicked, and I bit my lip, thinking about what I planned. "Just, um..." she started, looking back at the panel, and making all my happiness from a moment before run down the hall toward the stairs.

"Just, what?"

"Well, all the rooms are pretty close together, and I just think you should know that the Second Prince shares a wall with our King."

"Oh." I didn't know what else to say to that. Yes, I should know.

But looking toward the panel, knowing what lay beyond it, a shiver ran down my spine even though we had neighbors.

"Inara, do we have meetings, and a lot of formal affairs planned for our few days of travel?"

"No. Second Prince Nevan hates the sea." She looked toward the circular window, shaking her head as if she would never be able to understand that.

"Why did he agree to come on this trip, then?" There had to be some other way we could have shown him whatever she thought made this trip necessary.

"Because the Lighthouse is on a small island. There is no way to avoid the sea entirely on the way. Even if we got closer via land, then ferried out to the Lighthouse, it would take far too long. And it is…" she waved a hand like she was going to pluck the right words from the air in front of her. "…difficult to explain if someone does not see it in action."

Raising my brows, I looked more closely at her as she adjusted her wooden leg.

"Is it magic?" I asked, my voice low.

Pushing herself off the bed, she got to the door before looking over her shoulder at me and said, "Some things seem impossible. It makes us believe in magic, when the entire time they were just something we did not fully understand. Maybe one day we will. Until then, we remain thankful they exist."

She let herself out of my room, and I stared at the door after it shut behind her, trying to understand what she meant.

Magic was real, we knew that now. As terrible as it was, it did exist in some way in this world. Even if the Dragon King magic was gone, some remained.

Had Inara and her people found more, and were keeping it quiet?

What, exactly, were we about to reveal to the Amethsyts? And would their support in this war be worth the risk?

CHAPTER 20

ANYTHING

It was impossible.

Twisting and turning, trying in vain to get my hands on the ties at the back of my pants was not working.

Growling in frustration, I gave up and slipped the lacy little nightgown on over my naked top.

I wanted to wear something that made me feel pretty, take down my hair, crawl through the panel, and wait in Tristan's room.

Only part of my plan was going to work.

Brushing the braid out of my hair, I put my things away in the trunk. If I didn't keep my room tidy, everything was so cramped I was likely to walk down the hall trailing a pair of panties on my foot.

Sighing, I scooted across the bed to the panel, and put an ear to the wood, hoping I wasn't going to break into the middle of some kind of meeting with Second Prince Nevan or the Captain.

Careful and slow, I turned the piece of molding, and swung open the panel.

No one was in the room.

I let out a breath, shaking my head. Stumbling around trying to learn how to be a queen I didn't want to be when I had the benefit of Tristan helping me would be worth it just so we wouldn't have to sneak around to be together. That and being able to order people to leave me alone with my King when I wanted to be.

With my husband.

The thought screwed me up, and I snagged a foot on the edge of the hole as I crawled through it, dumping me abruptly on the floor of Tristan's room with a thud.

Pausing there, I waited for someone to run in because of the noise, for someone in another room to yell, for anyone to notice the sound I made.

But nothing happened. I just swung the panel shut, and took in the room around me in the light from the large windows.

When Inara said this room was larger and had the best view, she didn't exaggerate. Not only did it have the best view because the back of the ship allowed for the entire horizon to be visible, but these windows took up almost the entire back wall.

In front of the windows, a table big enough to seat four and a desk took up the space. The rest of the room was large enough to dance in the middle, and the bed along one side was just as oversized as mine at the castle. Only this bed was set into a carved-out alcove in the wooden wall.

There was nothing for me to do.

For the first time since we came to the castle, there was no Madam or Jacquetta or Gus to talk to, to adjust a bandage, or to dress me. No meetings to attend. No Prince to be intimidating for.

Even my face felt so much better. I didn't have to think about my injury.

My hands longed for some blades and a training area.

But in that, too, there was nothing for me aboard this ship.

I didn't even have to spare a thought for Brix. Tristan was with me on the ship. He couldn't question Brix from here. He couldn't have all his belief in me destroyed from here.

Sighing, rubbing the tight knot that formed in the back of my neck, I went to the desk in front of the windows, and leaned forward to see even more of the view.

Now that I knew they were there, I could see the lines strung across the window on the outside to protect it from the Corvids.

How much would Tristan be able to plan and attend to when it came to the war while we were at sea?

And who was in charge while we were gone?

General Pace? Did she come with us?

Leaning even further forward, I tried to spot people on the dock. Maybe I could get a clue about what was going on above me and when we were likely to take off.

Behind me, a low chuckle ran over my skin like a caress.

I looked over my shoulder at Tristan, who leaned back against the closed door behind him, his arms crossed, and a smile on his face as he looked me up and down.

"For some reason," he said, his voice quiet and rumbling, "I thought walls would be a bigger problem for you on the ship."

Turning around, I leaned back against the desk behind me, and crossed my arms, too.

"And here I thought you knew me," I said.

He reached behind himself and threw a bolt, locking the door, before he strode across the room to me, and grabbed me by the waist, his hands an inferno that sent my own temperature soaring in response.

"I have the feeling there is so much more to learn," he said, kissing me with lips that danced along mine in barely-there touches.

"Tristan," I said, my voice thin as I reached for him, to pull him closer to me.

"Cinder, we have time." He ran a hand along my leg, the other toying with the small strap to my nightgown. "I want to know you more. Tell me something."

Even trying to think of something I could tell him about me that wouldn't be a lie was daunting.

Running a hand into my hair, taking out the few remaining pins carefully, one by one, he kept up the kisses along the skin of my face, my neck, and my shoulder. Kisses as light as the falling ashes of home.

Home.

"We used to have roses that grew along the walls and ramparts of the manor." Why I picked that detail from my life to tell him, I didn't know, but there was so much I would never be able to share. Maybe that was something I could, so I did.

Air, warm and sudden, puffed along my collar bone as he laughed a silent laugh between kisses.

"Lovely, but that isn't what I meant. I want to know you."

"You already know me." His hand on my thigh, running up my leg to my hip, the other combing through my hair...this was dangerous. I couldn't afford to be too distracted while I answered these questions.

"More. I want to know more."

His hands kept running over me, his lips barely touching me, and I was willing to tell him anything just to feel him on me.

I grabbed for him, but he took my hands and placed them back on his shoulders.

"No, Cinder, not until I know more of you."

My breath grew ragged, and need coiled in my body, a thirst begging to be slaked.

Anything. I needed to tell him anything that was true and wouldn't let him know too much.

"When I was young, I wanted to be Captain of the guard."

He picked me up off the desk and kissed me, long and deep, letting me roam my hands over his chest and tangle in his hair.

But when I reached for his buttons, he turned me around and bent me over the desk, pressing my hands to the wooden top.

"Tell me more." His hands roamed up the exposed section of my ass until he got to the top of the laces. He began to untie them.

"Under the manor are great bathing pools, directly over the hellfire water source. They're so hot most people can't stand to be in them for very long. But I could spend days down there." His hands, as hot as the baths, slipped under the back of my pants, pulling off the first section he had unlaced, getting so close to my sex I sucked in a breath.

He followed his hands with his mouth along the small of my back, his kiss soft, causing a shudder down to my toes.

"More." His voice was rough and low, making me curl my toes as his hands continued to unlace me.

"The heat of the hellfire source...It soaks into my bones, curls around my soul, and cleanses me of the past coating my skin. Like the warmth of your hands does."

"Hmm." He stood up, stopped unlacing me for a moment, leaned into my back, then reached around to slip his hands between my thighs, sweeping across my sex, and using the wetness to rub against my clit. "You, hot and wet in the pool...I need to see that. Tell me something else about you."

Pulling his hand away from me, he licked his fingers and went back to my laces. My mind sputtered out nonsense while I tried to avoid anything that would give me away.

"I had a cat once. Her name was Mia. She was the first being I loved that I wasn't related to."

Kissing down my legs, his low laugh came again. This time the sound ran through my body, and I bit my lip as I gripped the edge of the table tight.

"The first, but not the last," he said, slipping my pants off, one foot at a time.

As soon as I was free, I whirled around.

He looked up at me, an easy smile on his face as he stood up.

"Cinder," he said, reaching out a hand to run along my jaw before he tangled his fingers in my hair, "did I say I was done?"

"You want to know more?" What was he doing? I couldn't keep thinking about details I could afford to tell him. Not while he drove me past the breaking point.

"Everything." His mouth fell onto mine, hard and claiming, while I tangled my hands in his jacket until he pulled his head back. "I want to know everything."

I looked past him to the alcove bed, planting my feet and preparing myself.

"Tristan," I said, my voice like a coo, and his gaze intensifying in response, "tonight, I bow to you."

Grabbing him around the middle, I lifted him and carried him across the room to the bed, tossing him back against the covers.

He laughed, loud and long, and propped himself up on one arm, curling a finger at me.

"Come here, Flame. You made your point."

"Shhh," I said, putting one finger to my lips, "we need to be careful that no one hears us through the walls."

"We? Don't you mean you?" His whole face morphed into a wicked grin that made me want him to tease me more, but I had work to do here.

I climbed onto the bed, straddling him, my fingers flying over the buttons on his jacket and shirt while I shook my head.

"Not that it won't be hard for me," I said, rubbing my sex against the bulge of his cock in his pants, putting emphasis on the word "hard." "But tonight, I think you're going to have a difficult time staying quiet."

He shook his head, as I slipped his shirt and jacket off him.

The second he was free of the sleeves, he sat up and grabbed my hips, pushing his cock harder against me as I rubbed myself on him.

"Feeling you," he said, his voice low and heavy, settling deep within me, making me throb, "being inside you, fuck yes, I want to be loud."

Lifting one hand from my hip, he slipped it under the edge of my nightgown and rubbed his thumb against my clit, making me gasp.

Rubbing against him harder, I dug my nails into his shoulders, my breath speeding up.

He closed his mouth on my neck, a low growling noise I felt more than heard going through my skin and into my veins.

"Tristan," I said, my voice a hush, even as my pleasure built, rising higher and higher as his thumb and the rhythm of us moving against each other made me want him more.

"Cinder, I want you to burn for me."

Just the feel of him saying the words against my skin on top of his thumb, rubbing against my clit perfectly, exactly as I wanted it, while I grinded against his cock, got me so close, my legs started to shake.

"Yes," he said, his kissing on my neck growing hungrier, "burn for me. I want you as wet as you were before."

And I broke, a hushed moan coming from me no matter how hard I tried to hold back.

"Cinder." His voice was barely audible, and strained like he held himself back even as he pressed me tighter against him and his skilled thumb. "I want you."

Grabbing his face, bringing his lips to mine, I took his words into my mouth, swallowing them whole, wanting them to become a part of me.

He made the rumbling noise into my mouth, and I shuddered with the last of my orgasm before I pulled away from him and shoved him backward against the bed.

"Now it's my turn to tell you to come here," he said.

"What did I say?" I asked, untying his pants and starting to pull them off him while I looked across his chest to find his eyes riveted on me.

"You want to bow to me?"

"You're my King."

CHAPTER 21

EVERYTHING

Slipping his pants down to his thighs, I freed his cock.

Looking at him, laid out before me, I throbbed, wet with my want of him.

But I bit my lip and tugged his pants the rest of the way off, dropping them onto the floor.

"Cinder," he said, pulling on my hand as I crawled back toward him, "when you bite your lip while you look at me, I want to fuck you until you can't help but scream."

"Tristan," I said, my voice calm even as my stomach exploded in butterflies and I curled my toes, "you really shouldn't have said that."

I wrapped one hand around his cock at the base, and it was his turn to suck in a breath as I worked my hand up and down his shaft.

When I cupped his balls with the other hand, my fingertips rubbing against the soft place behind them, I whispered, "Tell me what you want."

He opened and closed his mouth, his eyes unfocused.

"Did you forget the words? How about this?" I leaned over

and licked around the head of his cock as he shuddered, and that rumble turned into a louder growl.

"Shh," I whispered, and took him into my mouth, closing tight around him.

Tristan jerked and made the same low rumbling noise in his throat, tangling a hand into my hair.

I started slow, using my mouth on him in the same way he entered me before, slow and careful, a little more every time, while I used my tongue to swirl on the underside of his shaft.

Looking up along his body, I found his eyes on me, molten and golden. He breathed with my movements, and tightened his hold on my hair with one hand, gripping the covers with the other.

Watching him, I kept massaging his balls, running my other hand up and down the base of his shaft, as I took him as deep into my mouth as I could. He shook and shuddered. I grew wetter still.

The skin on his legs turned into goosebumps, and his balls tightened in my hand.

Erupting, his eyes squeezed shut, head thrown back, and he moaned as the warm wetness of his release tickled my throat.

Once he was done, his body still shaking, I licked the last drop of his pleasure off the head of him and let go, climbing up his body to rub my sex against his cock.

"Cinder," he whispered in a hushed croak, opening his eyes and grabbing onto my hips, rubbing me harder against his cock as it started to soften.

"Tell me what you want," I said, licking my bottom lip.

He sat up, surging up to me, crashing his mouth onto mine as his cock jumped against me, growing hard again.

I moaned into his mouth, and he pressed harder into me.

"Why don't you tell me?" he said into my mouth.

"You know what I want." I always wanted him. "Everything. I want you ready for me again. I want to ride you until you spill every drop of your pleasure inside me. I want everything with you."

He groaned, his mouth closing on my mine, and picking up my hips.

I reached between us, taking hold of his shaft.

"Cinder," he said, his voice low and plaintive, like he was begging for me.

Rubbing the head of him along my sex, his tongue caressing mine, I moaned into the kiss, and he shuddered.

Finally, I placed him just at my entrance, and slowly, one tiny measure at a time, lowered myself onto him, his mouth on my neck, sending shivers down my body.

Once I was down to the hilt, every part of his cock inside me, I moved.

He met my rhythm and my pattern, up and down at the same time we moved back and forth rubbing along each other as he moved in and out.

Pulling his mouth away from my neck, he looked into my eyes.

His pupils dilated, dark taking over the burning gold with green shards.

My breath grew ragged, small noises creeping past my ability to stop them on every exhale as we built together.

"I love you," he said, one hand in my hair, the other holding onto my hip.

"I love you." And, there, with him inside me, moving with me, climbing toward that shattered height with me, holding himself back just enough not to scream, it had never been more true.

We kept moving, the rhythm growing a fraction more frantic as we got closer and closer.

He kept himself back, he was waiting for me. And I was waiting for him.

"You belong with me. You feel so right, so perfect," he said.

Letting a small moan out, I pressed tighter against him.

None of the men I had been with felt as good as he did, stretched me as much as I wanted without hurting me, and managed to touch every part of me the way I wanted.

And I knew he thought the same thing.

When he said I belonged with him, at first, I thought it was just something loving to say.

Being with him like this, with him inside me, I wondered if he was right.

Tangling my fingers into his hair, maintaining his constant eye contact, I leaned closer, my lips brushing his, and said, "Tell me what you want."

A shudder ran through him, and I throbbed with a low moan into his mouth.

"I want you," he said, his voice a soft groan. "Everything. With you. Always."

His words, his voice ringing through me, the promise in it, I broke.

We looked each other in the eyes as we both shattered, dying little impermanent deaths, and coming back together again, more ourselves and more than ourselves, a pair, one, together.

Touching my hand to his cheek, he leaned into my palm and brought his hand to my face, brushing a lock of hair away from my eyes.

"I will always love you," I said, and I added silently in my head that I didn't deserve him, knowing it was true, and wishing I could prove myself wrong.

He smiled, soft and perfect, and kissed me on the palm again, his eyes never leaving mine.

"And I will worship you until the day I die." He kissed me then, his mouth forming to mine as he wrapped an arm around my waist and swung me into the covers of the bed, tucking his body alongside mine.

This. This incredible man was exactly why I needed to kill Brix as soon as we got back to the castle.

He worshipped and loved me, but would he be able to do either if he knew the stories that I couldn't tell him tonight? More importantly, could he still feel that way if he found out I was supposed to add his name to my kill list?

Even as he stared into my eyes, with wonder and profound adoration, I didn't think so.

CHAPTER 22

SAY NO

Days of making love, of exploring each other, telling stories of our lives, left me not wanting this to end.

After we took a bath together in the tiny private bath in his room, I laid sprawled on the bed while he was propped up on one arm next to me.

"How do they get the water on the ship?" I asked, shaking my head, trying and failing to come up with something to explain it that wasn't magic.

"That's one of the things Duchess Inara is going to show us at the Lighthouse," Tristan said.

"She can show us, but I'm still not sure I'll understand it." Not that I wasn't happy about it. Bathing in sea water as we traveled would have sent Jacquetta and Madam into fits over my hair when we got back. And not bathing at all was not an option with the way Tristan and I were spending our time.

"Cinder," he said, trailing a finger along one of the lines of my abdominal muscles while he leaned over me, "why don't you ever talk about the time since the last war? After the explosion?"

His voice was soft, but the words still hit me like a blow. I wanted to curl my shoulders in and turn my stomach away from him in case he somehow saw the echoes of the punches it had received.

"You already know about my life after that. Every waking moment was filled with training until I came to the palace and met you." Please, I begged silently, let this be, and focus on us together now.

"Did you do it to become the Captain of the guard?" he asked, leaning down to kiss along the outline of the muscles on the side of my stomach.

"No. My brother gave that position to someone else." Someone who was in a cell waiting for me to kill him. "But I didn't want to be in the position I was during the last war. I wanted to know how to fight."

"What about when you're Queen, and you have to spend less time with a blade in your hand. Will you still be happy?" He glanced up at my eyes, biting on his bottom lip, and went back to staring at my abdomen while he put his hand flat across the well-defined muscles there.

Part of me twinged with the thought of losing my sole purpose, my single-minded focus. But looking at him, I chose to pay attention to the rest of me that thrilled to a future with him.

"Tristan, will I still get to train?" I asked, finally willing to admit to myself that I needed to know for sure before I put on a crown.

"Of course. I don't want you to be less the warrior Queen. But there will have to be some time spent away from it. Not the constant schedule you've kept for all these years." He still wouldn't look at me, and his hand shook slightly where he brushed against my skin.

I pushed myself from the bed and went to the panel in the wall, while he sat up behind me.

Once I was in my own space, I found what I was looking for in my trunk right away. Along with my mother's shoes—safe now at Madam's—it was more important to me than any other item I could hold in my hand.

Climbing back through the panel, Tristan sat on the bed, his face in his hands, and his knees pulled up to his chest.

The look of him, naked, broken and crumpled even though he sat there whole, made my throat close as I sat in front of him and put my hand to his cheek.

"My King," I whispered.

A shudder ran through him, and he pulled his fingers away from his eyes, letting me see the pain etched into the lines around his eyes and downturned lips.

"Cinder, I don't want to change you." He grabbed the hand on his face, and held it to his chest, pulling me in closer. "I don't want to take anything from you. But it's just part of being Queen. I'm sorry."

"No, Tristan. I understand." I pulled my hand back from him, and slipped the sigil ring he gave me onto one of my fingers. "I just wanted to wear this."

His face lit up, his eyes turning from hazel to burning gold, and he pulled me into him, wrapping his arms around me. He planted a kiss on my forehead, the heat of him so intense I shivered.

"You are so much more than I ever thought to want," he said, running a hand down my back.

"Part of me refuses to believe you when you say things like that." I snuggled further into his arms, smiling despite the flare of doubt that always rose in my mind when he was more perfect than I deserved.

"So, I get to spend the rest of my days making you believe."

Wrapped in his arms, in the tight bubble of the quiet Captain's quarters, a knock finally came to the door announcing we were close to the Lighthouse.

He helped me into one of the outfits that Madam packed for me, and I got to watch as he tossed aside his formals for something closer to what he wore at the palace, even if there were more embellishments along the sleeves.

"This is nice," he said, touching the shoulder of overlapping dragon scale-shaped pieces of leather that covered one of my shoulders and trailed down my arm. "Although I wish you had it on both shoulders."

"No one ever designs armor for someone who fights with two blades. I've always hated any kind of clothes that limited arm movement," I said, swinging that arm in a circle. "This isn't terrible, but I would prefer not to have it at all."

"Cinder," he said, shaking his head with a smile on his face, shaded in frustration, "remember when I said I wanted to wrap you in fifty layers of heavy armor?"

Nodding, I bit my lip.

Understanding his inclination, wanting to do the same to him, to protect him, did nothing to quell the instinct that rose in me to tell him no.

"Panels like this, something small, doesn't limit your ability to fight. Can you try and wear things like this more often? Just to make my heart ache a little less when you insist on putting yourself in harm's way?"

"You're going to be a huge problem." I ran a hand along his cheek, shaking my head.

"How am I a huge problem?" He grinned at me, pulling me into him.

"First of all," I said, looking down at where he pressed my hips against his own, "we don't have time. And second, although getting enough of you is a challenge, that's not what I meant."

Laughing and giving me a fraction more space, he nodded like he wanted me to keep explaining,

"Even when I don't want to listen," I said, shaking my head and marveling at him, "I find it very difficult to say no to you."

Scooping me up and holding me above him, he grinned and stared into my eyes.

"Nothing is wrong with you finding it hard to say no to me, especially since I want to give you everything and do everything you want."

I smiled and lowered my mouth to his, knowing that there was one thing I wanted desperately that being with him likely made impossible. And hoping he never found out that I wanted my brother to remain my family. Or why it was so dangerous if he did.

CHAPTER 23

SECOND PRINCE

Waiting in my room long after another knock came at Tristan's door, and the panel between our rooms swung shut, I started to think about how I was going to get Brix to tell me what I needed to know.

During my attack on him in the cell, he didn't seem to care about the pain.

In fact, he weirdly seemed to enjoy it.

How was I going to get him to answer my questions without a layer of bullshit coating everything he told me?

Shoving myself up off my unused bed, I paced along the gleaming wood floor, turning after only three steps.

Maybe that was it.

I curled my nose at the thought, but it seemed like the only way he would give me what I needed.

He enjoyed fucking with me. He enjoyed making me hate him, torturing me with the details of what he did and who he really was, and how much of a monster my brother allowed into our home for so many years.

But if I could hold back my rage for long enough, maybe I

could bargain with him, let him tell me the disgusting things he wanted to say in exchange for information.

Dropping back down to sit on the bed, my hands curled into fists, I had to admit it was as good a plan as any, even if it would be hard to keep from vomiting while I listened to him.

After I got the information I needed, I was going to carry through on my threat, no matter what he told me.

Even Brix, as twisted a fuckhole as he was, had to feel it when I ripped apart every single thing that dangled from him.

Grinning, I leaned back on the bed. Maybe it made me twisted, too, that I was going to enjoy inflicting pain on him. But I would lose zero sleep over making him suffer after what he did.

Beyond the door to my room, the sound of what seemed like pounding footsteps and shouts made me jump to my feet and grab for the spikes on my thighs as I tore open my door and ran into the hall.

The hall was packed full of sailors and people in fine clothes, shoving past each other in opposite directions, some crying, others yelling.

None of it made sense.

"Get out of the way," I screamed, shoving at the people in front of me, heedless of who they were or where they were going.

But mine was just another panicked voice, lost in the maelstrom of noise and humanity around me.

I couldn't pull my spikes here and risk some innocent person being wounded, but, dammit, I needed to get past them.

Right now.

Growling low in my throat, I shoved more people far enough out of the way to press between them.

Tristan was somewhere on this ship.

And I needed to get to him. Right fucking now.

"Move," I yelled, shoving some fine Amethyst lady back into the dining room as she tried to sneak in front of me.

Grabbing two more people I knew were somehow important to Inara's retinue, I threw them through the door after the Amethyst woman, gaining myself a short distance further into the hallway.

From somewhere above me on the deck, a reverberating boom almost knocked me off my feet.

"What the fuck was that?" I yelled, while people around me screamed and cried out.

Scrabbling at the wall, I righted myself. Using the fact that everyone else was thrown off balance, I leapt over some who crouched down low, shoved others aside, and finally reached the turn toward the stairs.

The stairs were worse than the hallway.

Clogged full of Amethysts streaming away from the deck of the ship, I squeezed my way between people coming down the stairs, pushing past and taking up the space they were just in.

Looking up the stairs, there was no sign of Tristan.

But there was a lot of purple hair.

"Out of the way," I yelled, and managed to startle some of the fleeing Amethysts into hugging themselves along the walls.

Running up the steps, I almost made it out of the open door, the change in light blinding me for a moment, before arms wrapped around my middle, and pulled me back against someone's chest.

"You can't go out there," Nevan yelled right next to my ear.

Clawing at his hands, trying to unlatch his grip on me, I was shocked to realize he was somehow bigger than I thought.

Gone was the thin, wiry build of the soft Second Prince. Instead, I was held by an immovable wall of muscle.

"Let me go." I squinted out into the light, trying to make sense out of the pandemonium on the deck.

Sailors ran by, some with spears in hand. There was blood

spattered on the boards, and a few straggling nobles pushed past me into the narrow stairs on their way down.

"Corvids are attacking. I can't let you out there," Nevan said, grunting as I elbowed him in the gut.

But looking back up again, in the middle of the deck, I found what I was looking for and screamed.

My King stood in a puddle of blood and black feathers, some of them spattered on him and stuck in his hair, firing arrow after arrow into the sky.

"Tristan," I screamed, bucking and trying to twist out of Nevan's grasp.

Tristan looked my way for a second, before turning back to his task, shooting and shooting from the two quivers on his back, one of them almost empty.

"Stay there, Cinder," he yelled.

"Fire," Inara's voice called out from somewhere on deck.

Another massive boom ripped through the air, sending Nevan and me slamming into the wall and pulling a grunt out of Nevan. His grip didn't let up.

Tristan stumbled, recovered, and kept shooting.

"What was that?" I yelled. "Let me go. I need to protect him."

I was no longer making as much sense, panic constricted my throat, making it hard to breathe, making my mind conjure all manner of terrible magic that would make sense out of the sound.

"We're firing cannons at the Corvid ship. You can't go out there. He wants you in here." Nevan grunted again as I slammed my other elbow into his other side.

"He doesn't always get what he fucking wants. It's my damn job. Let me go."

"No." He tightened his hold, making it harder for me to move.

"Don't make me hurt you," I snarled, but I couldn't reach my spike now at all. Even bucking and flinging my legs up in front of me, my arms wouldn't reach around his.

"You can't hurt me right now," he said into my ear, his voice lower and harsher than it had been.

I tried to look behind me, to see his face, but I couldn't manage to turn far enough. I could barely move.

"The fuck I can't," I finally said, swinging up a fist and nailing him in the nose with the backs of my knuckles.

"Ow, fuck, stop. I'm only doing what he asked," Nevan said in that strange voice.

"He didn't mean it. Let me go." I grabbed at the edge of the door frame, pulling us both forward as I gritted my teeth at the weight.

"No ally would break word with the King."

"Don't make me punch you harder." I tried to ply his arms off me again, the sleeves of his jacket in ribbons that tangled in my fingers. "Tristan," I screamed again.

On the deck, Tristan looked at me, a pained expression on his face and turned away, continuing to fire.

A strange twang bounced through the air. Even though I didn't know what made the sound, my struggling increased and my heart leapt into my throat.

"Tristan," I wailed, as a crow flopped onto the deck of the ship right next to him, broken in pieces, and no longer a threat.

But if one got through, more could follow it. "Look out."

Punching up again and again. I pummeled Nevan, and he grunted as each blow landed harder than the last.

Finally, Nevan let me go. I ran to where Tristan stood, still firing, but focusing his shots at the hole in the webbing of fishing line protecting the ship. The rest of the webbing was littered with blood and feathers, clear attempts of other crows to get past.

One crow had made it through Tristan's barrage of arrows, and flew in a tight circle, coming at him from behind.

I threw myself at the crow as it neared Tristan's back, spike first, and slammed into its eye, toppling to the side with it. It crashed to the deck boards of the ship, already slick with blood.

Another boom sounded, and a cheer went up from the sailors, who still fought with their spears through the fishing lines.

The remaining crows in the sky around the ship veered off and flew out to sea.

"What happened?" I screamed, shoving up from the body of the crow I killed, yanking my spike out, studying Tristan where he stood still ready with his bow and arrows, breathing hard. I tried to figure out how much of the blood splattered on him was his own.

He turned to look at me, finally lowering his bow, his jaw clenched, and his eyes stormy and dark.

"You didn't stay below."

CHAPTER 24

PROMISES

"Are you out of your mind? If I stayed below, this crow would have killed you." I gestured to the body by my feet, wiping my spike off on my pant leg, and slipping it back into the sheath at my thigh.

"Look," Tristan said, pointing to where two sailors were gathering up a net. "We had a plan to capture any that got through the barrier."

"Repair the lines, prepare the cannons in case any come back, and clean this deck," Inara shouted to the sailors, standing on the roof of the stairwell to below, her wooden leg stuck out of her skirts.

"Fine," I yelled at Tristan, throwing my hands up and turning away. Stalking toward the stairs, I called over my shoulder, "Maybe next time you'll let me in on your little plan, so I don't think I'm going to watch you die."

Ridiculous. He was ridiculous.

He really thought it was okay to be angry with me for not knowing his stupid, risk-his-own-neck-needlessly, plan.

Making my way below, the stairs were clear, and Nevan was

nowhere to be seen—neither the thin version nor the oddly strong version.

"Cinder," Tristan said, grabbing my shoulder when my foot hit the top step.

"You are the King. I won't apologize for protecting you." My voice was a snarl, but his hand on the shoulder that wasn't covered with leather scales grew hotter.

"Will you come speak with me about this plan?" he asked, slipping into the formal, clipped tones of the King addressing his Fighter.

"Of course," I said, letting my own voice match his as I squeezed my feelings into my tightly curled fists.

He let go of my shoulder and stepped past me, leading me down the stairs and through the hall to his room.

The sound of muffled crying and shouting came from almost every room we passed on the way there, but the only people still in the hall were sailors darting around.

All the Amethyst nobles and Inara's people must have been cowering in their rooms, as far from the threat as they could get.

Finally, he slammed open his door, and I followed him inside.

He shut the door and whirled on me, tossing his bow where it clattered on a table.

"Damn it, Cinder," he said, his voice a rough whisper, "will you ever fucking stop risking yourself for me?"

"No, I won't." I crossed my arms over my chest, "and you can't ask me to. Every damn time we talk about this, you say you know me, accept me, but then you ask this of me. And you can't do that anymore."

"Yes, I can when I set up a situation that means you don't have to put yourself out there."

"Which you didn't bother to tell me about," I yelled,

throwing my hands in the air. "And you didn't bother to have your little accomplice tell me either."

"Shhh." He waved his hands at me which made me want to bite him. "Accomplice?"

"Prince Nevan. He said you asked him not to let me go out there, but he didn't say anything about why."

"Because I didn't say anything to him. I asked some of the sailors." He turned and looked into the middle distance, thoughts running across his face as clearly as the feathers stuck in his hair.

"What?" I asked, bracing myself for a blow even if I didn't understand why.

"Exactly what did Second Prince Nevan say to you?"

I rolled my eyes and stepped back, crossing my arms again, but looser this time.

"He said you didn't want me out there. He held me still and fought to keep me in the stairwell. He said an ally would listen to the King." I smiled a wicked-edged grin and went on, "And he said I couldn't hurt him, then yelled, 'Ow,' when I punched him in the face."

Rubbing his hands into his eyes, Tristan shook his head.

"I don't know whether to be happy that he said 'ally,' or furious he touched you, or angry at you for punching him in the face." Brushing the long black feathers from his hair, he gave me a humorless smile.

"You should be apologizing for trying to keep me out of the fight. Again." His course of action seemed obvious to me. I didn't know why he was struggling with it.

Tristan reached for me, his hands scalding and his eyes that bright green, but I shook him off.

"Don't, Tristan." I stepped back from him, not trusting myself if he was touching me. "You can't keep saying you accept that I'm going to fight for you, always, and then try and stop me from doing it. That isn't how this is going to work."

"Cinder." His voice had that low, rasping, growl tone to it that reminded me of other moments, and made my blood heat in the wrong way because it was too damn distracting. I wanted to remain angry, to finish this, to make my point, and not let the fact that I wanted to throw him to the bed and kiss him until we both forgot get in my way.

"Here," I said, pulling the sigil ring out of my bustier and slamming it into his chest, "if you can't handle me with a blade and a crown, then you don't get me with a crown, because I am not giving up the blade."

"Damn it." He grabbed my hand holding the ring, and pushed it back at me. "You said forever. Just because we argue, you can't throw everything away."

"Of course I can." I shook my head, and tried to yank myself free of his grasp.

But he growled low in his throat and wrapped me up tight against him, claiming my mouth in a punishing kiss.

It didn't matter how angry I was, how high all the tension in me was after watching him at risk, I relented and kissed him back, grabbing onto his jacket with both fists.

"You and I belong together," he whispered into my mouth, pulling back a fraction. "And forever means a lot of arguments. As long as we can agree that angry doesn't mean throwing away everything else between us."

No, angry meant fists and bruises, tender and bleeding. Angry always meant destruction. Ash taught me that. My shoulders tensed, their want to fold in said it wasn't wrong.

Staring at him, at the bright green of his hellfire eyes, I didn't know what to say. I didn't know how to process a different way to be.

"Tristan."

He closed his eyes on the sound of his name and put his forehead to mine, his body relaxing against me.

It didn't matter what I thought angry meant, or what he did.

It didn't matter how many times either of us expected to argue in the future.

With his warmth against me, his forehead to mine, and just his name on my lips sending sensation rippling through his body, I didn't want to let him go.

"Promise me you won't stop me from fighting for you," I said, and a shudder went through him.

His eyes opened, and he ran a hand along my jaw.

"As long as you promise not to ever hand this back to me," he said, pulling my hand off his jacket and unfolding my fingers to let the ring glint in the light.

This time a shudder ran down my spine, but I nodded and kissed him, all the while having no idea how to trust either of us would do what we promised.

CHAPTER 25

PROTECTORATE

"This is the Lighthouse," Inara said, looking out at the small island with the stone tower jutting up into the sky.

Sailors were busy setting up the walkway that would allow the Amethysts gathered around, Tristan in his clean clothes without the feathers and blood, Duchess Inara, and me to go inside.

Only an hour after the attack from the Corvids, we were about to walk into the Lighthouse, and discover the reason we came here.

Marquessa Ziya, just on the other side of Prince Nevan, swallowed and swayed as she clamped a hand down on the railing and focused on the Lighthouse.

"Is there something wrong with the Marquessa?" I asked Inara, leaning her way.

Grinning and biting her lip, trying to stifle her smile, Inara said, "She is not the only one. Quite a few Amethysts are struggling with seasickness. Especially since the attack drove them all from the deck to hide below."

"Seasickness is real?" I looked back at the Marquessa and

tried to figure out why anyone would even come to Breakwater at all if they were allergic to the sea.

"Cinder," Inara said, laughing, "not everyone has the same control of their bodies, and ability to move with the world around them that you do."

"Moving with the world has something to do with being allergic to the sea?" I looked back at Inara as she fell forward, laughing so hard she could barely stand as she held onto the railing.

"Fighter Cinder," Second Prince Nevan said, suppressing a laugh himself, and making me narrow my eyes, "seasickness happens because people can't stand the way the boat moves on the waves. They aren't allergic."

"Oh." There was nothing else for me to say when I felt too stupid to be allowed to speak ever again.

I stared ahead at the island and the Lighthouse, trying to ignore Nevan standing next to me, back to his normal body and his sleek clothes.

But he leaned forward, resting his arms on the railing, and I couldn't help comparing the thin arms to the massive ones I couldn't reach around.

"Prince Nevan," I said, glancing at him out of the corner of my eye as the first of our group walked across to the island, "may I ask you a question?"

"Anything, Fighter Cinder." He bowed his head to me, the cocky grin back on his face.

"Why is it you seemed…" Was I really going to just blurt out the question? There had to be a different, more palatable way to ask him, but maybe using a blunt question would mean I could get past this feeling I was missing something obvious. "…larger before."

Standing up straight with his smug grin and adjusting his jacket, he looked at the fingernails on one hand then past them to focus on my face.

"Lady Cinder," he said, and the small hairs at the nape of my neck stood on end like the change in my title on his tongue was a threat, "not everyone is best served wearing our secrets for the world to see."

He dipped his head, and went to the walkway onto the island, leaving me with no more an idea what happened to him than before.

The island itself looked barren and inhospitable. The Lighthouse was a large stone tower that wasn't made of the same kind of worn and pocked stone as the castle. While the castle looked as if it were part of the landscape, shaped by it in some way, this tower was almost at war with the sleepy rock and sand-strewn island that seemed only to be home to birds and the Lighthouse.

When was this built? How was it built?

Along the coast, too far away it seemed for it to be a same-day commute for the people who worked at the Lighthouse, a town of considerable size sat looking out toward us.

"My Flame," Tristan whispered behind me, "are you ready?"

"Yes," I said. Looking up at my King, I found all the unease of what Nevan said and the oddity of the island slipping away from me. Looking at Tristan was like going home. "But don't call me that where someone might hear you."

"I'm starting to care less and less about someone hearing me." He gestured for me to walk ahead of him, his voice dropping to an even quieter whisper. "Especially if it means that I could see you wear that ring, and Second Prince Nevan would know exactly how to refer to you."

A thrill went through my body. I wanted to be done with this visit and back in the room with him.

"How should he refer to me?" I whispered back, turning my head a fraction toward him.

"Someday, everyone will only call you Queen."

The hard little lump of the ring, tucked safe against my

breast in my bustier, was usually something I hardly noticed. But right now, it seemed to grow as my want to wear it so everyone could see grew as well.

Once we crossed to the island, he went to the front of the group with Second Prince Nevan. I was left to trail after them, the solid feel of the land beneath my feet almost too hard after so long on the ship.

Sailors lined up with spears, their eyes trained on the skies, as we all made our way inside the stone tower.

"Here at the Lighthouse," Inara said, once we were all inside, "we make the systems that Breakwater and our ships rely on."

"Interesting," Nevan said, although the look on his face made him look exceedingly bored, "but I am still confused as to why you're showing us this."

"Patience, Prince Nevan," Inara said, smiling coyly.

She was so good at this. When I was Queen, I was going to have to bring her to the palace to teach me how to handle the diplomatic intricacies of the job.

Anyone who managed to be a Duchess bold enough to come to the palace for her people, lead her lands in a time of war while winning over the trust of her people, and do it all while still a teenager was a formidable diplomat in my opinion.

Maybe we could talk her into doing international work on behalf of Onyx.

We walked through a series of doors and offices, up flights of stairs, and finally we found our way into what looked like the world's most out-of-control kitchen.

Stations of people working on long tables full of gadgets and some organic materials were littered all over the large, circular room.

It seemed as if there were multiple floors within this windowless building lit by stone lights because more than one set of stairs reached up from where we were. They were massive, extra wide, and could accommodate more than five people walking side by side.

What did they move through here?

"You see," Inara said, walking up to a strange, oven-looking thing that a woman was working on, "one of these, all put together, is on every one of our ships. It is small in size, and yet mighty in what it affords us."

She touched a finger to a small dial that was on a table full of little parts.

"And what does this do?" Nevan asked, leaning in closer, all his boredom erased.

"This is a desalination engine. The beauty of it is, it uses the salt and the water passing through it to power itself." Her smile was subdued, but the calculation in her eyes was obvious.

My friend was smarter than even I realized.

Nevan raised his brows and looked at Inara only to get closer to the engine and study it further.

I didn't bother to look closer. It was as much magic to me as the Corvids turning into crows, and no amount of staring at the parts would change that. But I did appreciate how genius it was.

"Fascinating. I don't understand how it works," Nevan said, shaking his head.

"We had help from a Protectorate Priestess to make the first one, and show our crafters how to make more," Inara said, smiling as everyone turned and gaped at her, including me.

Help from a Protectorate Priestess?

All my life, the people of the Protectorate Mountains were called witches, and spoken of in hushed, half-frightened tones.

But Jocelyn was from the Protectorate. And the woman who didn't speak to anyone but smiled at all of us when she came to be a potential Queen was from the mountains, too. And one of them came out of hiding to help Breakwater at some point.

Realizing I was wrong about something I had always

assumed was fact was starting to become far too commonplace for me.

The people gathered around me, though—especially the Amethysts—seemed unused to the sensation.

Small, muttered conversations broke out. Some of them with vehement head shaking.

"My trainer is from the Protectorate," I said into the growing disquiet, which earned me silence and even more open-mouthed shock than Inara's pronouncement had earned her. "She has been with us for years, and her and her partner saved many lives during the last war."

I wasn't going to add that she was the reason I was able to kill as well as I did. They didn't need to know the particulars of what she trained me to do.

"We have been able to learn much from the lessons we were taught," Inara continued into the silence with a tilt of her head to me in thanks, "and I believe we can offer the Amethyst kingdom an avenue to power your systems much like the one we use with Hellfire water, without taking from Lehar."

For some reason, the way she said "Lehar," as if she was speaking of a family member and not lands on the other side of Onyx, made me look closer at the engine.

"Duchess Inara?" I asked, quietly, hoping she would understand.

"Yes, Fighter Cinder," she said with a smile, "this is what I was talking about."

CHAPTER 26

BACK TO BASICS

Going back to the ship, Tristan, Inara, and Nevan were in close conversation. But all I could think about was how soon I could get some engines back to Lehar to help clean the air.

I didn't need to know how it would work, just as long as there was a chance it would.

My people, the lands I loved, might get to be what they once were.

Ash would be thrilled.

But as much as I couldn't wipe the smile from my face thinking about bringing clean air and the possibility of green plants and life back to the duchy, my hands shook while I wondered if Ash would accept something that came from me. If he would take the chance to believe, to allow himself to be thrilled.

The thought of facing my brother made my old wounds ache and all my scars itch.

We had days more of travel to get back to Sandstone Castle, days where I could do nothing except wonder at what Brix would have to tell me about my brother.

No one stopped me from retreating to my little room while Tristan and the others went to his.

Their meeting must have been spirited, because occasionally I heard a raised voice through the wall.

But they needed to work through the details, to have some kind of understanding before we went back to the castle and the Chamberlain ironed out the rest.

And I needed not to think anymore.

Leaving my room, heading up to the deck, I found Amethysts all over the place.

"Well, this isn't what I was hoping for," I said to no one, planting my hands on my hips.

"Is there something I could help you with, Fighter?" a sailor asked, pausing as he walked past.

"Probably not." I shook my head and smiled, looking at all the purple-haired people wandering around and in the way. "I was hoping to do some training, but there are far too many people up here."

"Do you mind a slick deck?" the sailor asked, grinning.

"No." My answer was tentative even though the question had me grinning back. I didn't know what a slick deck had to do with all these people, but I couldn't help finding it funny for some reason.

"Just follow me then, Fighter," the sailor said.

He went to a cupboard in the wall near the door to the stairs, and took out a bucket and a mop.

Laughing, I trailed after him, pulling my spikes from the sheaths on my thighs, turning them in my hands, and feeling the comfort of the grip. It felt like my hands should always be this way.

Sure enough, as the sailor started to mop, the nobles fled the slopping water and the slickness it left behind.

It gave me the space to start small at first, going through the motions of forms and moves that Jocelyn had trained me with.

Once the sailor had mopped further, giving me more room, I used the slippery boards to practice slides and turns, and challenge my own ability to land jumps and leaps.

My legs started to burn, the muscles between my shoulder blades aching with the work after neglecting my training too long and overdoing it to such a great extent before the break.

I doubled my efforts, working through the muscle fatigue and the strain, my breathing returning to a comfortable pattern.

Years of practice, years of recovering quickly after a beating, years of not missing the day of training after, left me more than prepared to work my body through the moves. Just being lazy for a while and driving myself to exhaustion chasing after Gus wasn't as bad as working through the things Ash made me work through.

Eventually, my mind reached that place. The one where the world around me became fuzzier and more distinct at the same time.

I stopped seeing the sailors hovering at the edges of the space I moved within. I grew less aware of the darkness of the night falling around me. But at the same time, I was more aware of the now dry deck boards beneath my feet, the movement of the ship along the water, how it affected my body, and the way I had to adjust to it.

After running through all the patterns and movements Jocelyn had me train with, I started on the long list of improvised combinations I used that came from other disciplines and moments in a fight when I discovered something new.

Finally, sweat trickling down my back, collecting under my breasts, and coating my skin, I moved on to the dances that Madam taught me, using the steps as I memorized them, my weapon real instead of imagined.

Only after that was done did I sheath my spike, and start on the fluid stretching moves that Jocelyn taught me, my muscles screaming as I forced them to loosen against their will.

Laying out on the deck boards, stretching my entire body at once and breathing deeply, footsteps approached from the side of the stairs.

I peeked through one eyelid, not stopping the stretch as Tristan crouched down just past my hand.

"You have amassed quite the audience," he said, his voice low and carried away by the wind as soon as the words were past my ears.

Tilting my head, I looked past him and spotted Second Prince Nevan, the Marquessa, and half the Amethyst contingent making no secret of their attention.

Along with them, sailors all over the ship sat sprawled along the roof of the stairwell, leaning against the railings, and even hanging from rigging by the mast, staring my direction.

"Well, they can watch." I grinned at him, and he shook his head with a smile.

"Not that they can't," he said and tilted his head, his eyes trailing down my body. "Are you ready to go in now?"

"To my room?" I asked, sitting up.

"Only as long as it takes you to open the panel, yes."

"Give me a short sword, go to your room, and I'll meet you there shortly," I said, my blood thrilling to the thought of him.

"How about I stay for a little while longer, and watch how you handle that thing." His grin was wicked, and the innuendo enough to make me curl my toes in my shoes. "Then I'll follow your plan."

Pulling a short sword out of a sheath on his back, Tristan handed it to me, hilt first.

"When did you put that on?" I asked, narrowing my eyes.

"I was going to come up here and ask you to spar," he said.

"Really?" My smile was massive, and I pushed myself up to my feet.

He laughed as he stood up with me, but he shook his head.

"Yes, but now I just want to watch everyone grow more impressed with you, my Hellfire Queen."

Turning on his heel, Tristan went to stand next to Nevan, turning back around to watch me and giving me a tip of his head.

With a shake of my head and a small laugh, I twirled the short sword in my hand and passed it to my other one to do the same before I pulled one of my spikes and started through more patterns and movements.

My movements and patterns consisted of some of the same moves and some specific to the sword. But I added to the list, going through them all.

Even though I knew this time that people were watching, that Tristan was watching, I still managed to get into that place where they were nothing more than a blur at the edges of my awareness.

Until one of the figures jumped out at me, a blade at the ready.

CHAPTER 27

FLIRTING SHARPLY

I twirled and met their blade with the short sword, bringing the spike up to the edge of their chest before I had any idea who it was that I was about to skewer.

"Prince Nevan," I said, breathing hard, stepping back from him, and pulling the spike away, a drop of red on its tip.

"Ow," he said, dropping his arm with the sword in it, and touching that side with his other hand, his fingers coming back red.

"I didn't mean to. I thought I stopped before it would touch you." How did I calculate that so wrong? I was usually so perfect with the placement of my blades.

"Not your fault, Fighter Cinder," he said, laughing and cringing at the same time. "I deserve this."

"Will you be okay? Do I need to do anything to help you?" Oh, shit. What was I going to do to fix this? I wasn't even Queen yet, and just caused an international incident. Did I just screw this all up, and start another war?

"Really. It's fine." He shook his head. His smile was kind as he stepped back, and Tristan came to my side laughing. "You were right, King Tristan. I shouldn't have done that."

"At least she pulled back, or you would be dead," Tristan said, smiling at me.

"Entirely my fault in presuming I could catch you off guard." Nevan handed the sword to Tristan and smiled. "But I would love to see you spar with *someone*."

"Is that your cue?" I asked Tristan, swallowing down the fear running through me that this wasn't as okay as they seemed to think.

"Seems like it," he said.

Nevan nodded and grinned, stepping back to stand with the others who started to fuss over him. But he waved them away.

"Well, if he's alright enough to watch…" I swung my short sword, and put my spike back in the sheath.

"Are you sure you don't want two blades?" Tristan asked, twirling his own sword.

"No, I'm pretty sure I'll be fine." And I lunged, attacking and grinning as his blade met mine with a clang.

He turned out of the clash and laughed. The fight was on.

We didn't have blunted edges this time, so I had to be a little more careful. But his buttons weren't safe when I was around. I sent three flying.

"A death to you," he said.

Going around with him, not using my flips and tricks, I relied just on my ability to keep the fight fairly even. That is until he took a step into a move he had never done with me, and followed up with a pattern he had never used. I decided if he was going to start using tricks on me, I was free to return the favor.

The next time he lunged at me, instead of parrying with my blade right away, I dropped back, bending in half, catching myself with my hand on the deck, and thrusting the sword up to block his downward strike. I pushed myself into a roll, and turned before he could make a move to catch up to me.

Next thing he knew, I grabbed his free arm, pulled myself up onto his shoulders, and wrapped my leg around his neck, letting the other hanging down his chest.

Holding the sword to his chin and tilting it up at me, I smiled down at him.

"Dead again," I said.

"Get to your room," he said, his voice that low growl that made everything about my position different no matter who was around, "now."

"Yes, my King. Now hold still."

I jumped off him, flipping in the air to land in a crouch.

When I stood up, I tossed him my sword, hilt first, and bowed.

"Thank you for a skilled fight," I said, "but I need to call it a night."

His eyes grew golden, and he bit his lip, bowing with a sword in each hand as he maintained eye contact.

"Amazing," Nevan said, shaking his head, and clapping one hand against the back of the other where he was holding the wound in his side. He walked over to us, and smacked Tristan on the shoulder.

Tristan bent forward a bit, his eyes widening, before he straightened again.

"King Tristan," Nevan said, "I have never understood you more." Then he turned around and headed to the stairs and the waiting Marquessa who looked like she wanted to kill all of us.

"Does he seem oddly strong for such a..." Tristan started, staring after the Prince.

"Soft person?" I asked.

He looked back at me, his brow low, all the humor gone from his face. "I was going to say, 'slight.'"

"Either way, yes. He's weirdly strong, and when he held me back from coming out here to protect you, he was bigger than he seems."

"I'm not sure I like anything you just said." Tristan's jaw clenched and I laughed.

"You're cute when you're jealous," I whispered as I passed him.

He made a snarling sound low in his throat, and I wondered if he was going to be able to wait until I was through the panel between our rooms before he reminded me who I belonged with.

Grinning, I made my way down the stairs past the collection of people still staring at me. As I moved through the crowds, soreness started to seep into my muscles, and the sweat on my skin began to cool and grow uncomfortable.

Tristan had the bath in his room, and I needed it now.

Once I was in my room, I didn't bother to take off my clothes before I crawled across the bed and opened the panel.

Before I was even through the wall, Tristan was there helping me, crushing my lips to his.

He pulled back from the kiss then shut the panel, smiling at me and shaking his head.

"You just had to wrap your legs around my neck, didn't you?" He picked me up and carried me toward the bath as I grinned down at him.

"Well, you look so good with my legs as a necklace. I couldn't help it."

"The only problem with it was that you were wearing far too many clothes."

"Really? I thought the only problem was that we had an audience and none of them are supposed to know about us." I raised a brow at him, and he bent his head to kiss my stomach as he let out a long breath before setting me down next to the bathtub.

"I know. And that's the real problem." He ran a hand along the sweat at my hairline, brushing the small hairs back from my face. "I wanted you so badly when you were wrapped around me. It was everything I could do to stop myself from kissing you out there."

"No one is here to stop you now," I said, wrapping a hand around the back of his neck.

He grumbled low in his chest and held me tight against him, pressing his mouth to mine as his hands pushed against my back making our bodies form together.

But a second later, he pulled back and gave me a short kiss before he bent to the tub and started filling it up.

"One day," he said, straightening up and helping me undress as I fished out the ring from my bustier, "you're going to be my Queen, and then I'll be able to kiss you whenever I want in front of whoever is looking."

"Maybe by then you'll have had your fill of me," I said.

He shook his head and took the ring, slipping it onto my finger.

"Not possible. No matter the scars," he kissed next to the stitches in my cheek, "the calluses," lifted my hand to kiss my fingertips, "or if you get round and soft," he grabbed my ass and pressed my hips to his, "you'll always be my brightly burning flame."

"Tristan," I said, running a hand along his jaw and staring into those shifting eyes, "I love you. Even when you're a pain in the ass. I love you."

"You belong with me." He went back to helping me take off my clothes, and I returned the favor before we climbed into the bathtub.

But it wasn't the heat of the water that chased the aches of training away. It washed off the sweat and refreshed my skin, but it was his hands, the hot touch of his fingers running along my body and kneading into my muscles, that banished all the soreness from my body.

CHAPTER 28

PERFECT

"At some point," Tristan said, rinsing out my hair, "we're going to need to spar under new rules. You can't wrap your legs around my neck."

"Do you think you could beat me if I didn't do that move?" I asked. "That's cute."

He splashed me in the face and laughed as I giggled.

Wrapping his arms around me, settling my back against his chest, he kissed my neck and took a deep breath.

"You are objectively better than I am. And I love sparring with you, and showing off your skills. But…"

"But what?" I ran a hand along his arm and braced myself. 'I love you, but…' was never a great way to start talking about something.

"I can't say it isn't still difficult for me to even think about you out there with Corvids, or any other enemy targeting you." He buried his face in my neck, and I tightened my hold on his arms around me.

The feeling was mutual. Watching from the sidelines while he fought the Corvids attacking the ship while I wasn't able to stop it was my worst nightmare.

"Just don't do what you did today, please?" I asked, my voice low. "I can't handle that again for the same reasons it's hard for you."

Nodding, he relaxed and started to kiss my neck.

His mouth, hot enough to rival the steaming water around us, sent waves of sensation through my body.

Pushing myself tighter against him, I discovered that being naked in a bath with him had an effect. He was ready for me.

Reaching a hand behind me, I grasped his hard cock in my palm and stroked him, relishing as he sucked in breath and groaned into the skin of my neck.

He dipped his hand down my stomach and softly rubbed my clit.

"Tristan," I said.

"Don't forget," he whispered, reaching his hand down further and entering me with one finger. "We need to be quiet."

"I don't want to be," I said, my breath coming faster as his finger sped up, his palm pressing against my clit. I responded by stroking him in time to his movements.

"Neither do I," he said, his voice that thick, gruff growl that made me throb. "Especially when you do that."

"You like that?" My voice a breathless moan.

He picked me up as he stood, sending water splashing out all over the floor, and carried me to the bed, laying me down, soaking wet, and hovering over me.

"I don't like that. I love it, like everything you do," he said, spreading my thighs with his knees, and rubbing against me.

At first, the water from the bath made us almost stick together, the friction almost too much. But his cock rubbing against my sex made my own wetness enough to combat the bath water. He finally entered me, driving into me in one thrust that made me shatter around him, crying out.

"Just like that. I love that, too," he said, his voice rough enough again to make me whimper.

He kissed me, and I savored the taste of him, the warmth of his skin on mine, the feeling of him moving within me.

If I thought the stretches after my workout helped relax my muscles, I was wrong. When his hands rubbed against me, it turned my body into liquid. And if I thought his hands were capable of remaking me, turning me into hellfire water, they were nothing compared to him inside me, moving with me.

Pulling back from me, he smiled, and I grabbed for him.

"Tristan," I said, "don't stop. Come back."

"Cinder," he said, kissing my palm, "I'm not going anywhere."

With one hand, he braced himself above me, with the other he pressed down with barely-there pressure on my lower abdomen and suddenly, that spot he managed to hit inside me that sent me over the edge was even more sensitive.

I cried out as it drove me past the limit, and I went tumbling down the other side of that cliff of pleasure.

"Cinder," he moaned, falling down after me, crashing into my own wave of pleasure with his.

My throbbing matched his again, and it was as if the feeling was never going to stop.

But eventually, his growling moan ceased, and he collapsed into my arms, wrapping his around me.

"Tristan," I said, running a hand through his hair, sleep tickling at the edges of my mind and my vision, every part of my body still wet from the bath, warm from his heat, and as relaxed as I had the ability to be.

"Maybe I can pass a law that says we can be as loud as we want," he said into the skin of my neck.

"Do you think that would get us out of the trouble I'm pretty sure we just caused? Because if Second Prince Nevan was in his room just now, he heard that."

When Tristan laughed, his whole body rumbled against me, and my toes curled as I smiled.

"Good," Tristan said, and I shook my head.

"Not good. No one is supposed to know, remember?" I kissed his forehead.

"Cinder," he said, pushing himself up so he could look me in the eye, his chin sitting in his hand. "Why can't they know?"

"Because the Marquessa wants you, and that's a good bargaining chip to keep them on our side in this war." He knew this. Why was he asking this?

"The Marquessa doesn't want me." He shook his head, his eyes softening as he looked at me. "She wants the crown. I'm just attached to the crown. Same thing everyone else thinks."

"Not true," I said, shaking my head. He squinted at me. "That's true of her. And I'm sure lots of other people. But, honestly, I would prefer it if you weren't King. I loved you before I was willing to even begin to accept the crown that went along with it."

"I know, Flame." He took his other hand and ran a finger along my jaw, closing his eyes on a small smile. "That's part of why I think you'll make a good Queen. You don't actually want to be Queen."

Furrowing my brow, I tried to make sense out of that. Instead, I kissed him and decided he lost his mind.

"You need to sleep," I said.

"How about I sleep right here," he said, lowering his head back down and wrapping his arms around me again.

"Perfect."

CHAPTER 29

CONGRATULATIONS

The day we returned to the castle, I was still dressed as the deadly Fighter Cinder, but I wasn't able to do much with my hair other than pull it back into a braid.

Part of me wondered if Madam would be upset with me when I got back.

But as the carriage pulled to a stop in front of the castle, I had to admit I was too happy just to see my friends again to care much if I got scolded.

Going back to them, my friends and Madam and the General, was as close as I imagined it would be to going home if my parents were still alive.

During their lifetimes, I never went anywhere without them to be able to go home to them. They left occasionally, and they would come home to me if they didn't take me with them.

But it had been a long time since going home didn't make me brace myself for a beating. Now, going back to the women who had become like family, even the thought of their frustration or scolding, or anger, never made me think they would actually hurt me.

Even when I was such a failure at first learning to dance, Madam never lashed out at me.

My mind was on all the ways my life was so different now than when I first went to the palace. I didn't pay enough attention to who was in front of me in the hallway.

Until I noticed Prince Nevan's purple hair, and tried to avert my gaze as I made my way past him.

"Congratulations, Lady Cinder," Second Prince Nevan said.

If he had not said my name, I would have been looking around to see who he was talking to. What was he congratulating me for, exactly?

"Excuse me, Prince Nevan?" I asked, thinking that was neutral enough to cover all manner of strange thing he was referring to.

"I wanted to be among the first to congratulate the future Queen of Onyx." His smile was as close to genuine as I thought his face could be, and I still opened and closed my mouth on words that wouldn't come.

"King Tristan informed me on the ride to the castle once I agreed to his terms." He leaned in closer, and I was too much in shock to stop him from whispering in my ear. "Not that I couldn't see it anyway. Or…hear it."

"You…Um…" Good job, Cinder. My first conversation with a foreign official as the future Queen and I couldn't speak.

He heard us?

Oh, Gods and Goddesses, this was bad.

"Don't worry. I understand why you both tried to hide it. And I'm only a little jealous." He smiled and walked away, leaving me in the middle of the hallway as the activity of everyone returning flowed around me.

Making my way in a daze to Tristan's room, I didn't bother to check what the voices inside were saying before I swung open the door.

General Pace stepped back from the maps on the table in

front of her, the piles of paper that were probably full of reports fluttering.

The Chamberlain gave me a tight smile from a chair set along one side, ever-present notebook and quill in hand.

And Tristan beamed, leaving the table to come and take my hand, leaning in to kiss me on the lips in front of the Chamberlain.

"What are you doing?" I asked, my voice thin because nothing felt real still. "Prince Nevan knows."

"He knows because we have our agreement with Amethyst." Tristan said, tucking a loose piece of my hair behind my ear. "There's no reason to hide it anymore."

"Congratulations, Lady Cinder," the Chamberlain said, grinning, and only managing to make everything even more surreal.

"But you hate me," I said, the filters on my words broken in the strange new reality I found myself in.

The Chamberlain cringed while General Pace and Tristan laughed.

"My apologies," the Chamberlain said. "All I wanted was an alliance with Amethyst because they are Corvid's strongest allies, and it would be a way to slow the slave trade. I thought that would come through the Marquessa and a marriage. But this is a much better solution."

"An all-Onyx throne benefits everyone," the General said. I was dizzy, lightheaded with the change in my circumstances.

"Cinder," Tristan said, running a hand along my jaw and making my eyes slip shut from the heat of his fingers, "as soon as this war is over, we are going to have a massive party to celebrate, and top it all off with a wedding and a coronation."

I snapped my eyes open again. The full weight of what a wedding and a coronation would mean came crashing down on me, threatening to pull me under.

My brother...

"First, though," I said, taking in a shuddering breath, "we need to end this war."

Tristan's mouth tightened into a firm line, and his eyes grew grave.

"Yes."

"May I question the prisoner? See if I can find out what that letter meant?" I was on my knees begging him in my mind, but I had to keep my voice steady.

"Among these," General Pace said, her voice tired as she waved at the piles of papers, "is a report from a physick. He thinks the prisoner is well enough to be questioned now."

"Good. We will question him tomorrow after I get caught up." Tristan looked back at me, his face still worried. "Are you sure you want to be part of the questioning?"

"Of course." I nodded.

"Then you can come with us tomorrow." His eyes softened and he smiled, tucking an arm around me to put a hand on the small of my back. "Do you mind if I come to your room tonight?"

At that I smiled, my stomach flooding with bubbling nerves and my heart picking up its pace.

"We don't have to spend anymore nights apart," I whispered, forgetting the two other people in the room as I kissed him deeply and thoroughly.

Tristan pulled back and put his forehead to mine.

"Do you still have the ring?" he asked.

I pulled it out of my bustier, and he slipped it on my finger, biting his lip.

"Seeing you wear that, having everyone know," he said, shaking his head like he was as surprised as I was, "it's hard to accept being this happy when we're at war."

"That, I understand," I said, putting my hand to his chest, but an errant thought made me snap my eyes to the Chamberlain and the General. "But I can't wear this yet."

"What?" Tristan said, and he may as well have been speaking for all of them based on the Chamberlain's open mouth and the tiny line between the General's brows.

"Not until you speak to the other potentials waiting for the bride hunt to start up again."

"Oh," Tristan said, laughing. "You're right. How about I get you a chain to wear it around your neck until we get back to the palace and I can tell the others? The Marquessa already knows."

"I would like a chain," I said, touching the ring with my other hand, and less willing to take it off again than I thought I would be.

"Tonight. I'll bring it to you, tonight."

Smiling, I kissed him again and left, making my way to my rooms, and wondering how I was going to protect the future the ring represented from Brix while Tristan and the General were there.

CHAPTER 30

WANT AND DESERVE

Opening the door to my rooms, I took in a deep breath and held it, waiting for the explosion of screams when I told everyone about the news.

But no one was in the main room.

They were probably spending time in Gus' room.

"Careful, careful," Jacquetta said, her voice floating through the door from Gus' room with a note of panic in it.

Who was she talking to?

Rounding the corner, I found Gus out of bed, her leg wrapped tight in layers of bandages, her bad arm supported by Madam Valentin under her armpit, and the other by a wide-eyed Jacquetta.

"You're walking," I yelled and ran forward, holding my hands out in case she needed me.

"For the second day in a row," Madam said, beaming with pride for our girl.

"A little bit. Not too much," Jacquetta said, like she was trying to convince herself.

I smiled while Gus gritted her teeth and kept taking slow, deliberate steps toward the bed.

They got her to the edge of it, Jacquetta and Madam both taking a moment to breathe and pause.

"You ready, Gus?" I asked, while she leaned against the mattress, trying to take the weight off her leg.

"Ready?" Her eyes widened as I bent down, got her around the waist, and hauled her up while she squealed.

"Cinder," Jacquetta yelled.

"Just grab her feet and sweep them to the side," I said.

Madam and Jacquetta did as I asked, and I lowered Gus back into position without even popping the tape on her bandages.

"See?" I said, turning to look at all of them, and patting Gus' hand while she gaped at me. "Sometimes I'm useful to have around."

They laughed, slowly at first, their giggles trickling out of them. But the sound built until everyone was past the tension of worrying about Gus as she tested out her leg.

"You do make a very pretty people mover," Gus said, laughing and settling back into her pillows.

"Hopefully as people find out I'm going to be Queen they'll think I'm useful for more than that." I shook my head and plopped down into a chair at the table.

"Everyone knows you're also very useful for stabbing people, too," Jacquetta said, perching on the edge of Gus' bed.

"And for terrifying our enemies," Madam said, smiling as she sat across from me and took a deep breath.

"Maybe we should wait until the war is over to tell the Kingdom," I muttered, turning the ring around on my finger, and doubting that anything they listed would be particularly great recommendations for the Queen. They didn't sound like the any of the noble women I had ever met, let alone a Queen.

"Lady Cinder," Madam said, leaning forward and narrowing her eyes at me, "I thought that was already the plan. Has something changed?"

I smiled. It didn't matter how much just thinking about the

judgement of the entire kingdom made my heart heavy in my chest and sent tremors wanting to shake through my hands. The thought of being able to kiss Tristan and be with him openly was enough to etch my smile into place, and have it never fall from my face again.

"Tristan made a treaty with Amethyst," I said, my voice low.

Jacquetta and Gus looked at each other. Gus shrugged and Jacquetta shook her head, but Madam's smile widened, taking up her entire face.

"Wonderful. So, I will need to start planning very soon." She drummed the fingers of one hand on the table in front of her, and her eyes took on a faraway look that made me wonder for the first time what she would prepare for the wedding.

"Cinder," Jacquetta said, "I feel like Gus and I are missing something."

"He's going to tell the other potentials as soon as we get back to the Obsidian Palace. The Marquessa already knows."

And there they were. The screams.

Gus and Jacquetta screamed, and Jacquetta jumped up and down, clapping her hands.

"We get to plan your wedding," Gus yelled.

"First," I said, grinning at the idea of being a bride, which once upon a time wasn't something I thought I would ever want, "I think we should plan yours."

"Oh, Gus," Jacquetta said, climbing up next to her on the bed and wrapping her arms around her, "do you think the King would marry us?"

"He's too busy for that," Gus said, slipping her hand into Jacquetta's.

"No, he isn't," I said. "I am sure he would be more than happy to marry you."

More screaming.

The way they planned their day, the detail with which each

of them added their opinions and hopes to the picture Madam painted, made me think about my own.

I didn't want anything more than Tristan standing beside me, telling the world he was with me forever, and a long life of loving him.

The life part of that equation was something I was comfortable without just a little while ago.

Now, though, I had to think about the day. A whole day dedicated to the hope of life instead of the finality of death.

What did someone do when they were inspired to live after spending their entire adult life delivering death, and expecting they would die young because of it?

More than that, how did someone like me celebrate that inspiration in a day?

"Cinder," Jacquetta said, and I had to shake my head to focus back on the conversation happening around me.

"Yes?" I asked, hoping I didn't miss too much, and that they wouldn't be upset with my preoccupation.

"Do you know what kind of flowers you're going to want for yours?" she asked, her smile unfaltering just like everyone else's in the room, as if none of them noticed how absent my brain had been.

Good. I didn't want them to think I didn't care about their day.

I cared more about theirs than my own. My friends deserved the best.

But I actually had an answer for her on this one.

"There is only one kind of flower that I want," I said, looking down at my sigil ring with the flames of Lehar on the side, picturing them in my mind, the color as rich as the one Tristan associated with his mother and his personal color.

"I want crimson roses like the ones that used to grow in Lehar. They even had bright green stems, and leaves as if the hellfire water below the ground made them that way." And they were my mother's favorite.

"Does that kind of rose even still exist?" Gus asked, looking to Madam.

Madam smiled, soft and sad, and I swallowed, knowing it was likely they didn't.

In all the places I had been for kills, I never saw roses exactly like them.

"We will find them. I know they are very rare now, but our Queen deserves to have what she wants."

Part of me didn't think that was true. I was already getting so much more than I deserved.

But that didn't stop me from tipping my head to her in thanks and hoping she would be able to find the roses I remembered.

CHAPTER 31

KISS

For the first time since Tristan and I saw each other nude, I had a chance to prepare for him to come to my bed.

Madam and Jacquetta helped me take a bath, dry and brush my hair, and then it was up to me.

Standing in my room, staring down at the pile of nightgowns Madam had made for me, I wondered if wearing nothing would be the better option.

But looking at my reflection in the mirror, at the muscles and hard planes of my body, I wanted to look softer. I wanted to look like a queen. Like the kind of lady my mother had been.

One of the nightgowns was a short, silver, flowing piece of organza that shimmered in the low light of the hellfire lamps turned down. It had an empire waist, and little pieces that draped along my arms.

Putting it on, it did exactly what I wanted it to.

I was...pretty.

Not powerful or terrifying. Not even the scar on my face—the stitches for which Madam had just removed—lessened the effects of the nightgown.

The only other thing I needed for a perfect night was Tristan.

Sitting on the bed, I looked out at the dark night and the even darker sea.

Out there somewhere, hidden among all those shades of black, riding on top of the deceptively calm depths, were Corvid ships waiting to strike again.

Hopefully, the war would move off the water soon. Then we could fight somewhere I was more comfortable, and the Corvids would be more at risk of my blades.

They had already hurt too many of Inara's people...my people.

Every person in Breakwater and across the other lands that made up Onyx were my people now. I needed to think about them that way.

I took a deep, shuddering breath, and wrapped my arms around my knees, still listening to the sound of the waves crashing against the bottom of the castle and watching out to sea.

At some point I must have curled up and fallen asleep, because the next thing I was aware of was the searing heat of Tristan's hands as he scooped me into his arms, and pulled back the covers on the bed.

"Tristan," I said, his name like a sigh, wrapping a hand around the back of his neck.

"Shhh, go to sleep, Flame. I'll be with you all night." His voice was low and gentle, like a loving caress as he laid me down in the bed.

"Come here," I said, tugging on his hand.

He huffed a low laugh as he took off his clothes, and climbed into the bed, wrapping me in his arms before he pulled up the blankets, enclosing us in a cocoon of his heat.

"You really should pick something else to say to me when you want to sleep," he said.

"But I don't want to sleep." I pressed myself against him, breathing in his breath, basking in the warmth of his body as it sent shivers along my skin. The aches in my muscles eased.

"Not sleeping sounds good to me." His hands roamed along my back, running his fingers through my hair, and sliding along the silky fabric of my nightgown.

"Then kiss me." I played with the hair at the nape of his neck, and felt his smile against my lips as he leaned into me and placed the ghost of a kiss on my lips.

"You want me to kiss you?" That smile was in his voice, and I groaned making him laugh.

"Why are you so mean to me?" I ran my leg along his, and wrapped it around his waist. My want of him grew by the second while his hands trailed heat up and down my back.

"Mean?" He leaned into my neck and kissed it, opening his mouth and playing his tongue along it, the fire in it making me suck in a breath. "Is this mean?"

One of his hands dipped low and reached around my back-side, the side of his fingers pressing against my sex from behind.

I moaned as a throb went through me, wanting him.

"Cinder." His voice had that low, gruff, growl quality to it again, and it made my need grow.

"You are so wet. Did your dreams do that? Do you want me to let you sleep? Tell me what you want." He kissed along my neck still, not letting me cover his mouth with mine.

"I always want you. Always."

He growled and turned me, sending my front into the bed, climbing between my legs behind me, continuing to run his hand along my sex as he spread my legs apart.

"Stay right there, Cinder. I want to watch that perfect ass move while you get even wetter."

"Tristan." Now his name sounded like begging, and I didn't even care. I would beg if it meant he would finally be inside me, filling me the way I wanted—needed him to.

Moving his hand, he ran it along my sex, spreading me and rubbing my clit with his fingers at the same time.

With his other hand he pushed the short night gown further up along my spine, and pressed down on the small of my back.

"Is this what you want?" he asked as he drove me closer to the edge.

"You," I said, my voice thin, my breaths coming faster and faster. "I want you."

"Why do you want me? Because you like this?" He kissed along my ass and the small of my back, making me buck.

"Hmmm," I was beyond words, I was so close to the edge.

"Because we belong together?" He adjusted, his legs trapping mine, which were spread just enough.

"Yes." With one more rub against me I was gone, falling off that cliff, breaking apart. He was slamming himself into me, making me cry out as he moaned. And I broke again.

Still moving within me, he bent over and took my chin in a gentle hand, turning my face to his, playing his lips over mine, and still denying me the kiss I wanted.

I whimpered, needing his lips on mine.

"Tell me," he said.

"You belong with me," I said, and he throbbed inside me, making my legs shake beneath him. "Your tongue belongs in my mouth. You belong inside me."

"Cinder." His growl on my name was louder, his movements inside me harder, and his hand moved to grab my hip as he slammed into me.

"Tristan," I said, turning my head again, needing that kiss, needing to taste that sweet tang of his mouth.

Finally, he claimed my mouth with his, his tongue caressing mine, and I broke apart again, moaning at the same time he did, our mouths echoing each other's pleasure.

But he didn't stop, even as I felt him throb inside me, which sent me over that cliff again and again, he kept on, moaning into my mouth.

His thrusted faster, deeper, harder, until he bit into my shoulder, and growled into my skin through his teeth. I called his name while we both shook and sagged against the bed.

Not bothering to pull out of me, he rolled us over and pulled the blankets up high again, kissing along my neck as he curled himself around me.

Part of me wanted to roll over so I could kiss him, but another part didn't want to move.

"I love you, Cinder," he whispered into my neck, sleep heavy in his voice.

Before I could say it back, or turn and get that kiss, his breathing was even against my back, and his arm limp across my middle.

"Good night, my King. When you wake up, I'm getting that kiss."

CHAPTER 32

BURN

I woke up to that heat trailing along my hairline. It was his favorite way to rouse me, and one I hoped he would continue so long as I awoke next to him.

"Be careful," I said, my voice muffled by sleep, "you keep waking me up like that, I'm going to get used to it, and not be able to wake up without it."

"Good," he said, laughter in his voice, "because I don't see any reason to wake up without you next to me from now on."

Opening my eyes, I met his, burnished brown and gold with flecks of hellfire green, shining down at me.

"Tristan," I said, his name enough to make my heartbeat faster and my hands reach for him, to touch the searing heat of his chest.

"Cinder." He closed his eyes and kissed me, finally, his lips soft and tender. "I want to stay here."

His words played along my lips as he kept his to mine.

"Stay, then." I smiled as I said it, knowing it was impossible, and yet the fact that he wanted to stay made me feel more like a queen than any crown could.

"Now I know why my mother and father kept separate

bedrooms." He laughed and pulled back from me, still running his fingers along my face.

"They kept separate bedrooms? Do we have to do that?" Something sunk in my stomach even thinking about it.

"Would you mind if we had the same bed? You could still have a space just for you to get ready, somewhere to get away from me. But I would like to share a bedroom with you."

He looked so unsure, his words stumbling, and I snuggled in tighter to his side.

"My parents shared a room," I said, running my hand along his chest to his jaw. "I want that with you."

Smiling, his eyes shining, he bent to kiss me again. This one more insistent, even as a knock came at the door, and he turned to groan into my neck.

"Unfortunately, I can't stop that from happening." He sat up and pulled me up with him, playing with the little piece of my nightgown hanging down my arm. "Do you always wear things like this to sleep?"

"No, this was for you, and because it made me feel pretty." I shook my head and looked down the nightgown flowing along my front. It was an embarrassing thing to admit.

"You are beautiful no matter what you wear." He smiled and kissed me, climbing from the bed, and throwing on pants before he headed to get the door.

I believed him. It didn't matter to him that I was 'far too muscular' according to Madam. And as proud as I was of my strength, the things it allowed me to accomplish, and the protection I could offer my King and my country, feeling beautiful without all the work Madam and my friends put into my looks was still a challenge. But the way he looked at me, even smiling over his shoulder as he put a hand on the door, chased away my doubt.

"King Tristan," the General said, stepping inside and shutting the door behind her, "Lady Cinder." Her nod my way was small, but made the fact she stood in my bedroom while I was in my nightgown and he was shirtless, a tiny bit less weird.

Although I still pulled the blankets further up onto my lap.

The whole world would soon know beyond any doubt I was sleeping with the King. It was time for me to get over thinking that it was strange for everyone to know my personal business.

"General, it's early," Tristan said, coming back to the side of the bed and slipping his shirt on.

"Yes, but there are reports from the guards who arrived in Thirteen Rivers Valley that you need to see." She handed him a few sheets of paper, and he sat on the edge of the bed, reaching one hand back to me to thread our fingers together as he read them.

Looking over his shoulder, they seemed to be reports of rumors from the people of the Valley. But…

I sucked in a breath and looked at the General as she stood straight next to the door, chewing on her lower lip.

"Do we know who it is? Can this be right?" I asked, trying to deny to myself what they said, unwilling to look at it too closely. Because I couldn't. Not yet. Not before I had proof.

"The last one in the stack details a slaughter at a farm on the outskirts of the Valley. It seems some of the forces the people believe are staying in the hills and stealing from them at night got tired of scraps." The General nodded to the where Tristan was still reading, his hand tightening on mine.

"No attacks from the air, yet?" Tristan asked, handing the papers toward me as he looked up to the General.

"So far, it is just ground forces. And unfortunately, aside from clearly staying at that farm and taking it over for a time, we have no idea who they are or what they are doing in the area."

"Could they be Corvid ground forces coming from the opposite direction to fight alongside their winged troops once the birds get past the coast?" I asked, looking through the papers and reading a terrible account of a family destroyed so forces could set up camp in their home. It was so like the little town Gus was kept in that my cheek ached with memories.

"Possibly," the General said, "that is what we have to assume regardless of whether we find proof of that."

"We need to send more guards to the Valley," Tristan said, running a hand through his hair and making it stick out at odd angles. "Get as prepared as possible."

"And set up sentries and patrols along the border," I said, earning me the attention of both Tristan and the General.

"That might upset this fragile alliance we have with Amethyst," he said.

I nodded. He was right, but it didn't mean I was wrong.

"Doesn't mean it shouldn't be done," I said, my voice low, even as I wanted to go down the hall and punch Second Prince Nevan in the face until he answered some questions.

"Careful sentry and patrols," Tristan said, looking away from me to focus on the General. "They need to understand how tenuous their position will be out there. We don't want Amethyst even knowing they're there."

"Yes, Sir," she said, nodding.

"It's also time for us to ask our prisoner some questions," he said, his voice growing hard. "As soon as I get dressed, that's what's next."

"As soon as we both are dressed," I said, flinging back the covers and climbing out of the bed.

"Cinder," he said, standing and rounding the bed to me, taking my hands, "Are you sure you want to be a part of this?"

"One hour from now," the General said, opening the door, "I will be ready to question the prisoner."

She shut the door behind her, and I narrowed my eyes at Tristan, tugging my hand from his and crossing my arms.

"Why would I not want to be there for this?" I asked,

straightening my spine and preparing the list of wounds I wanted to give Brix. "He hurt my friends. This is personal."

"I know." He folded both hands behind his head, closing his eyes and tilting his head back for a moment before he looked back at me. "But there will be things I'm going to do that you might not want to see."

Laughing, I wrapped my arms around his middle and leaned my head against his neck.

"Tristan," I said, unable to stop smiling, "nothing you do in there is going to be somehow worse than what I want to do to him."

His hands fell onto my back, running his fingers through my hair as a single huff of a laugh moved through his chest.

"You're right," he said.

"My King," I said, smiling, "I think when it comes to blood-shed, you'll get used to saying that eventually."

His laughter that time was longer and louder, his entire body relaxing against me.

"Again, you're right."

"Oh, I know. Now," I unwrapped my arms and pushed at him, "go, get dressed. We have work to do in an hour."

"Flame," he bit his lip and kept his hands on my shoulders, his eyes pinched like he was still worried.

"What?" I put a hand on his cheek, for the first time in a long time wondering if he didn't like my enjoyment of violence.

"Just don't…" his hand strayed to my face and the worry etched around his eyes softened into something else, "don't burn him so bad he isn't able to tell us anything."

I smiled and turned him toward the door. "I'll try."

CHAPTER 33

CELL

Almost every weapon I could wear at once while still being comfortable was strapped onto me as I walked toward the stairway to the cells.

"Are you going into battle?" Prince Nevan asked as I walked through a room where he was holding court, smiling and telling tales I was sure he thought were charming to all who would listen.

"Of a sort," I said, not stopping. I had work to do, and if he wasn't careful, I was likely to say something nasty that would upset Tristan and their agreement.

"Please tell me, Fighter Cinder. I find you very interesting when you're bristling with sharp objects." His dark purple hair matched the deep, velvet jacket he wore, the lace around his face and hands a pale lilac. The whole thing was a bit too much purple, but I wondered if mentioning his clothes negatively might get him away from me.

I cut a glance his way, narrowing my eyes.

He was fucking with me. He had to be.

"That has to be the worst line," I said, "and possibly the stupidest, I've ever heard."

Prince Nevan blinked at me, his mouth falling open, and then he laughed, boisterous and explosive, until he touched the corner of one eye like he was wiping away a tear.

"Having words with you is a kind of diplomacy I was never taught." He laughed again, and I shook my head, still not sure what he was doing.

"Good thing you talk mostly to hear yourself speak." I needed to get out of here, but part of me wondered if he would follow.

The laugh that answered my dig was sharper than the last.

"You should be part of more of our negotiations." His voice was hard and heavy with meaning that I didn't understand. "That is, if you really are as straightforward as you seem."

He didn't know me. He knew nothing about me.

This ended now.

I stepped up next to him in one swift move, my mouth at his ear and my chest a breath away from his.

He stiffened and all the conversations around us hushed.

"Don't worry, Second Prince Nevan," I whispered into his ear, my voice as close to another blade as I could make it, "I would never risk your *fragile* negotiations with the presence of me and my blades."

Slipping one of my spikes from the sheath at my thigh, I stepped back and touched the point of it with the finger of my other hand, looking past it at him.

"One never knows when one of them might slip because of a careless word I take as a threat."

Pursing his lips around a smirk, he tipped his head at me and cocked one eyebrow.

I turned around, put my spike away, and left the room to find my way down to the cells.

He always blurred the lines between calculation and some strange attempt at sincerity and friendship.

But I had enough friends. I could be that Goddess of Death he labeled me. I didn't want to be anything else to him.

Whatever game the Prince thought he was playing, I didn't want to understand it. I had more important things to worry about.

Around two more corners, I came to the top of the stairwell. General Pace stood there waiting for us with two guards next to her.

"No King Tristan?" I asked, standing alongside her.

"He will be here any minute." Her eyes narrowed as she perused the short sword strapped to my back, the hilt showing over one shoulder, the two spikes on my thighs, the dagger on each hip, and the throwing knives tucked into a strap on each cuff.

She lifted her brows, and waited for me to explain myself.

"You never know when someone might need to lose an appendage," I said.

One corner of her mouth twitched. Her brows lowered again, and she turned away without saying a word.

Good. Maybe I would actually be able to gut Brix, and get this over with.

Although, even after running it through my head a thousand times, I still wasn't sure how I would find out about my brother without Tristan knowing as well.

Standing there, waiting for Tristan to arrive, I allowed myself a moment to hope that he wasn't coming.

If this was just me and the General, it would be best. Better yet, she could just allow me to question him by myself.

But the hope died in my throat as Tristan came around the corner, adjusting a cuff full of throwing knives.

For the first time in a long while, I didn't want to see my King.

I swallowed, and turned toward the stairs.

He came up beside me, touching a hand to my arm and

kissing me on the side of my head, looking toward the stairs with me.

"Are we ready?" he asked, and I knew the question was another way for him to give me a chance to walk away.

"Of course," I said, turning my gaze on him.

He nodded, his face all lines and angles, nothing soft about him. The General stepped past the guards as they moved aside.

Making my way down the stairs this time, with Tristan by my side and the General in front of us, I both knew more and so much less than last time.

And this time, I knew exactly how much I had to lose.

Everything.

We walked down the rows of cells, all of them empty now. I allowed a moment to look at the back of the General's head, and wonder what happened to the other prisoners.

Finally, standing in front of his cell, I got my first look at this version of Brix.

I built him up in my mind for so long, the idea of this monster who sat on his bed, one arm still in a sling, one hand bandaged, and his nose no longer on his face straight. But looking at him now, he was just Brix.

Just the same person I had known all my life. My brother's best friend.

There was no stopping the screaming in my head. All I could do was curl my hands into fists and keep the questions inside my mind.

Were you always this, Brix?

Did Ash know?

How many people did you kill? Torture?

Why were you there?

Did my brother approve?

And what was he planning?

"I see you brought your assassin," Brix said, looking right at me, his mouth in a line, but a smile in his eyes.

Cold rushed through me.

He couldn't say that. He couldn't call me that. Not in front of Tristan.

"Just in case you think it would be a good idea not to talk," Tristan said, his voice low but as hard as the sword on my back.

"Right," Brix said, leaning back in his seat. "So, what do you want to know?"

"Let's start with where you're from," the General said. Somehow, she managed to sound bored.

I wanted to look at her, to see her face and try to understand her angle so I could play along with her. But I couldn't look away from Brix. I couldn't break his eye contact. If I did, he might say something else. He might tell them the truth about where he was from. And destroy me in the process.

"You know," Brix said, smirking at me, "I don't think you actually care where I'm from."

My breathing became a conscious effort. Not too fast, not too slow. I couldn't react.

"Tell us what you think we care about," Tristan said.

It was a challenge. A question like that, so open-ended, meant Tristan was already giving Brix enough rope to hang himself with.

Enough to hang me, too.

CHAPTER 34

HANG

"You care about your country," Brix said, and I swallowed, waiting for him to say it, to tell Tristan the truth.

Brix looked at me and grinned, that leering, sharp smile I saw too much when Ash beat me in front of him.

Oh, Gods and Goddesses.

I sent up a prayer to my mom and dad, begging them not to let this happen.

"Of course, that's boring," Brix said with a laugh. "What do you really care about?"

He narrowed his eyes, and looked at the General, studying her.

"You want to know about the Corvids, and why me and my group attacked at the same time. If we were in with the Corvids, or something separate."

I couldn't breathe, but my heart crashed against my ribs as hard as the waves outside slammed into the bottom of the castle.

"And you, King," Brix said, looking Tristan up and down and

shaking his head, frowning, "you care about what I did to those two girls. But more than that, you care about her."

He looked back to me, turning his entire head to focus on me, the move slow and deliberate, leading Tristan and the General to move, too.

Every eye in the room was on me at once, and I had to force my lungs to continue to take in air. Slowly, deliberately, I breathed while my fists clenched so tightly that my knuckles popped.

"You..." Brix stared at me. His voice was thick with threat, and Tristan went as still as the stone around us, "...all you care about right now is what I'm going to say, and when you can kill me."

I couldn't stop the sneer that formed on my face, even though he smiled when I did it.

Fuck. This fucking asshole knew he got to me.

Tristan grabbed for the door to the cell, and the General fiddled with a key, working on unlocking it.

Brix only smiled wider, more feral, his eyes still on me.

A growl built in Tristan's throat. The General finally got the door unlocked.

He took three steps, and roared as he punched Brix in the face, blood spraying from Brix's re-broken nose as he was thrown back against his cot, laughing.

"Don't ever talk to her," Tristan said, his voice what I imagined a dragon would sound like.

"No, Tristan," I said, running inside the cell and grabbing his hand before he could swing again. We couldn't give Brix what he wanted.

The look Tristan turned on me was equal parts rage and terror.

"I'm fine," I whispered, looking into eyes that were the brightest hellfire green and surged in a way that made me think the color was moving in them, until he looked back to Brix. But he held back, his hands curled like claws at his sides.

"Yes," Brix said, wiping some of the blood from under his nose, and looking at the red that stained his hand before smirking up at us, "*Tristan*, she's fine."

I sucked in a breath, and it was my turn.

Reaching past Tristan, I pulled my spike in one movement, held it under Brix's chin, and forced his head to tip back.

"Give me a reason not to kill you," I whispered, my voice a hiss. "Fast. Tell me something that is worth letting you keep your life for even one more minute, you fucking monster."

He laughed, and I pushed the tip of my spike into his skin, drawing blood that dripped in a line down the spike to fall across my fingers.

The laughter died in his throat.

"Fine," he said, his voice thin and squeezed through his teeth and his clenched jaw, "Corvids only thought I was working with them. All those people you killed were Corvid people."

Even as my own blood roared in my ears, flooding through me faster than it should, I heard every single word he said, and took more from them than either Tristan or the General did.

Maybe my brother didn't know.

"But the people I actually work for wanted me there," he said.

And my world turned black.

I could still see through it, feel through it, breathe through it.

But nothing looked the same.

"Why?" the General asked from over my shoulder, and I stiffened, making Brix suck in a breath through his teeth.

"Not yet, Cinder," Tristan whispered, his voice still sounding like he was breathing fire as he put a hand on the small of my back, his touch as light as air and so hot my entire body broke out in a sweat the second he made contact.

"So we would know what the Corvids were doing. So we could know the right time to make our move."

"What fucking move?" I asked, forcing my voice to remain low so none of them heard it shake. This was it. This was everything I needed to know.

Yes, I wanted to know if my brother was aware of who Brix really was, but he wasn't going to tell me that. He wasn't going to give me what I wanted. This is what I needed. I needed to know what the fuck Ash was planning.

"Not everyone wants him as King."

I dug the tip of my spike a tiny fraction further into his skin and snarled. Too fucking close. He was way too fucking close to saying it.

"And not everyone wants you, someone who is only worthy with a blade, as Queen. Some want you dead." Brix said.

Shaking my head, I didn't know what the fuck that had to do with anything. A second later Tristan roared and pulled me away, turning back to punch Brix, again and again.

He loomed over the bed, his fists flying, the blood from his strikes flinging all over.

General Pace tried to grab one of his hands and pull him back.

"King Tristan," she yelled as he continued to pummel a now unconscious Brix with the other fist, "you have to stop. You'll kill him. We still need information."

I slipped my spike into its sheath, ducked a flying fist, and stood right in front of Tristan, my hands on his face, and my eyes on his.

"Stop, Tristan," I said, and he froze under my hands, one arm stopped mid-struggle with the General. She pulled away and held one hand as if she had injured it, his other arm part way through another swing. "You need to stop. He doesn't matter."

Tristan took in deep, shuddering breaths and closed his hellfire eyes, touching his forehead to mine as his hands wrapped around me.

"He…can't…talk…that way…to you." His words came in between his massive intakes of breath.

"I'm okay," I whispered, kissing his lips, the heat from him still making me sweat even as it sapped me of the fury and agony running through me moments before.

While Tristan pulled me in tighter, I nodded to the General as I led him toward the door. The part of my heart that Ash owned, the part where my only living family, my entire world for seven years was housed, began to burn into dust.

Pausing at the door to the cell, I waited until the General bent to check whether Brix was alive.

I hoped he was dead.

Even if I didn't find out what my brother was planning. Nothing mattered as much to me anymore as Brix dying, and being able to hold onto the man in my arms and the friends that I had waiting for me.

General Pace straightened and nodded, following us out of the cell and locking the door.

So he was still alive.

All that meant was that I would have to come back and kill him.

Next time, before Brix got a chance to get as close as he did to giving away all my secrets, I was going to drive my spike into his chin.

Tristan clung to me, his face in my neck, as if he wasn't sure I was still here.

"We need to get out of here," I said.

He nodded and stood up straight, looking me in the eye as he ran a hand along my jaw, just under the scar on my cheek.

"I want him dead for hurting you. For plotting to kill you."

"And I will kill him as soon as we learn what we need," I said, wiping a spot of blood from Tristan's cheek. There was still so much more that sprinkled his body and his face. Some was in his hair, too.

Killing Brix was going to come sooner than Tristan could know, but we needed to get out of there while the General looked on. He seemed in a daze from his rage.

"He said he was working for someone," the General said, passing us and heading for the stairs. "I need to know who."

Swallowing, I held Tristan's bloody hand as we walked away from the cells, trailing after the General.

That was one thing I thought I knew the answer to. But there was no way I was going to let the General find out.

CHAPTER 35

LET GO

"I don't want to let go," Tristan said, wrapping me up when we got back to his rooms, the General still with us.

"No one is plotting against me," I said, taking his face in my hands and staring into his eyes. "He's fucking with you so you'll kill him, and he won't have to answer any questions."

"Cinder," he said, his voice full of warning and doubt.

"Tristan, please. Trust me. I saw it in his face. That damn grin. He wanted us to attack him. It was all a twisted game." He needed to believe me. I wasn't wrong, but it was hard to convince him when I couldn't explain why I was so sure.

"Sir, I think she's right," General Pace said, marching back and forth not far from where we leaned against the big table.

"I don't care if it was a ploy or not." His voice was low, and his arms tightened around me.

"Well, you should. Because as long as you're worried about a plot against me that doesn't exist, you're not focused on the war like you need to be. And you're definitely not thinking about the threat looming around Thirteen Rivers Valley." I raised my brows and refused to look away from his bright green gaze until he shuddered and nodded, his arms loosening their grip a fraction.

"And that's what we need to understand more than anything else. All we have now is confirmation of what we already suspected." The General was just speaking her thoughts out loud now, her heavy footfalls like exclamation points to her words.

"Right." I kissed his cheek, and stepped a little further from him.

He squeezed his eyes shut and let me go, only holding on to one hand with his.

"Fine. I fucked up." He ran his other hand through his hair, the blood in it making it stand up even more wildly than it normally did when he did that. "What do we do from here?"

I had never seen him act so lost, so unsure of himself and his next move. It made my stomach flip over, and a chill ran up my spine.

"Obviously," I said, about to use my best chance to fix this, "the next time he's ready to be questioned, I go in alone."

"Absolutely not," Tristan said, pulling me tight against his side.

"Good," the General said at the same time, finally pausing in her pacing.

"Yes, Tristan," I said, shaking my head and squeezing his hand to reassure him at the same time. "He wanted to fuck with me to get to you. He doesn't care about me at all. It's a game to him. One I'm better at playing now that I know his rules."

That part was a lie. I wasn't good at this game, and it was pushing it, maybe even over selling the case. But this was the best chance I had.

"It's a good plan. Lady Cinder would never be in any danger. She would be armed, and he wouldn't. And if she questions him soon after he regains consciousness, he might not have time or capacity to come up with a new angle to his game."

Nodding to the General, I looked at Tristan, waiting on his word.

Having the General on my side for this plan was helpful, but he was the most important voice in this room. And we all knew it.

My breaths were shallow while he looked at the floor and clenched his jaw, his grip on my hand tight.

Finally, he breathed out, and went from leaning his ass against the table behind him to slumping.

"Okay, but I want someone posted at the top of the stairs just in case. So all she has to do is scream." He looked at me. There was a line between his brows, his mouth tensed.

"I'm going to be fine. And when I have answers and he's dead, you're going to laugh about this." I smiled and leaned against his side, not wanting him to see the part of my statement that was a blatant lie.

While I was going to find out the answers, and get as many details as I could, he would never know.

"Good," General Pace said, turning to face Tristan head on, "now that we have a plan for that, we need to talk about the details surrounding the latest reports."

"Right." But Tristan didn't seem to be paying much attention to the General, or what they needed to do next. He was still focused on me next to him and not letting go.

"You should change your clothes and wipe the blood off your face," I said, stepping back from him again, giving us more distance than before.

He looked down at his hands and found the blood coating him, the blood he had almost painted me with in the process of holding me close.

"We're both a mess," I said. "And I'm going to clean up. So should you. Then have your meeting with the General."

I nodded. The General frowned, but didn't argue.

"Okay," he said with a sigh, "but I will see you soon."

My kiss on his mouth was short, but that was only because I needed to get out of his room before he thought to have me stay and get cleaned up with him.

He really did need to get to his work, and my presence would distract him. That was obvious.

Although, once I was walking the halls back toward my own rooms, I couldn't help but second guess myself.

Was this a good thing? This preoccupation he had with a threat to me when we were at war?

Maybe it was a way for him to do something he knew he could be successful at—protecting me—in the middle of so much he wasn't sure he could accomplish for the rest of the country.

But it felt like I was bad influence, whatever the reason.

Finally, I got back to my rooms and opened the door.

"Lady Cinder," Madam said, her mouth falling open, "what happened to you?"

She sat at a little table making notes in a notepad.

"It isn't mine," I said, looking down at the blood all over me.

Part of me wanted to tell her that the King had a lot more on him, but that wouldn't be any more reassuring than saying I was covered in someone else's blood.

"You need to get cleaned up. We have events to prepare for." She smiled at me as if there wasn't a red crust of dried blood along the skin of my hands.

"Events?" I asked, trying and partially failing to keep the frustration from my voice.

Now? Did we really need to have a bunch of events in the middle of a war while I was trying not to have my whole world fall down around me?

"Of course. The entire castle wants to have a celebration for you, and for the treaty with the Amethysts." Her smile was kind, even as her gaze allowed no room for argument.

Unfortunately, that reason for an event made perfect sense, no matter what else was going on.

"Right." I smiled back and headed toward my room, wishing it didn't make sense so I could argue with her. "I'll just take a bath and clean all this off before I get ready."

If only it was possible to clean off Brix, his knowledge of me, and the stain he threatened to show to Tristan just by existing.

CHAPTER 36

BLACK

"No," I said, looking at the dress laid out on the bed, swallowing around the lump in my throat as I held onto the ring on the chain around my neck.

"Gold is the color of weddings," Madam said, putting the last gem in my hair. "It is appropriate to wear it for tonight."

Appropriate it might have been, but it also felt like tempting fate. And after the way questioning Brix went, just looking at the color sent my knees quaking for reasons I couldn't entirely explain to myself, let alone Madam.

"Maybe, but I would rather wear the crimson one, his color." That was a good enough reason.

She pursed her lips and raised a brow at me, but she put away the gold dress and helped me into the red one.

It was the rich, dark crimson he loved, shoulderless with thick straps of fabric that almost looked like sleeves on my upper arms, and a line of black gems like scales down each.

On the bodice, more black gems made two dragons over my breasts, their tails wrapped around the sides of my ribs and down my back where the dress was cut into a low vee.

"What does this one say?" I asked, my voice hushed as I

looked at myself, standing in the beautiful gown with gems in my hair that mimicked a crown around the pile of curls on my head.

"The gold one says we are celebrating a wedding," Madam said, standing back and looking over me. But her face softened, and she met my eyes in the mirror. "This one says you are his."

"His."

She smiled and left me holding onto that.

While Tristan said we belonged together—and deep in my bones I believed him—the part of my mind that was still bruised and battered by Ash and his lessons, struggled to fully accept it.

I left my room and made my way to Gus' to helping her get into her dress while Madam helped Jacquetta.

"Gus," I said, looking at her standing there, hanging on to the edge of the bed with her red hair shining in a complicated series of braids with gold cuffs throughout, and looking like she was already dressed in gold. "You look beautiful."

"Maybe, but I'm going to look pretty naked if you don't help me into this thing." She screwed up her face as she looked at the gold and hellfire green brocade dress in her hands.

"Come on," I said, grinning and taking it from her, "you know that if you're too much trouble while I get this on you, I'll just toss you over my shoulder and force you into it."

She laughed and gritted her teeth as she picked up her bad leg as far off the floor as she could, which wasn't even to the knee of her other leg.

There was so much strength she still had to get back, her poor leg muscles still healing from the holes and tears Brix caused her with his poison.

I slipped the dress under her, helping her as fast as I could so she would be in less pain. I wanted to kill him. Right now.

We managed to get the dress on her, squeezing and tugging to get it over her ample ass.

"You said take a bite out of mine, but Gus..." I said, shaking my head at the round shape of hers in her dress, "...your ass looks better than mine ever has."

"Oh, shhh," she said, waving a hand, but her cheeks turned pink, and she grinned. "Do you think Jacquetta will like it?"

"Gus," I said, tying the last tie on the back of her dress, and slipping her arm through mine. "Jacquetta is going to love it."

This was as much a celebration of their upcoming wedding as it was mine and the treaty with Amethyst.

Everyone, the entire castle full of people, especially those from Breakwater, needed a break from the horrors of everything happening around us. We needed to look at Gus and Jacquetta, a beautiful, glowing couple, and find hope for the world after this was all over.

"Maybe I should change," I said, looking down at the dragons on my breasts.

"No." Gus rolled her eyes even as she smiled at me. Her smile wasn't as broad as it used to be, but it was getting better. "King Tristan won't be able to take his eyes off you in that. It's the perfect mix of soft and dangerous."

Soft and dangerous...Looking at her, that's what she had become. After everything with Brix, after training and fighting, coming back from an injury, and putting herself in harm's way for Jacquetta— she was the real warrior.

"Gus, when we get back to the palace, after you're all healed up, would you like to keep training?"

"Yes." Her eyes brightened as she turned to me, away from focusing on her careful steps. "Cinder I want to be able to fight back better than before."

"Perfect. As soon as I can."

She squeezed my arm and we kept walking, making our slow and deliberate way toward the grand ballroom of Sandstone Castle and the celebration of everything we were looking forward to, everything that wasn't found at the edge of a blade.

"Jacquetta won't like it," Gus said. "Maybe don't tell her."

"We need to tell her." I narrowed my eyes at my friend. Why would she want to hide something from Jacquetta? "Why won't she like it?"

Gus cut a sideways glance my way, and sighed.

"She's struggling with anything that makes her think about danger." Gus shook her head. "After what happened, she doesn't want to hear about the war. She even broke down the other day when I mentioned the training grounds."

"Oh." I missed so much. All this time spent worrying about Brix, and about my own problems, even after I knew that I was so checked out that my best friends fell in love in front of me and I didn't notice. I still didn't see how almost losing Gus was affecting Jacquetta.

"Maybe when we get back to the palace, maybe after the wedding, I can try and get her to train with us." I wasn't sure what else I could do.

"No, Cinder. That works for you and me, but it would just make it worse for her. Let her be. She's friends with you. Eventually, she'll be able to get past the fear."

"What does being friends with me have to do with it?"

Making our way down a set of stairs meant Gus leaned further into me, her other arm gliding along the banister on her other side.

Part of me didn't expect her to answer, her focus was so completely taken up with trying to step correctly and not hurt her leg.

"No one who knows you, who you really are, can entirely hate violence," Gus said, and I almost lost my own footing.

"I'm not sure that's a good thing." I wasn't sure what it meant, about me or anything else. But it made my heart hurt for what my very existence put my friends through.

"Death is a part of life, Cinder. Just like night is a part of day. We can't ignore midnight if we love the stars. Sometimes, we just get scared in the dark."

At the bottom of the stairs, the celebration spread out before us. People from sailors with salt in their hair and clothes stained with the sea mingled with nobles in their finery in shades of the blue of the sea and the purple of the night sky.

But standing at the threshold of what felt like a whole breath for everyone around me, I was never more aware that my blood was darker than the black obsidian sigils of the Dragon King on the guard uniforms.

CHAPTER 37

CROWN

Jacquetta was radiant in her hellfire green gown with gold gems dripping down her lithe frame. Standing next to Gus, matching her and yet opposing her in so many ways, they made a vision that was so striking it was as if the entire party was for them alone.

"Your Ladies bring light to this affair," Second Prince Nevan said, coming to my side, and looking at them with a soft smile on his face that I wasn't sure he was capable of before that moment.

"Careful, Prince, I might start to believe you are nice," I said, smiling when he choked on his sip of wine.

"Now that would be a terrible thing to say about me." He wiped his mouth, his grin turning back to the kind he normally wore, insincere and full of calculation.

"Of course, for someone who spent so long in a Kingdom that traded in slaves, kindness would always be questionable." I looked sideways at him, and watched as that smile faltered and fell from his face, his eyes cast down into his glass of wine.

"Lady Cinder," he said, turning to face me, his perfectly groomed beard—which never seemed to get past just the hint of facial hair along his narrow face—making him look far more serious than I thought he was, "may I have the next dance?"

My brain emptied of any thought.

Did he really ask me that? Now?

I looked around the room, expecting Tristan to arrive and lead me out to the dance floor himself, to save me from this awkward moment.

"King Tristan isn't here yet." Nevan set his cup on a table behind us, and held out a thin, ring-covered hand that barely reached past the layers of lace coming out of his sleeve.

Taking his hand, I had a moment where I would have sworn my eyes lied to me, and the little hand holding mine was actually three times the size with thick fingers and callouses.

He led me out onto the floor, swinging me into place in front of him, holding me at the perfect distance for a valz.

With a nod to the musicians in one corner, a valz started, and I stepped into the movements of the dance, my other hand on a shoulder that didn't feel as bony as it should have under my palm.

"Prince Nevan..." I started, unsure how to finish the questions swirling around in my head.

"You aren't imagining things, Lady Cinder. But I want you know that my country is...complicated. And no one person knows everything about the people around them." He gazed directly into my eyes. Even when he was supposed to turn his head as the dance required, he kept those purple irises trained on me.

"That sounds like a warning." And it sounded like something he thought I should understand, although I had no idea.

"My mother is only part Corvid. The rest of her lineage is from a small country that managed to break away from Corvid's stranglehold on their trade. You see, they didn't want to trade their own people for slaves anymore." He looked away from me then, and I tried to keep up, tried to puzzle out what he was talking about.

"Perhaps you've heard of that small place at the edge of the continent." His face may as well have belonged to someone commenting on the weather of a bland day, but the pounding of my heart told me that this went far beyond that.

"What is the name of the country?" I asked, my voice a tight whisper, not sure I wanted to know.

"Gemiscrye." He looked back at me, his face still impassive to anyone watching. But his purple eyes bored into me, and I couldn't breathe.

Years ago, one of the first hired kills I did was for a noble-woman in Gemiscrye. She had me kill a series of people for her, organized through my brother. He said it was enough money to replace some ruined homes for our people.

"Queen Phailin, she is from Gemiscrye?" He nodded, and I wetted my lips, forcing myself to keep trying to learn what he knew of me. "And she still has some connections to her family from there?"

"Some. But I have more contact with them because of my position. She doesn't care to spend much time on foreign affairs, even if the foreign place is her own home country."

I sucked in a breath, and turned my head away as the dance required, although the movement was stiff. I struggled to follow the right steps with my feet.

He knew. Nevan knew about me.

Maybe not all of it. No one other than Ash, Brix, and I knew about my mission to kill Tristan, but Nevan knew I was an assassin.

Sneaking a glance back at him, he nodded once, as if he knew what I was thinking. And maybe he did. Maybe he could see the horror on my face, or feel the fear ricocheting through my veins.

The song stopped, but he didn't let me go. He waved a hand at the band, and they played another valz.

Nevan kept moving me in the steps of the dance, and I was too distracted to stop him, to walk away.

"For many years now, I have wanted to make a change in the way Amethyst works in international settings."

What? What was he talking about now?

"But I needed to make this treaty work a certain way to convince my brother, the crown Prince, that it would be good for the country."

I turned toward him, not caring that it was wrong for the dance anymore.

"You..." He always planned to stop the slave trade. But... "What about all the hellfire water stuff? The proposal?" None of this made sense.

"Again, I needed to make it a positive move for my country. Hellfire water was the obvious way to do that." His smile was back to smug, and sure, and bullshit.

It was all bullshit.

"I knew you didn't want me," I said, shaking my head and reexamining everything.

"Oh, I would not kick you out of bed, and I do want someone like you fighting for my country, but..." His grin turned lascivious, and it was everything I could do not to roll my eyes.

The truth portion of the night was over.

But even as he kissed the back of my hand before walking away after our dance was done, I couldn't figure out why he offered me any truths at all.

From the corner past his shoulder, I spotted eyes boring into me.

Marquessa Ziya stood seething as we danced.

"Wait, Prince Nevan," I called, catching up with him as he headed back to the refreshment table.

"Careful, Lady Cinder. When the King does come to this party, I have a feeling he would not appreciate thinking I am still trying to get you to leave him for me."

The laughter in his voice as he slowed to allow me to fall in beside him was obvious, and I didn't worry about Tristan thinking I wanted anyone other than him. He knew better.

"Very funny," I said, picking up a glass of wine as he did. "I was wondering, what does the Marquessa have to do with any of what you told me?"

He may have been here for his own ends, but the Marquessa wanted to marry Tristan enough to poison me. And at the same time that was true, she was still here. None of it made sense.

"Oh," he made a sad sighing noise and glanced toward her corner, holding the glass of wine in front of his mouth and pointedly turning away from her to look out on the others dancing. I followed his lead. "My cousin was engaged at one point. Did she tell you that?"

"No." *That* I would have remembered if I had heard rumor of it.

"Well, it was a secret at the time, and quite the scandal for a while. We had to manage a feat of will, diplomacy, and bribes to make it to go away so that it didn't taint my brother's reign."

"Your—" My mouth fell open behind my wine glass, and I couldn't speak.

"Believe it or not. They were both children at the time. Just a folly caused by one of them being a stupid, gullible teenager, and the other's parents being grasping, terrible people who were stripped of their titles. No one with any taste speaks to them if they can help it."

I sucked in a breath and tried to do the math in my head.

"How old are you?" My voice was a hushed and strained croak as the full weight of the ugliness her parents put her through as a child pressed against my chest.

"Ah," he touched the side of his nose with a finger and

winked at me. "Now you understand. I am twenty-eight, one year younger than my brother. My cousin is twenty-six."

"When was she secretly engaged?" I wasn't sure I wanted to know the answer. I didn't need to feel bad for the Marquessa.

She hated me and tried to poison me. Hating her back was easier than understanding her.

"My brother was sixteen."

The Prince of Amethyst was sixteen, and the Marquessa was thirteen.

Her parents convinced the two young children they were in love enough to enter into a secret engagement all to elevate their daughter to the throne.

When Tristan said she didn't want him, she only wanted the crown, I didn't know how far her parents had taught her to go to get what she wanted.

Looking back toward her corner, she was gone.

CHAPTER 38

NAMES

"Why are you telling me this?" I asked, half afraid to breathe.

"Because my cousin is…confused. And my allies need to know the people they will be dealing with as we both try and improve my country."

Improve his country?

Looking closer at him, I wasn't sure how much help we would actually be on that front. Sure, as part of the treaty, Amethyst couldn't trade in slaves with Corvid anymore. But, beyond that, how were we supposed to have any influence there?

My mind reeling, I made my way out to the edge of the party. Standing next to one of the large openings in the wall, I let the chill wind off the water sweep across my face.

Woefully unprepared. That's what I was for the world I found myself in. The world I was supposed to navigate just by loving Tristan.

Holding my drink tighter, I tried not to worry about being a colossal failure at all the things a queen was supposed to do, all the things she was supposed to be.

"Flame," Tristan said behind me, his voice like a wish.

Turning around, I found him in his formals, perfect and as beautiful as any human had ever been. I used his voice to boost my own hope that I would be able to be the kind of queen he needed me to be. Because even navigating things I couldn't fathom about other countries was worth it to be with him.

"You took so long," I said, not even caring that I sounded like I was whining.

He took one of my hands and placed it against his chest, folding his over top of it, and claiming my mouth with a kiss that reaffirmed to me that love was real, no matter how much it was battered by stories like the Marquessa's.

"I'm sorry. I wanted to do all the things I needed to so I could spend all night with you and our friends." His forehead on mine, he sighed, and a tension fled his shoulders as he touched my cheek with his other hand.

"Tristan, don't apologize. You're King. And I would wait for you forever." I kissed him in a quick flutter of lips, because, even though that was true, I didn't like waiting. And in a perfect world we could be like this all the time.

"Cinder, I don't want to wait. I want to marry you tomorrow." His kiss was more than mine, a promise of more to come.

Keeping my wine glass from dropping from my fingers as he pressed himself against me took more control than I would have believed I had.

But he pulled back and looked at my hand with the glass in it, laughing and shaking his head.

"I probably need to be more careful." He tipped his head at my wine, and I laughed with him, holding onto his hand. Dropping our arms down from his chest, I turned toward the party.

"Are you ready for a night where everyone can pretend nothing bad will happen again?" I asked, my voice low because no one else needed to hear my melancholy.

"More than ready. They don't get to spend time with you in

bed. They need this." His grin was wicked, and I turned away from him, laughing again.

"You probably should not run around telling everyone that." I wasn't sure how many people knew we shared a bed, but it was probably already too many for it to be appropriate by some rule of royalty I didn't know.

"Why not?" He kissed the back of my hand, grinning at me over the knuckles, laughed, and pulled me back toward the party. "Come on, we should at least go check on Augustina and Jacquetta."

"Maybe you should dance with Jacquetta for a few songs," I said, thinking of how sad she would be if she didn't dance at all tonight because Gus couldn't.

"I will do that. But first, Prince Nevan needs to leave her alone." He came closer to my shoulder, and nodded at where Jacquetta and Nevan were dancing a spirited quartanza, her smile breathtaking.

Gus sat to the side, everyone around her laughing and chatting, her good leg tapping on the floor.

Inara sat next to Gus, her wooden leg extended out, and swaying in time.

"You have made great friends," Tristan said, squeezing my hand.

"We do have great friends." I smiled and leaned my head on his shoulder, knowing that all of these women looked out for him the same way they looked out for me.

But I did wonder where his friends were. Was being King so lonely?

Lifting my head and watching him as he stayed back to bask in the glow of everyone else's happiness, I took the chance.

"Tristan, where are your friends?" I asked, my voice as light as I could make it, hoping I wasn't hurting him by asking.

"Of the few people I include on my list who aren't far older I am, like General Pace and the Chamberlain, most of them are leading the guard regimens somewhere. But one of them…" he looked around, straightening and standing on his toes, trying to see over the heads of everyone else in the crowded room.

"Cinder," he said, smile wide, "come with me. There's someone I want you to meet."

We weaved through the crowd, people stopping to smile or nod to us as we went. For tonight, the entire crowd in this room felt different than it had at the palace.

Maybe it was Inara. Maybe it was the distance from the capitol and the throne. Whatever it was, Tristan and I moving among them felt no different than anyone else.

Here, we weren't a King and his future Queen. We were just Cinder and Tristan.

If I could have bottled the feeling and carried it with me, I would have.

Finally, we reached the back of a tall man with dark brown, curly hair and dark bronze skin showing around the sleeveless tunic of teal he wore.

"Rath," Tristan said, and the man turned around, his face splitting into a wide grin of bright white teeth, his eyes crinkling at the corners.

"King," Rath yelled, grabbing Tristan roughly by one shoulder and pulling him in close to wrap his other arm around him.

He called him King like it was his name?

"You made it," Tristan said, patting Rath on the shoulder, and stepping to the side to include me in their little circle.

"I couldn't miss this. I'm more than willing to admit when I'm wrong about your stupid ideas." Rath jostled Tristan, who just shook his head and laughed.

"This stupid idea wasn't mine. And it was the best thing I ever did." Tristan's eyes turned to me, his smile softening.

"Ah," Rath said, flinging his arm around Tristan's shoulders.

"Hello, I'm Rath, spelled with an 'r,' but sounds menacing. And you must be the flame I hear so much about."

Cutting my gaze to Tristan, it took me a minute to accept that this wasn't just Tristan's friend. This was someone he knew well enough to talk about what he called me in private.

"It's nice to meet you. I'm Cinder," I said, wondering how this sailor and Tristan met and became friends.

"Nah," Rath said, jostling Tristan and grinning at me, "you're something. But a little bitty cinder isn't nearly big enough to describe it."

"Rath," Tristan said, his voice full of warning.

"Was that supposed to be an insult?" I asked, the polite and awkward smile falling from my face. My hand pulled from Tristan's, and curled into a fist at my side.

"I wouldn't insult you. Just making an observation. King here likes that you can look him in the eye." Tristan stiffened next to Rath, looking at the floor instead of me.

"Mmm hmm." My mumble wasn't agreement. It was a delay while I figured out how to respond. Exactly how much could I look this friend in the eye?

"Okay, Rath," Tristan said, shoving at Rath's side, "ribbing her to rib me isn't going to work."

"Come on, King. Trial by fire. The crown is harder than I am."

I stepped up to Rath, a breath from his face, and lifted one brow, my mouth tight.

"You think I'm just here for a crown?" I asked, my voice low and steady, as flat as I could make it.

"No, that isn't what I think at all." His grin disappeared. Now he studied me as if he wasn't sure what to make of me.

Tristan froze at his side, his eyes wide and darting back and forth between us.

"Believe me, I would prefer no throne. But that isn't the

problem here." I looked him up and down, not moving my head, and not stepping back.

"And what is the problem?" His voice was careful, and he was starting to lean away from me.

"That you think some stupid insults from a guy who is afraid of me is really going to be some kind of *trial*. You need to find a new target. Because when someone comes for my *rib*, they end up losing more than one of theirs."

CHAPTER 39

MAGIC

Rath threw his head back and laughed. Unwrapping his arm from Tristan's shoulders, he wrapped me up in a hug so tight I couldn't breathe.

I shoved back at him, none of this making me like him more.

"Perfect. You're right, King. This flame is perfect for you." He kissed me on the cheek with a wet smack, and I cringed.

"Eww," I mumbled, breaking free and wiping his kiss off my skin.

Tristan took a deep breath, his entire body relaxing, and laughed with his friend.

"How is the Baby?" Tristan asked, and I was even more confused.

Who was this guy? And what baby? Someone had children with him?

"*My* Baby is still the best out there. You should see the new sail."

"Are you talking about a ship?" I couldn't help it. I didn't want both their eyes to turn my way. I didn't want to be in this conversation anymore, but this was too weird.

"Of course," Rath said, smiling with a far-off look in his eye. "The Princess is the world's most perfect ship."

"We'll have to go out on her sometime with Rath so you can see her." The look on Tristan's face was almost the way he looked at me, but he was as far away from me as Rath was.

It was as if Tristan was in love with a boat named Princess.

"And you know this Baby well?" I asked, not sure at this point if I was capable of being more confused. But I might as well ask and completely lose my capacity for understanding.

"King gave me my Baby." Rath flung that meaty arm over my shoulders even though I tried to step out of the way. He leaned in, and, like he was telling me some well-guarded secret, said, "Imagine if I introduced you to King. He gave me the love of my life."

"Okay." Nope. That didn't clear it up at all. I still didn't know what was going on.

But a second later, Tristan and Rath were deep in a conversation about some time they were out on the water with the ship and had to lose an anchor.

All I could do was shake my head and squeeze Tristan's hand before I went to find Gus and Jacquetta.

Inara was still by Gus' side.

Jacquetta was still dancing, this time with a guard. The General and Madam Valentin were dancing along with them in the crowd of others.

"Did I see you talking to Rathmoreland?" Inara asked, waving me to a seat next to her.

Sitting down gratefully, I looked to where Tristan and Rath were talking with hands flying, laughter, and the occasional shout punctuating the conversation.

"Is that his whole name? Apparently, he is one of Tristan's friends." An odd friend. But as long as Tristan loved him, I was going to let him enjoy his time.

"He's also one of my best sailors, and one of King Tristan's cousins." Inara smiled and shook her head, looking their way.

"Cousin? I didn't think he had any family."

"Not on the Dragon King side. And his mother was Queen Tanith's stepsister, so only his cousin by marriage."

More connections that I should have known. More reasons my mother told me to pay attention when I ignored my lessons.

"But when I was young, I remember every summer, King Tristan, who was only the Prince then, came here and spent months on the Lady's Spark with Rathmoreland and his father."

"The Lady's Spark?" I asked, trying not to laugh, but not managing to shove the smile off my face.

"I told you," Inara said, grinning, "everything with the sea is female."

She did. She told me that, but I had no idea.

Gus laughed next to her, wild and free, watching Jacquetta dance, but she cut her gaze our way. "And that is one more reason I love Breakwater."

Now it was my turn. Inara and I both laughed.

All night long, we danced and laughed and talked with our friends and anyone else who came into the circle of whatever conversation we were having.

By the time the first rays of dawn were peeking through the windows, the yawns were more pronounced, some people were asleep on the floor or propped up in chairs, and I had never had more fun.

"What are the chances we'll be able to repeat this feeling for our weddings?" I asked, leaning against Jacquetta as she rubbed her feet, sore from so much dancing. Tristan held my hand while he talked to Rath on his other side.

"Maybe it's better if we don't," Jacquetta said, her voice soft and tired.

"But this was so much fun." In the middle of a war, at night, we all managed to find fun and light. I couldn't imagine a better feeling.

"Yes, but if it was that easy to repeat," Jacquetta said, smiling at me, Gus following her look on her other side and smiling, too, "it wouldn't be magic."

Now it was my turn to smile and look out at the last people on the dance floor, General Pace and Madam Valentin, dancing a perfect valz.

"Magic."

When I first went to the Obsidian Palace, I didn't believe magic was real. Sometimes I still doubted any kind other than the Corvids shifting into crows.

But at that moment, surrounded by my friends and loved ones, with all of us safe and happy, it made me believe.

CHAPTER 40

LIGHT

As dawn took over the room, the sun shining on the blurry and faded faces of the exhausted people all around me, I yawned.

"No matter how much I don't want to do this," Tristan said, squeezing my hand, "I think it's time we all go to our rooms and get some sleep."

"Good plan, King Tristan," Gus said, but her face looked skeptical as she stared down at the floor, her mouth screwed up to the side, "but I'm not sure I'll be able to get there."

"Oh, no problem little one," Rath said, standing up on Tristan's other side, and making his way to plant himself in front of Gus with his arms out. "Your carriage awaits."

"Um…" Jacquetta muttered, looking back forth between Gus and Rath.

"Little one?" Gus asked, her smile back.

"He has a strained relationship with concepts of size. Just go with it," I said, shaking my head when Rath beamed.

"As long as he doesn't have a strained relationship with understanding how much he can lift," Gus said, shoving herself out of her seat, all her weight balanced on her good leg.

"Nope." Rath scooped her up with one arm under her back and the other under her knees, the muscles in his exposed arms flexing larger than I expected. "Like I said, little one."

Gus laughed, Jacquetta smiled behind a hand, and Rath grinned as he turned and carried Gus out of the room with Jacquetta on his heels telling him where to go.

Madam Valentin and General Pace spotted them as they left, and followed them up the stairs, too.

"Well," Inara said, stretching, "I need to at least try to sleep."

She stood up and turned back to me and Tristan, her smile softening.

"You two also need to actually sleep tonight. It was a good night, but I don't want my King and my Queen to hurt themselves." She pointed at us and grinned before patting my leg and walking away.

After all this time, it took a party for her to finally drop the formal speech around us.

"That's our cue," I said, leaning against his side.

"Everyone cleared out fast when I said something. Maybe I should have stayed silent."

"No, it wasn't you." I let my eyes slip shut. "It was the day coming to end our night. The light of the stars always gets outshined by the sun, and when it does everyone knows the world we had in the dark sleeps until we can be there again."

"Cinder." He ran the heat of his fingers along the back of my hand and stood up, pulling me with him.

"I want you to take me to bed," I said, leaning in close to whisper in his ear.

With a sweep of his arms, he carried me the way Rath carried Gus, and I couldn't stop smiling.

"You're going to be too tired by the time we get upstairs to my room." I ran a hand along his jaw, marveling at the soft lace. "Did Madam get you lace that doesn't itch?"

"First of all," he said, looking down at me and not taking the way to my room, "we're going somewhere closer than your bed."

Smiling, I leaned my head against his chest.

"And second, I will never be too tired to take you to bed." He kissed me on the forehead, and a small laugh rumbled his chest next to my cheek.

"Is there a third?"

"Yes. She did get me lace that doesn't itch. So I hope you meant it when you said you liked this."

Inside my slippers, I curled my toes at the thought of always seeing him in the formals.

"Tristan, someday seeing you in these clothes is going to get us both into a lot of trouble. As long as you're okay with that." I leaned up and kissed along his jaw.

"More than okay with that." He opened his door and kicked it closed behind us, not putting me down until we got to his bed.

"But, Cinder," he bit his upper lip once he laid me in the blankets and leaned over me. Before he closed the distance and kissed me the way I wanted him to, he said, "I need to apologize."

"Apologize?" My voice was thin, of all the things I expected him to say as he carried me to his room, it wasn't that. The joy of the celebration began to trickle down the hallway away from me.

"Yes. I wasn't..." He collapsed to sit on the bed next to me, and ran a hand through his hair. "Today when we questioned the prisoner, I wasn't a good version of myself. And, even now, I can't get the images out of my head."

"Images?" I couldn't seem to do anything other than ask one-word questions. I still didn't know where this conversation was going.

"When he said that about you. I saw..." His voice closed off as if he choked on the words, as if he couldn't physically push them away.

Climbing across his lap, straddling him, I held his face in my hands until he looked at me.

"Tristan, nothing is going to happen to me. Please believe that I am safe, we are safe. And I will never let anyone hurt you."

"Which means you can't let anyone hurt you, either," he said, cupping my good cheek with one hand, and running a finger of the other right underneath the skin of my scar.

"No one who wants to live will get close enough." I kissed him, but his kiss back was still sad, still full of reverence. It felt as if he were trying to protect me with his kiss, give me enough love that it would cover me and keep me safe from harm.

He didn't need me to make love to him tonight.

After laughing with our friends, finding some joy in this mess, all my King needed were my arms.

So I undressed and then took his clothes off for him in silence, continuing to kiss him, until we climbed under the blankets, and I wrapped him up with my arms and legs.

"Tristan, I love you. I'm right here. Safe in your arms." He tightened his hold around me, the muscles in him slowly starting to relax, until his breathing evened out, and sleep found us in the early morning light.

CHAPTER 41

HOPE

After Tristan was asleep, he didn't let go of me. Even after I woke up from a scant few hours of sleep, I spent an hour wrapped in his arms, trying to extricate myself from his grip, knowing I needed to try and get down to the cells to finish Brix off. By myself.

The night before, the celebration was a welcome and needed break from our reality. But it was a new day, and I needed to face it.

My brother was plotting against the country.

It was so far beyond a personal vendetta now.

The last war came because of the hellfire water stores. I knew that now. And Ash had always known, so why did he make me believe Tristan needed to die?

Why was he still working to destroy our King?

"Cinder," Tristan mumbled, pulling me in tighter, his skin an inferno.

"Shhh," I said, running a hand along his cheek.

Brix and his bullshit had managed to rip into Tristan's mind in a way that even time spent surrounded by the joy of our friends didn't release him from.

And that was reason enough for me to kill the bastard.

Knocking sounded on the door and he jerked, groaning into my skin before he flopped over onto his back.

"Yes?" he called, his voice thick, his eyes still squeezed shut.

"There's news from Thirteen Rivers Valley," the General said from the other side of the door.

He opened his eyes at that and sighed, but his hand stayed locked around mine.

"And Captain Rathmoreland's other ship has arrived," General Pace said.

"Fuck." He threw back the covers and tore into a trunk, dressing in seconds in clothes much more fitted to training than his formals. "I'm on my way."

"What does that mean?" I asked, sitting up and wrapping my arms around my knees, his frantic movements making my stomach churn.

"Rath does a lot of special work for me." He leaned across the bed and kissed me, one hand cupping my cheek. "Get dressed and come find me. I'll explain everything."

He was still buttoning his jacket when he swung the door open on General Pace.

"Madam Valentin is on her way down here," the General said, looking around Tristan, and then leaving with him.

Rubbing my hands over my face, I tried to figure out where everything got shoved off the track of my plan.

Brix needed to die. Now. Soon.

And every damn time I planned to do it, something made it impossible.

Fine.

No more letting that happen.

Madam would get me dressed, and I would stop at Brix's cell first. Whatever Tristan was doing would have to wait until I had my answers.

Or I was likely to lose my mind before Brix and his information lost me everything else.

It didn't take long for Madam to have me ready in more Fighter Cinder clothes.

I hoped that the black of them would hide any blood that managed to get on me. I made my way down to the cells with all my weapons on again, not bothering to hide them.

Getting close to the guards at the top of the stairs, every possible excuse for my presence poured through my mind. None of which I still thought were any good.

But they didn't stop me. They let me pass with nothing but nods of their heads.

Nodding back, I tried to school my face to keep from looking as surprised as I was while I walked down the stairs.

Of course, as soon as my feet hit the stone floor, it was obvious why they let me pass.

I wasn't alone down here with Brix.

Voices broken by the sound of the surf underneath the castle bounced along the stones of the room.

Maybe they were down here doing something else. I could just stab him though the heart and be done with it.

None of my questions would be answered, but I would rather be blind to the answers until I could find them some other way rather than risk Tristan talking to Brix for one more minute.

But all my hopes for today were destroyed as soon as I got closer to the cell.

Inside, messing with Brix's face, were a physick, and two more guards.

The chances I could kill him without the physick knowing while they stood right next to him and examined him were so bleak, they made the ashes in Lehar look vibrant.

Shit.

Now that I was down here, though, I couldn't just turn around and leave without raising some kind of suspicion.

Instead, I walked into the cell and leaned on the bars next to the guards, staring down at Brix.

"Fighter Cinder," the physick said, "now is not a good time to question the prisoner, and he will be recovering all day today from what I need to do."

"What do you need to do?" I asked, my voice cold. "Because if it is a matter of pain, let him suffer."

The guards bit down on the smiles curving their lips.

"No. It is a matter of keeping him alive long enough to be questioned."

I narrowed my eyes at Brix.

He had fevered spots of sweat on his forehead, his breathing was ragged, and he held the thin blanket before his barely-seeing eyes as if he was a child clutching a teddy bear.

"Pity. Right, Lady Cinder?" Brix said, his voice flat and shaking. "Sometimes it is hard to tell just how bad something is. Especially if someone has the kind of wounds others have all the time, so people think they know what those entail."

Brix managed to focus those eyes on me and nod his head a fraction before he slumped back and passed out.

"Good," the physick said, prying apart each of Brix's eyelids and checking his unfocused eyeballs. "Now I can get started on the surgery."

"I will leave you to that."

Making my way out of the cell, I ran through what little Brix said in my mind. He made such a point to look at me, to make sure I was listening to him...did he just give me a message? And if he did, what was it?

Something about it...

How would he have even been giving me any message? Especially one he thought I would understand when I had yet to ask him a single thing, and was talking to the physick about something totally unrelated to the questions I had for him?

Why would he think getting me a message about wounds would matter?

I…

Oh. It wasn't about wounds at all.

There was one question he knew I wanted the answers to. It was what I screamed at him as Tristan dragged me away from his cell the first time.

Did my brother know his best friend was a monster?

Brix just told me no.

Ash knew Brix was terrible, but assumed he was terrible in the same way Ash was. Not in this grotesque, inhuman, beyond-all-words, evil way.

For the first time in a long while, I was able to breathe a sigh of relief.

It wasn't everything. And I still needed to get back there and kill him as soon as I could. But it was something. If Ash had known what Brix was doing, there would be no coming back from that for him and I. All hope of repairing our relationship would have been dead.

This way, at least there was a small chance that one day I could talk Ash out of whatever mess he was in, and convince him to back our King.

All I could do right now, though, was find Tristan, and see what was going on with the war.

CHAPTER 42

INFORMATION

"Good. You found us," General Pace said as I walked in the door to the meeting room they had been in when we looked at the letter they found.

The whole room was packed full of guards who received orders from commanders and the Chamberlain, and then cleared out.

"Where is he?" I asked, not finding Tristan among the sea of people.

"In there." The General tipped her head to a closed door on the other side of the room, and started that way.

Trailing behind her, the level of energy in the room made me want to ask one of the guards what this was about.

So many other times, what I saw was just the few people at the top of plans. But this was close to mayhem with the number of people pouring through.

What was going on?

Finally, weaving through the crowd, General Pace and I tucked ourselves inside a smaller room.

Tristan's head popped up the second I walked in the door,

and he got up from sitting with his head close to Rath's. He came to my side and tucked me into him, kissing me on the forehead.

"It's better when you're here," he whispered into my skin, the warmth of him chasing away the last of the dread I felt down in the cells with Brix.

"Everything is better when I find you," I whispered back.

"Good, the Queen is here, too," Rath said, leaning forward in his seat, still rubbing his hands together, that wide smile not reaching his eyes.

"Rath," I said, and I heard the worry in my voice. It wasn't doubt of him.

Somewhere over the course of the party, I grew to trust him the way Tristan did. Completely. But this Rath was not the same person as just the night before. There was a weight to him now, and all my alarms went up.

"Flame, we have a problem." Rath's voice held all that weight I saw hanging over him, and it hit me in the chest as if he passed some of it to me, too.

Pulling Tristan with me, I made my way to one of the chairs clustered around Rath's. Tristan sat next to me.

General Pace took another chair.

"Tell me," I said, still holding Tristan's hand.

"First," Tristan said, holding up his other hand, "you need to know Rath runs information for me."

He put a heavy emphasis on the word "information," and I looked at Rath closer.

"And how do you do that?"

"Sailors move in and out of many ports. Most of the sailors have more connection to the sea, their ship, and their crew than they do to any kingdom." Rath raised his brows at me like he was willing me to understand.

I tried to imagine a world like the one he described, and I

kept getting stuck on one of the taverns I visited when I was on assignment in another country that was in a seaside town.

The people in that tavern all seemed to know one another. Their agreements and arguments all went back to things that predated that night. They referenced things that made no sense to me, and some of the crews were people from different nations all acting like a family.

Looking back at Rath, thinking about his open and engaging way with people, even if his way was odd to me, I started to understand.

"Which means that when you pull into a port somewhere," I said, "you learn a lot of information."

"Exactly," Tristan said. "So, now that you know all of that, he can explain the rest of what he knows."

"My other ship arrived with some strange news out of the lands of our new allies."

"Amethyst?" Cutting my gaze back and forth between all three of them, they all looked grave, and none of them told me I was wrong.

"Rumor has it Amethyst is struggling on the brink of their own war."

"What?" They were right. We had a huge problem if that was true.

"One of the nobles has their eye on a crown, to the extent that the other nobles and the royals are all concerned about them amassing some kind of personal army."

"Are they amassing an army? Because if they are, then, yes, it's a problem, and maybe we should do something about it. But if they're not, then there is nothing to do, and it could be as simple as bad blood between families."

"That, among other things, is what we've been talking about. What should we do about this? Because they are amassing the army. We have confirmation."

I sat back in my seat and looked around at them, wondering how many sides we would be pressed on.

"Do we know which noble?" I asked. "And is this related to the letter or the attacks in the Valley?"

"We were just getting to that," Tristan said, wrapping my hand up in both of his, chewing on his bottom lip, his skin growing hotter.

"Not yet, we don't know who," Rath said, rubbing a hand over his face, "but we're going to find out. And maybe they're connected? We don't know yet."

"That sigil was purple," the General said, and I nodded.

My first thought was of Amethyst when I saw that sigil on the letter. Now it made me want to throw Nevan out on his ass.

"Is it a good idea to try and find a diplomatic way to speak with Prince Nevan about this?" Tristan asked.

Brows high, I wasn't sure how to answer that. Maybe he could find a diplomatic solution. Clearly, I didn't have that ability.

"You can, King. If anyone can find a careful way to ask if he knows of a traitor in his midst, it's you."

Suppressing an inappropriate smile over the fact that Rath and I were thinking along the same lines, General Pace distracted me.

The look on her face was more a glower than usual.

"General?" I asked. She didn't usually show her feelings so obviously, especially not when she was concerned.

"How do we know it isn't Prince Nevan himself?" she asked, and my mouth fell open. "He is the Second Prince."

"I got the impression he didn't want to be King, and was more than happy to effect the changes he wanted from his current position." Why was I defending him?

By the way Rath studied me, I assumed he was asking himself the same question.

"Maybe I'm being naive," Tristan said, "but I'm inclined to agree with Cinder."

"Actually," Rath said, and I swallowed, waiting for him to expound on all the reasons his information said I was wrong, "I think she's right."

I exhaled and tried to hide my relief. Maybe I still had some of my ability to judge a threat.

"From what I've heard, he's a showboater, but he's working for his people. A war wouldn't be best for Amethyst right now. Especially not with the deal you just struck."

"Right." Tristan said, and the General nodded, the heaviness about her lifting. "If nothing else, maybe we just staved off something worse by doing this deal."

"Okay," Rath said, smiling and slapping his hands onto his lap, "so when are we doing this wedding?"

"What?" I asked, laughing and almost dizzy with the change in the conversation.

Tristan grinned behind a hand, and squeezed mine with the other one.

"Listen, Flame, I'm here and I'm gone a lot. So now is the perfect time." Rath ducked his head and lifted his brows, aiming what felt suspiciously like a dad-look at me.

I turned to Tristan and the General.

General Pace lifted her hands in the air and leaned back, shaking her head.

"No, Rath. We want to wait until we tell the other potentials to even announce it. And then we'll plan after the war is over." Tristan leaned back in his seat, the picture of ease. Except for the fact that he still chewed on his lower lip, and his grip on my hand was too tight.

"And maybe we won't have anyone but us in the wedding." I said, relishing when Rath's mouth fell open and Tristan's eyes opened wide, looking back and forth from me to his friend. "Maybe you wouldn't even need to be there, Rath."

By the time I was done speaking, Tristan caught on, and so had General Pace, both of them unable to hold back their laughter.

"That was so cruel," Rath said, shaking his head, but a second later he threw it back and laughed and I knew I was forgiven.

Better than that, though, was that Tristan was smiling again.

CHAPTER 43

MOVES

"Are you sure you need to leave already?" I asked, trying to hold myself as proper and straight as Madam did, but wanting to grab her and keep her safe with me and Jacquetta and Gus.

"You need me to be at the palace, preparing for your new role," Madam said, smiling in that way that made my heart clench tight in my chest, and tears threaten at the backs of my eyes.

"But you could wait and go back with us." It wasn't the first time I tried to get her to change her mind. I hoped mentioning it again would be the time it finally worked.

"No, dear girl, I have all the plans for the weddings right here." She patted the large folio tucked under her arm that she refused to show me.

"You know, I could probably get things faster than you think if you let me see the plans." I tipped my head at the folio and tried for a soft smile.

"I know what you want, and I know what Jacquetta and Augustina want. None of you need to stress about any of it now." She smiled and took a deep breath, putting one hand on my shoulder.

For the first time since I left them in our room after they said their goodbyes, I was glad they had not tried to come all the way down here and go back up.

The pressure of unshed tears building in me when Madam looked at me as if I were another one of her girls, just like Jacquetta and Gus, made it almost impossible to remain as held-together as Madam expected me to be. If Jacquetta and Gus were here with their own tears, there would be no way I could hold back.

"Madam Valentin," I said, my voice thin and strained, "thank you for all you have done, and are doing for me. I would not have Tristan if it were not for you."

Her smile, bright and gleaming, made my heart clench tighter.

"Lady Cinder, somehow I think you both would have found each other even if I were not involved. People who belong together always do."

She patted my shoulder, and I couldn't help it, I flung my arms around her and held her.

The hug she gave me back wasn't staid and reserved. It was strong, and squeezed me tight enough to hold me together.

When she released me, I nodded, using borrowed strength to keep my tears at bay.

"I will see you soon, my soon-to-be Queen," she said, smiling.

"Soon, Madam Valentin."

All the times I left people, whether it was planned and calm, or I was running after them, or into some danger to protect them, it wasn't the actual leaving that bothered me. The sense of growing distance between us didn't pull my heart taught against my chest until some unknown point when the tether snapped, and my body finally relaxed.

But when someone left me, the times I was forced to watch them go and do nothing about it, it made my entire body ache and my hands curl into fists to stop me from going after them and pulling them back to my side.

For the rest of the day, my mind wandered to Madam, and where she was on her journey back to Bridgeton.

It felt like I was doing something, checking in on her, making sure she was okay. But it didn't really make sense. I had no way to know for sure. Yet, I still did it. As if the act of checking on her in my mind would somehow keep her safe.

The next morning, after I was too distracted too many times, Tristan came to my side and laced his fingers with mine.

"Come on," he said, tugging my hand.

"What are we doing?" I asked, following after him, trying to shake off all the thoughts swirling through my mind.

"You need to take a break."

"No, we have too much to do. There's too much going on." I looked behind us, back toward the meeting room.

"*We* need to keep our Fighter focused. And I only know one way to do that." He shot me a sly smile over his shoulder, the only hint that he wasn't talking about stealing away to have some private time with me.

"One day, Tristan, we need to talk about the way you sometimes stumble into innuendo." I squeezed his hand and he laughed.

"Cinder, what we need to talk about is how you think they're always accidents." His smile this time was just as heavy with the promise of time spent alone as his words were.

A tingle went down my legs as we rounded a corner into one of the large, open rooms where long tables were sometimes placed down the center.

"I didn't know you wanted people to watch," I whispered leaning in close to his ear.

"Soon," he whirled around and cupped the back of my neck

with his hand, the heat of him making my toes curl along with the way his eyes shined looking at me as he licked his lip, "we are going to have to return to this idea of watching."

He stepped back, one second his warmth soaking into my skin and making it hard not to imagine things no matter who was around, the next he backed up and pulled a short sword from a sheath on his hip. His smile morphed into something less stirring, and more gleeful.

"For now," he said, twirling the sword in his hand, "maybe we should just do some training."

I pulled my own sword, moving it from hand to hand as I started to circle around him, feeling the stone beneath my feet, a grin spreading across my face.

Not waiting for me, he lunged, and I blocked his swing, the sound of the blades striking bouncing off the stone around us and turning into something more like the crack of lightning splitting the sky.

Circling again, he quirked an eyebrow at me, as if questioning why I wasn't attacking.

But I wanted this fight to last, and the only way to do that was to play defense, to let him come to me.

We parried and turned, clashed and swung. Our laughter joined the chorus of the storm from metal on metal, the untamed joy of pretending death didn't exist.

Tristan started to pick up on my moves, to anticipate them, and adjusted his attacks accordingly.

Eventually, one lucky break and a twist of his blade, my sword went flying through the air, clattering against the stones of the floor.

He dragged in heavy breaths that mirrored mine, his grin wide while I suspected mine looked wicked.

"Are you done, Cinder? You can pull another weapon. Or maybe you have some move I haven't seen yet." His grin shifted into something edged, and I bit my own lip.

"Oh," I said, settling into a loose circling stalk, hands held out at my sides, "I think I have more than a few you haven't seen."

I flew at him, getting past his guard before he started to swing his sword toward me, hitting the point in his arm that sent his hand spasming and the sword flying.

As soon as the sword cleared his hand, as his eyes widened, I swept his legs out from under him and held the back of his head and his waist. I stepped over him, straddling him as he fell between my legs, supported only by my hands.

"Like that move?" I asked, close enough that my lips brushed across his. "You haven't seen that one before."

But he shifted as he stared at me with his molten, gold eyes, getting his feet under him and grabbing my thighs. A second later he surged up, holding me to his waist as he carried me from the room and through a small door.

We were in some kind of service pantry with long counters on either side, and a window over one of them that he pressed me against as he kicked the door shut.

His mouth claimed mine and it felt like we were both falling now, together.

My hands roamed over his chest, his breathing still fast and hard, and he gripped my thighs tighter.

Pulling back, I kissed his neck and he sucked in a breath before he pushed me away, his eyes out the window past my head and rage taking over his face.

CHAPTER 44

NEXT TIME

"**S**tay here," he said, setting me more firmly onto the counter, "and I will be back."

One more kiss, deep and stirring, and cut too short, then he was gone.

I turned around as he opened the door, looking out the window. The sky over the water beyond erupted in light.

Shielding my eyes, I squinted into the flare. All I could do was watch in horror as black shapes dove on a ship, plucking other dark objects off the deck, and dropping them in the water.

Another two ships flanked the first, firing a volley of arrows on it and some kind of giant metal thing.

The first ship fired cannons that looked like explosions of light ripping through the other two ships in volley after volley.

Crows. That's what they had to be, although it was too far away for me to make out detail, continued to dive bomb the ship, until...One slammed into something and went pinwheeling down to the sea.

I cheered, even though they couldn't hear me.

My cheering only grew louder when another ship, from just

up the coast somewhere, probably from the dock past the castle, sped toward the battle.

That ship's sails were full, and a good wind had picked up in the right direction. Which meant that it was moving across the water at a steady clip, and would intercept the others in no time.

Which was the only way the first ship of ours was going to survive the onslaught of the other two ships at the same time.

Somewhere in the castle, Amethyst nobles were probably still ironing out some of the last details. Were they watching this? Would this sway their decision at all?

If we won this battle, would that change their minds?

And what if we lost?

Everything in me screamed to be on that boat, to be out there and doing what I did best.

But instead, I was here, in some damn pantry, waiting for my King.

I turned around, hopped off the counter, and stalked out of the room. If he thought this was the way I would be as Queen, he wasn't paying attention.

Whatever his reasons for telling me to wait here, I had a job to do. And part of it was to remind him who and what I was.

He wanted me for a queen. That meant that I was his, but I belonged to Onyx first, whether Queen or not.

It was time I acted like it.

Making my way out of the pantry, people gathered at the windows, various versions of terrified and sick. But I went toward the front doors, grabbing my dropped sword on the way.

Not knowing my way around, or how to get out to the water, made my plan seem stupid. But I needed to try.

"How do I find a boat to take me out there?" I asked a random guard, my hand wrapped around the collar of their jacket so tight they spluttered and coughed like I was choking them.

"Go down that hall and the last door on the left is the Captain," he said, his voice strained.

I let go of him and nodded. He scurried off, and I went toward the Captain's door.

On this end of the castle, guards streamed everywhere, and other people, who I took to be servants, ran past, too.

At least my weapons didn't stand out here. Unlike the royal wing, here I was just another person desperate for answers in the middle of a catastrophe.

Finally, I reached the Captain's office.

But the woman inside, long hair in a messy bun on the top of her head held up with what looked like sticks and...a fork, didn't look like a Captain of the Guard.

She wasn't wearing a guard uniform. Instead, she had on a white suit, and a white hat sat on her desk while she barked orders at the four guards in the room, digging through drawer after drawer.

Knocking on the frame of the door, I stepped inside.

"And you are?" the Captain asked, looking at me for only a moment before going back to whatever she was doing.

"Here," she said, handing a small stack of papers to them. "Make sure that call goes out to everyone."

"Of course," one of the guards said, and they turned on their heels and ran.

"Can I help you? Are you lost?" she asked, barely looking up from the stack of papers and things on her desk that she shuffled through and piled together.

"I am Fighter Cinder. I need to know when the next ship is going out to be part of the fighting, and how I can get on board."

Her hands froze in midair, and she looked at me through her lashes without moving her head.

"You're Fighter Cinder?" She didn't sound convinced, and I wondered what she thought I would look like.

Part of me wanted to yell at her, but instead of saying

anything, I pulled my spikes from their straps, holding them up for her to see, raising one eyebrow as my question mark.

"Hmm. Well, as interesting as you are, my orders are that you need to be notified when the prisoner is questioned, and, otherwise, you're going to be heading out soon."

Even though I didn't know anything about the timeline for our departure, I didn't ask because I was more focused on the fact that the Captain had yet to answer my question.

"What I need to know right now," I said, my voice low because I was holding myself back from snapping at her over things she had little control over it seemed, "is how do I get out to a ship."

"For right now, you don't. Every last war worthy ship I have control over is currently out. But after this crisis is over, then you can come back here, and I will find you transport."

Her dismissal was so final, she went back to moving the papers on her desk.

I curled my hands into fists and turned around, trying to come up with some way to push the issue. But if all the ships were out…fuck.

Standing around and waiting for this battle to pass me by wasn't going to work for me. They needed me to do a lot more than be a distraction for a foreign Prince, or spend my nights with my King, or plan a damn wedding.

Fuck, fine.

I grabbed another guard, this time by the arm, noticing the Dragon King sigil on their uniform. "How do I get out to one of the ships?"

"The only way I know of that's close, Fighter Cinder, is that dock you all took to the Lighthouse. But there are no ships right now."

Right.

Letting them go with a nod of thanks, I went to a window, standing behind others with no more power than to watch, to witness, as one of our ships sank along with one of the enemy's.

Next time, though, I wasn't going to be stuck in this castle. Next time, I was going to that dock. And I was going to fight.

While the world was distracted around me, everyone watching what remained of the ship falling into the water, and the other ship picking up the sailors they could from the wreckage, I stood impotent, fury flowing through me.

But…maybe there was something I could finally take care of.

Maybe now, the guards would be distracted. And maybe, I had a window to finish with Brix.

CHAPTER 45

COLD PLACE

Making my way through the doorway, I met no guards.

Walking down the stairs, I heard no one.

Every step I took between the rows of cells, the crashing of the sea outside drowning out any other noises, my hands itched to be done with this.

Brix needed to die.

No matter what it would say of my relationship with my brother, it needed to happen.

My brother...I swallowed.

Avoiding thinking about him wasn't working. Every step I took closer to ending this, Ash grew larger in my mind no matter what I did.

Killing his best friend, no matter how much of a monster Brix was, would leave me in an even worse position with Ash.

There was nothing else for me to do, though.

Ash made sure of that.

Ash.

Missing a step, my boot scuffed on the stone floor. For some reason that small sound landed on my ears like the last, rough exhalation of the dying.

It was only a second later that I stood at the door of Brix's cell.

He slept in the small cot, wrapped in a thin blanket, his face still battered and broken from the last time we were all down here. His chest rose and fell in easy breathing. If I didn't know he was a person with less humanity than most animals, I would have assumed him innocent.

Tightening my fists, my fingernails digging into my palms, I went to the cold place in my mind. The place I lived when I needed to kill someone who I wasn't sure deserved my blade.

Brix deserved it. But killing someone my brother called a friend still required the cold place.

In my mind, the drifts of ashes that coated Lehar were all over the world, muffling sound, air, heat, and turning my veins to ice this far from the Hellfire source.

The cold place welcomed me home, a nameless, faceless, soulless assassin, as I jammed my spike in the lock, twisted it, and slipped inside the cell.

Crouching down in front of Brix, he didn't wake up until I lifted my spike and touched the chilled point to his lips. A deadly mockery of remaining silent.

With a jerk, his eyes opened, and a single bead of blood formed on his nicked lip.

"You did that yourself. I suggest you not move again." My voice was as hushed and ominous as the cold place would have been to anyone who joined me in it.

"No one is with you this time." His voice was calm and lacked any sense of shock.

It wasn't a question, and there was no fear in his eyes.

He knew he was going to die, and he didn't care.

Tilting my head to the side to see him from a different angle,

I narrowed my eyes, but couldn't see into his black heart this time.

"Why did you attack the Shield House and go after the kids?" It didn't matter how deep I was in this frigid state, my voice shook on the words "Shield House" and "kids."

"Because it was the best way to guarantee I broke your heart." His face was blank. He showed no signs that he saw the bile rising in my throat.

Children died and were terrorized because of me.

"How did you even know about them?" I didn't even know about them before Tristan brought me there.

"From someone on our side. They know the place, the kids, and that you were there. They told me which one I should take. Just happened to fit my preference anyway."

Still nothing in his face changed, although I bared my teeth like a feral animal.

Cold.

Ice.

Frozen.

Quiet.

Blank.

Grasping for that place in my mind, it took me longer than it ever had before to return to it again when 'my fault' was running through me, screaming.

"Why take Gus?" If they already had Angeline, and knew she was enough to draw me out, Gus seemed like too much of a risk to go after.

"She just got in the way. They were looking for you in that tent, and when they went after the other one, she stepped in. But when they brought her to me to answer questions, I thought she would give me some more fun."

Fun. He called torturing them fun. Innocent people who had nothing to do with this. Fun.

Return to the cold place. Get back there, now. You need answers. Don't let him bait you into killing him too soon.

More reminders of ice and chill and silence finally allowed me to keep asking him questions.

But Brix stared at me, without emotion, as if he were studying me.

"How are you doing that?" he asked, his voice with an odd shake to it.

"You don't get to ask me questions."

"But you're not like me."

"Good." Of course I wasn't like him. What the fuck was he even talking about?

"Ash spent so much time convincing you the kills were worthy, righteous in some way, and I know you hurt for what happened to the kid and your friend. So how are you doing this?"

Wait…

"Did my brother lie to me about the people I assassinated?" I knew he did about Tristan, but I thought it was just about him. Just because of his own issues, and he had convinced himself somehow of the righteousness of killing the King. But if it was a pattern…How many people did I kill simply because it was convenient for Ash for them to be dead?

He told me…he told me that would never happen again after the first time.

"Of course. Do you really think he would risk exposing you, or himself, by hiring you out to that many people?" He narrowed his eyes at me, and looked skeptical that I didn't see it before.

But…I didn't see it. Never had. I missed so many things. So many truths.

"The deaths in other countries?"

"Safe. They didn't know who you were at all as Lady Cinder or Ash's sister. And they never knew the true identity of the assassin that stole into their midst to kill and disappear again. It was just a bonus that it furthered his story about the money."

"His story about the money?" Brix just kept talking, as if he knew the minute that he stopped, I was going to kill him. And now, at the end, he finally valued his life, and didn't want to die.

"Lehar has more wealth than Bridgeton."

I snorted a short laugh. Everyone knew how much Bridgeton valued money. There was no way that was true. But why would he lie to me now?

"Makes sense that you wouldn't believe me. Ask your Madam Valentin. She knows."

At times in the past, when I did certain things, or said certain things, Madam or others had reacted strangely.

Could Brix be right?

Not that it mattered. I could ask Madam, and I would as soon as I saw her again.

"Fine, Lehar has more money than I realized. Then why hire out my services at all? And where does it all go?"

Brix grinned, but it looked almost as if he were proud of a student instead of the usual skin-crawl-inducing leer he sent my way.

"Very good. Now she's asking the right questions."

I yawned. He could use the nudge. If he was going to play around, I could find some other way to get my answers. Madam Valentin was a better person to have a conversation with than Brix anyway.

"Your brother uses your kills to strengthen his international position for when he takes the throne of Onyx. He uses all the money Lehar makes, and what you make with your blades, to buy slaves."

Sucking in a breath, my hand jerked, and the tip of my spike snagged on the corner of his mouth, giving him a split lip.

He brought his hand up, and touched the tear on the edge of his lip, looking down at the blood on his finger.

"Don't fucking lie to me," I said. "If Ash had slaves, I would know. There is nowhere in all of Lehar he could keep them that I wouldn't hear about." My people were a lot of things, but slavers they were not. They would help the people escape to somewhere else in Lehar, and make sure that Ash could never be in a position to have them anymore if they knew.

"None of his slaves are in Lehar. He bought them for one reason. They can't fulfill that reason in Lehar. He keeps them in lands across the border in Amethyst, and they all think they'll be freed if they fight for him. Brilliant, really. He feeds them, and trains them, and treats them better than they ever experienced in Corvid, all the while convincing them to be the most moti-vated army money can buy."

"Why wouldn't they just walk across the border into Onyx? They have to know Onyx has no slavery."

"Your brother told them it's a slave country. They have no way to know otherwise. See? Brilliant."

I was going to be sick. My stomach churned, and it didn't matter how hard I fought to get back to the cold place in my mind, I couldn't find it.

"Ash wouldn't own slaves." My voice was a weak version of what it had been. Part of my soul floated away through the wounds Ash had given me, through all my scars and old bruises. Pieces of me flaked off and disappeared, as insubstantial as the version of my brother I believed in, as unreal. My voice fled with it, leaving me weak and screamless.

For so long, I let Ash hurt me, I devoted myself to him, to his ideas and missions, no matter how hard it got, no matter how bad.

And all along he was this different?

I shook my head.

"He does own slaves," Brix said. "He buys more every single year."

"But he can't think he's going to take over the country."

None of this made sense. This wasn't Ash, not the Ash I knew. He loved Lehar, but had no loyalty to Onyx as a whole. "He doesn't even like most of the country."

"No. He doesn't. But he thinks he would be better for it than a Dragon King with no dragon powers. And he hates Lehar more than the rest of the country."

"Ash doesn't hate Lehar." How much of what he said was a lie? Was it all a ploy? All my life I was told my brother loved Lehar, would be a good Duke, and care about it and the people.

But my parents told me that. They reassured me when Ash got in trouble for things and said things…

Did my brother count on that? Use my parents?

Looking closer at Brix it…didn't seem like he was lying. He never seemed like a very good liar. Even though he covered up his worst instincts, it was always clear he was rat bastard. Even when we were kids, I knew he was terrible.

"How much do you look back on the old Lehar and wish you could have it again?" he asked.

"Of course, I want that." I was going to have Inara send engines home to try and make it happen. No one in Lehar wished for the ashes to keep falling.

"For your brother, he thinks he deserves the Lehar of old. But he doesn't think it will ever exist. No one will even try to rebuild the manor since it sits on the source."

"So, what? He thinks he's entitled to the whole country because Lehar isn't as perfect as it used to be?"

He did the odd point of his finger again, and looked perversely proud of me.

But it was insane. It made zero sense.

I shook my head, unable to believe what Brix was telling me. If I believed him, it would mean that for seven years, while I clung to the only family I had left, while I made myself into this for him, he was using me and hurting me all for a fucking crown.

For long minutes, Brix let me run through everything he told me again and again, watching me as I did.

My hand strayed to the chain around my neck with the sigil ring on it, running it through my fingers, trying to connect to something I knew was true.

He must have seen the moment I decided not to believe him because he sighed.

"Ah, Cinder," Brix said, "don't be stupid. Why do you think he sent his own sister to kill the King? Although, even he was shocked when you decided to marry that worthless asshole."

"Stop it."

"He's going to use that to his advantage now, for sure. But he was surprised you would do it. Must have been the influence of those ridiculous friends of yours. We should have supplied your Ladies in Waiting, not let just anyone have that position. I told Ash that."

"Fuck you." My hands tightened on my spike. He didn't get to talk about my friends or Tristan that way. He didn't get to pass judgment on people superior to him in every possible way.

He laughed and the fucking leer was back, his smarmy, disgusting slime returning full force.

"You're already busy fucking the King. Is he so underwhelming that you want me?" He stretched his neck, pulling up from the bed further, and I wanted to wrap a hand around it.

"Shut your fucking mouth." The cold place was too far from me now. Even as I reached for it, I didn't think I was going to make it, and there was so much more I needed to know. But that fucking look on his face made my blood race through my veins. My hands itched to hurt him.

"I can tell you're fucking him. Can he tell that, while he's inside you, you're plotting to stab him in the heart with your little spike?"

With a swift slice, I cut one of the arteries in his neck and breathed into his face as he gasped for breath, his hands clawing at the cascade of blood pouring out of him, like he could hold it all in, his eyes wide.

"My little spike just killed you, and now I get to watch as you bleed out. Of all people, you should have remembered that I'm a killer."

A scuff on the stone floor, like the one I made, but followed by more stumbling sounded in the row between the cells.

Cold washed over me, not the comfortable nothing of the cold place. This was terror and wrong.

I dove for the door to the cell, leaving Brix to die alone.

Tristan stood between the cells, his face ashen, and a hand on his chest as he sucked down breath after breath.

"How long have you been there?" I asked, my voice a hushed whisper, torn through a throat that wanted to close as all my muscles clamped down, rendering me incapable of movement.

Every emotion crossed his face in seconds until they washed away, leaving him as frozen as the cold place.

"Too long."

CHAPTER 46

WEAK

"You're a killer," Tristan said, his voice flat and defeated, giving back to me the words I said at the training grounds before he had any idea what they meant. "And I'm a fool."

He turned to head back to the stairs, and my inability to move finally melted away.

"No, Tristan," I scrambled toward him, dropping my weapon, leaving it clattering to the floor, and ran toward him, every part of my body shaking as my blood turned to ice. "Please. This isn't what you think."

He whirled on me, his eyes cold, hazel and devoid of any of the warmth I always saw there, no matter which color they were.

"Really, Cinder? How is it not what it looks like?" He pointed to the cell behind me.

"I—I—I love you." I grabbed for his hand, and he threw mine away, his lip curling.

"Don't say that." His voice was a harsh snarl.

"But, I love you. Forever." He had to hear me, believe me.

"You don't get to say that anymore. Not when I know it's a

fucking lie. Not when it's just part of your game. You were going to, what? Marry me? Become Queen, and then kill me and take the country?" He shook his head, his hands curling into fists, and a tremor running through his shoulders.

"No. Nothing like that. Just listen." My mind raced from one word to the next, frantic to find the right thing to say. *Anything* to say to get him to believe me.

"Listen? So you can lie to me again? So you can find a new way to hurt me? To kill me?"

There it was. The fear that made tears heavy in my eyes. The same fear I saw in the eyes of my targets was stamped on his face, and it was everything I never wanted him to feel.

"I would never hurt you. Please." Oh, Gods and Goddesses, how was I going to make this okay?

"Too late." His voice lost the harsh tone. "You already hurt me."

I broke, a tear getting past my guard, falling down my cheek, and more racing behind it.

"I don't ever want you to hurt. I love you too much. Everything in me wants to protect you. Please." I didn't know what else to do but beg.

"Once, I thought that was true. But not anymore. I'm done." He turned to walk toward the stairs, but I grabbed his arm. It was as cold as the ice spreading through my heart, and he snatched it away from me.

"Please." My voice broke on the word, and tears streamed down my face in a torrent. "You have to believe me."

"Believe you?" He turned back to me, snarling with his eyes narrowed. "Fine, Cinder. Tell me something I should believe."

"We belong together," I said, and he shook his head even as his shoulders quaked.

"That's not what I meant." His mouth was pressed into a tight line, his jaw clenched.

"You are everything I always wanted and never deserved." Nothing was truer than that.

"Stop it," he yelled, holding up a hand.

Anything. I was willing to do anything, to give up anything to have him forgive me.

"Did your brother send you to kill me?" he asked, his voice flat and it was a dagger right into me.

I couldn't lie to him. Not now. Not when I needed him to believe the whole truth.

"Yes," he threw up his hands and started to turn away, "but everything is different now."

"How? Because you managed to make me fall in love with you, and your plan worked better than you thought it would? Because the crown is within your reach?" His eyes were so cold that I shivered, and the tears flowing down my face felt like sleet stabbing into my skin.

"No, Tristan, because I love you. Because he lied to me. Because I was wrong, and I know that now. Because we belong together." He had to see the truth. I needed him to see it. To see me.

A shudder went through him, his fists shaking at his sides, but his eyes didn't change.

The frozen muscles in my legs started to lose strength.

"Oh, you know that now?" His voice cracked on the last word. "When, exactly, did you figure out you were a treasonous snake? When you knew a crown was coming?"

"You know I fought for you when the Corvids first attacked. Tristan, please. Please believe me." I reached for him, but he recoiled.

"What about before that attack? Our first trip to Shield House?" His voice had a panicked edge, and his eyes widened. "Did I take a threat to the kids?"

"I would never hurt the kids," I yelled, but it was the wrong thing to say.

He went far too still, every emotion leeching out of him and creeping along the floor like a shadow dark enough to block out the sun forever.

I swallowed around my own frozen heart, hugging my arms to myself to slow their tremors.

"So, just me that night, then? You were just planning to kill me?" he asked, his voice hard.

And I couldn't tell him otherwise. Because I had planned to kill him that night. I brought my spike with me to do it.

"Please, Tristan. I love you. I've shown you more of me than anyone else knows. Please, tell me how to prove it. Tell me how to make you believe me." The shaking in my legs grew worse. Every muscle in my body began to quake.

"That wasn't you. It was who you wanted me to see." A shudder ran through him, but he leaned closer and looked me up and down like he hated what he saw, his mouth curled in disgust. "And I don't believe you."

My legs gave out and I collapsed to the floor, my entire body shaking, my breath hitching as I cried, my mouth open, trying to breathe.

"You made yourself the fucking hero of Onyx, and fucking Fighter Cinder like a cruel joke. So I can't even have you killed for treason. Your brother is as good as dead." He crouched down in front of me, and came close enough for me to feel his breath, as cold as I was, brushing over my skin. "But if I could, I would have you hanged for your crimes. Keep hold of your lies. You making everyone believe you're a hero is the only thing stopping me from killing you right now in this dungeon."

He stood up and walked away as I wailed.

"No," I screamed, unable to stop as I rocked back and forth on the floor near the cells, his footsteps ringing out on the stones of the stairs.

It didn't matter how far away Ash was, it didn't matter how

far I pushed my brother from me, he still caused me pain and left scars.

There was no escape from him.

Not for me.

My mistake wasn't loving Tristan, or defying Ash. It was in thinking I could get away from my brother, his influence over my life, and what he turned me into.

Even while I sobbed my tears into the cold stone floor of the cell-filled room in the bottom of the castle, even as I mourned the life I never deserved, my heart turning into ashes and flaking away into nothing, steps away, the blood of my latest kill spread along the floor.

The crashing of the waves beneath the castle and slowing drip of Brix's blood splashing to the floor were the only things besides my own voice negating this new reality.

Until my voice was a hoarse croak, my shivers were gone, and I didn't believe I would ever be warm again, I kept crying on the floor.

Finally, steps came down the stairs.

But they weren't Tristan's.

Even as they ran down toward me, I knew they weren't his, and my dry throat cracked around his name.

"Tristan," I said, although no one would have been able to understand what I was saying, my voice as weak as our forever.

"Cinder," Nevan said, pulling me up by the arm, "we need you."

CHAPTER 47

RISKS

"I can't," I said, the words barely there.

"You have to." Nevan shook me until I managed to look him in the eye. "There is an attack in Bridgeton, and your King's boat is taking heavy fire."

Madam was either in Bridgeton already, or on her way there. If she already arrived, or if she arrived in the middle of it, she could be killed.

But he was under fire...

"How do you know?" I asked, coughing out words.

"Ziya left for the palace at the same time Madam Valentin did." His voice was grave and low, but there was a tinge of... something in it that I wasn't in the right mind to place.

"And—" I couldn't ask about him. The question clogged in my throat. I couldn't say his name. Even though I needed to know, and my heart lurched at the thought of him in danger, I couldn't even call him by his title in my mind.

"We can see it."

I squinted at him and ran up the stairs, stumbling and catching myself with a hand on a step, my bones angry to be told what to do after spending so long crumpled on the floor.

At the top of the stairs, I didn't find the panicked melee I expected.

Everyone I spotted as I reached the main floor were gathered at the windows, muttering, crying, and looking past them. I understood why.

Just beyond where the waves broke and the first white-capped peaks appeared with any regularity, in the deepening red of the sky as night started to touch it, five of their ships were engaged with one of ours.

More of our ships were on the horizon, heading toward the battle, but I didn't know if they would get there in time.

As I watched, two crows toppled out of the sky, splashing into the water below.

I ran to the window, shoving people out of the way. It didn't matter how closely I tried to look, I couldn't see him on the deck.

But another crow keeled over into the sea. It was flying too far beyond the barrier of fishing lines for it to be a casualty of a sailor with a spear.

Even while we watched, our ship took two shots of that weapon that looked like it was a massive blade shot at speed somehow.

Our ship shot cannon fire at all the enemies surrounding them, but one of the oversized blades seemed to cut through a swath of the protective fishing line barrier, letting a crow in.

I turned and ran.

Fuck the Captain in her office. Fuck standing here and doing nothing. Fuck bothering to try and survive this time.

No one stopped me when I blew through the front door, across the bridge, and angled for a carriage unloading barrels at the edge of the lane in front of the castle.

They barely glanced at me as I darted past them, until I pulled the short sword at my back and sliced through the harness on one of their horses, vaulting onto the horse's back a second later, and kicking it hard to get up to speed.

While they screamed behind me, calling for my attention and for their horse back, I drove the animal in a line toward the dock. The same one we used to load onto the ship, where I pretended I could have him in my life.

It didn't take me long to get there, but every second of the ride I was praying to Mom and Dad to protect Madam and him at the same time. Hoping she would be out of the way of the attack happening in Bridgeton, and he would survive long enough for me to get there.

Coming over the rise, my heart lurched to see that a ship, much smaller and much more rustic looking than the one we traveled on, was about to leave the dock. They were throwing off the ropes from the tie downs.

"Ahhh," I yelled, my voice unable to give me anything close to an actual command for the horse, just a guttural scream as I kicked hard into the horse's sides, urging it to go even faster.

I had to make that ship.

Sliding down the last stretch of the dune, the horse didn't miss as it launched us onto the dock.

None of my training made me trust the animal beneath me as I pulled my legs up and balanced, standing on its muscular back, and trying to judge the distance from us to the ship as it was pulling away.

Please, horse, don't freak out.

When we were at the right point on the dock, I launched myself off the horse's back and flew through the air until I slammed hard into the deck boards of the departing ship.

"Fighter Cinder?" one of the sailors asked, leaning down to help me up.

"Get me to that ship," I said, my voice a croak, but my hand clear as I pointed toward the fight.

"We're headed that way," the sailor said, mouth in a grim line, looking toward the battle.

I looked at the ship around me, and spotted a strange number of cannons. They were out in the open on the deck, not in narrow halls down below.

But there wasn't any fishing line protecting this boat.

Pointing up at the clear, open sky, I made sure the sailor followed my prompt as I lifted my brows.

"We cut the lines before we pushed off." A nod to the massive number of people lining the railings of the ship and the two hanging from a platform on the mast. "Our archers aren't as skilled as King Tristan at getting their arrows between the lines."

Hearing his name made me suck in a breath and look back toward the fight.

Faster. We needed to go faster damn it.

But this was a ship, not a fucking horse. And even as I curled my hands into fists and my muscles itched to be there right now, I knew they were going as fast as they could.

No one cut the lines of their best protection if they were worried about themselves.

"Thank you," I choked out. "Can I have some of the cut line?"

"Uh, Fighter Cinder? I'm sorry, but I didn't catch that."

My voice failed me. Gathering a bunch of the sailors around, I showed them via pantomime what I wanted them to do, and that I was very thankful they were risking their asses to save the ship and our King.

By the time we neared the fighting, we were ready. A heavy smell of cannon smoke floated along the water between ships that were no longer moving.

All the sailors along the railing—the two up on the platform with me, and the other sailors manning the cannons—we were all ready with our eyes to the skies.

Still, just at the edge of the ships, the first crow spotted us, and sent up a cry to the others. A whole group of them headed our way.

They knew to get me closer to our main ship, but in the meantime, I had work to do.

When the first crow got within my range, I dove off the platform right at it, swinging the sword and cutting off its head. The weight of the blow reverberated up my arm and I twisted, grabbing the rope wrapped around my waist and legs, and swinging to keep attacking as the crows came.

The sailors shouted, arrows flew, and cannons blasted.

But the entire time I slashed and stabbed, threw my knives, curling myself into a smaller target when the crows got too close to me, and extending my body out to get more speed when I needed to.

After clipping one of the crows' wings, I climbed back up the rope and ran along the top off the main sail, swinging at anything that moved through my line of vision.

Once I was on the other side, close to the end of the beam I ran on, I spotted a Corvid as it focused on our other ship and flew that way.

"Not him," I said, as if saying those words would make it true even if no one could hear me or understand me right now.

Launching myself off the end of the beam, I landed on the back of the Corvid.

It squawked in protest, and started to fall from the sky.

Before it could recover from me dropping onto it, I stabbed my short sword into its eye.

With a push and swing, I separated from the crow, letting the body plummet into the sea, and launched back into the fight, blade first.

Getting close to the end of my momentum, an arrow shot too close to me, and I tucked my arm in without checking what was around me.

The move sent me careening into a crow, and then slamming back the other direction to bounce off the mast with a grunt.

Without my momentum, I released the rope and tumbled down out of it onto the deck. I grabbed a fallen arrow I landed next to, putting it between my teeth as I climbed up the pins on the mast to get to the platform again.

All around us the sounds of battle, the crows, the sea, the cannons, the cries, and the ring of weapons in use, created a kind of discordant symphony of war.

In the middle of it all, I heard someone scream, "Look out."

Twisting, leading with my sword, a crow flapped in my face, rearing back and managing to avoid being stabbed.

Putting the sword between my thighs, hoping it didn't fall to the deck below, I took the arrow from my teeth and threw it.

Of course, it didn't hit the crow, but it spooked it enough to send it back a little more. The archers below me finished it off.

Taking hold of the sword again, I continued to climb up to the platform.

Just as I was pulling myself into position, one of the archers up there with me called out, "Almost time."

Looking past them, our ship loomed.

A cheer went up below me, it was echoed from our bigger ship.

"What's going on?" But my pathetic croak of a question was impossible to hear over the cacophony around us.

It didn't matter. As soon as I turned, I found what had everyone cheering.

Two Corvid ships were sinking fast.

"You ready?" one of the archers screamed in my face.

Nodding, I sheathed the sword on my back, and grabbed hold of the fabric we tied up here earlier, wrapping it around each hand before I took hold of an arrow they handed me.

"Are you sure, because here comes one," a sailor yelled,

aiming the arrow on the other end of the fishing line tied around the one I held.

Gritting my teeth, saying a silent prayer to Mom and Dad that this would work, I nodded and held on tight.

CHAPTER 48

DARKNESS

The archer took a shot at a crow flying up above the line of the deck of our other ship.

With a jerk on the arrow in my hands, I was yanked off the platform and sent careening off kilter and uncontrolled after the bird.

Its wing was skewered by the arrow on the other end of the line, not the leg we hoped for, and it was going to crash soon enough. All I could do was hope that it would keep flying long enough to get me up onto the larger ship's deck. The world spun around me, and I struggled to place where I was in the blur.

Dizzy, I couldn't figure out where I was, what I was seeing, or when I was supposed to let go.

The sounds swirling around me didn't help. They were everywhere, and I couldn't even scream.

A second later, I slammed into something solid, and lost my hold on the arrow, sending me skidding along wet wood.

Blinking, I realized I was on the deck of the ship I aimed for, the fluid I slid in was blood, and the crow I rode was a crumpled, twitching mess at the other end of the deck.

Sailors pushed the crow off them, stabbing it with their spears for good measure, and went back to the fight.

I shoved my way up to standing, pulling the sword from my back, and looked around for Tristan.

He was here. I knew he was here.

Maybe a crow—

No.

Cutting off the thought before the tremor it caused in my hands grew worse, I didn't spot Tristan, but I did find a door to a weapons cupboard flapping open with the waves rocking the ship.

Lots of swords, a single spear, and throwing knives all along the floor were all that remained.

Stocking up on the throwing knives, leaving one in my hand, I looked for him again.

Finally, I spotted a loose circle of sailors sporting spears, and looking skyward with an archer with their back to me at their center.

"Tristan," I said, my small voice snatched away by the wind, even as his name was louder than the war in my own ears.

Running in their direction, spotting a crow about to get a sailor in the back while the sailor stabbed another one of its brethren with a spear, I threw my first knife.

Making my way to the circle, I took up a spot with the sailors, not bothering to let Tristan know I stood at his back whether he wanted me here or not.

Crows dove at us at such a clip, it was hard to keep up.

But it was clear what my actual job here should be.

While Tristan and the other archers shot the crows out of the sky, I ran from one to the other as they landed, cutting off their heads.

Even after they landed, wounded, and in some cases dying, they thrashed and tried to kill everyone around them.

My short sword dripped with their blood before I let them wet their beaks in ours.

One of them, though, got past me, taking out one of the sailors around Tristan.

I jumped on the body of another, avoiding slipping on the red-soaked deck boards, and leapt onto the fighting crow's back, screaming my hoarse croak of a scream.

Tristan must have felt the weight of the giant bird coming close, or maybe he heard my strangled wail, because he turned as he reached back for another arrow.

But before the bird's lunge could bury its beak in Tristan, I slit its throat, spraying blood all over my King.

"Cinder?" Tristan asked, as I picked myself up from the fallen Corvid, his voice was low If it was anyone other than him, I wouldn't have heard it.

He was different.

Even now.

Among the terrible noise around us, I could still hear him.

I heard the tone of half disgust, half surprise, and all fury.

"Get down," I yelled, grabbing his shoulder and shoving at him, using his body to launch myself past him, swiping at a crow that got too close.

Tristan went back to shooting them out of the sky, and I stayed at his back, hacking away at any other crows that managed to get through after I ran out of my throwing knives.

After so much time spent healing and focusing on time with Tristan, my arms ached with the effort. Even my eyes couldn't seem to take in all the threats swirling around us. It felt like playing catch up instead of fighting on offense.

But I gritted my teeth as I slammed my sword into another bird's leg, driving it off.

Running after Gus, I was in good form after training the guard. And it still took so much out of me.

Now, I was in less-than-perfect shape, and my body let me know.

This time, though, Tristan was at my back.

And I was never going to let these fucking crows hurt him.

It didn't matter that he hated me, that the sigil ring hanging from the chain around my neck was nothing more than a token of memory now, or even that my Dragon King had gone cold.

"Fuck you, Corvid," I screamed at another crow as it flapped above me, grabbing onto its leg, stabbing it through the gut, and sending a torrent of blood down on my own head even as I let it fly out of control into the mast.

"What are you doing here?" Tristan yelled back at me, glancing over his shoulder.

"My fucking job. Protecting you." I swiped at my eyes, clearing them of the blood and adjusted my stance, trying to calculate a better way to kill more of them faster.

There were too many casualties already, too many close calls for my King.

"It's not your fucking job," he yelled, although I didn't know how he understood me.

A massive boom split the air, larger than all the others, and knocked me from my feet.

Scrambling to get up, I tried to spot what just happened.

On the other side of the Corvid ships, more of ours just arrived.

Huge ships flying flags with the Dragon King and Breakwater sigils fired on the Corvid ships again.

I couldn't remain standing, sinking down to my knees again.

But the crows around us went berserk, slamming into each other and shaking, far off their intended flight routes.

"Yeah," I cheered, raising my sword in the air toward our ships as they pummeled the Corvid ones with a relentless barrage of cannon fire.

The enemy ships started to break apart.

From somewhere, though, something slammed into the deck of the ship I kneeled on next to my King.

All around me, pieces of wood flew through the air, turning into shards so sharp they were weapons. A river of sea water followed the wood, soaking me.

"Tristan," I screamed, turning as I flailed through the air, trying in vain to find him in the maelstrom around me.

Slammed against some other part of the ship, every bit of the air in my body disappeared.

My vision blanked, torn from me.

My sword, too, gone to some other place.

I opened and closed my hands, took stock of the feeling still in my legs, the amazing reality that I was whole.

"Tristan," I croaked, my voice already destroyed, now weak and thin.

But the answer wasn't him, wasn't his voice, or seeing his face.

The only answer I got was the continued bombardment, the deafening drowning of the enemy by our back up forces.

And blessed darkness.

CHAPTER 49

MIDNIGHT HEART

I was drawn out of the dark, not by heat trailing along my skin. Not by the sound of familiar voices. Not by anything that made me think that my world had been put to rights.

The things I grew used to waking up to were absent in a way that made my blood run slower in my veins, even though I wasn't sure why for a moment.

No, it was none of the things I wanted and had experienced so many times since I came to the palace that forced me out of the dark.

What woke me was a dripping sound.

A damn dripping sound managed to break into my mind from the real world, and I started dreaming about a leak I needed to fix.

It annoyed me awake.

For a few seconds, a scant few blissful seconds, I didn't remember what world I was waking up to. And then it was all there, stabbing me in the heart all over again.

Blinking, I had to squint into the sun shining into my eyes.

Well, that was better than having no vision at all like before.

Only seconds later, the rest of my surroundings rushed in on me in a tidal wave of sound and sight and sensation.

Sitting up, I looked around the massive room in Sandstone Castle.

I was only one of many wounded, dying, and dead laid out on the floor, the tables, and the chairs.

The dripping was blood and sea water falling to the stone floor next to me from a soaked guard sitting up, and holding an arm with a deep and angry slice down it.

But that guard was in good shape compared to so many of the others in the room.

Grabbing the hand of another guard as they passed, I asked in my still-broken voice, "What happened?".

"Fighter," they said, sighing, "there was one last cannon shot from one of the Corvid ships."

"They don't have cannons." My voice cracked, and my throat squeezed almost shut with the effort to speak.

"Not like ours, but they have something. Some kind of metal weapon." The guard patted my hand, and kept going to whatever they needed to.

How did the Corvids get something like a cannon? Was that what I watched attack the ship before I got out there?

Although it didn't really matter how they got the ability to shoot at us, we knew they had it now. We could be more prepared than this last battle.

Maybe we could, anyway.

The damn Corvids twice took the chance to attack one of our ships that they thought didn't have any backup. They managed to best us that way *twice* that I knew of.

Of course, they were right at first. The ship was all by itself on the water for too long.

And would we all have been so willing to drop everything and rush to the ship's defense if we didn't know the King was on it? The first one they tried it with was sunk. What about this one?

Looking around at all the carnage the battle caused, I hoped we all would have been willing to go out and help our fellow Onyxians.

But, like every other time I thought about Tristan being anywhere without me, I knew that I would always be more likely to be willing to take stupid risks to get to him and protect him.

Protect Tristan…

I shoved myself up to stand on shaking legs. The ice inside my body only made colder by the water rendering my leather stiff.

Someone would have told me if Tristan were dead. No one would be acting nearly as normally as they were if we had lost our King. Right?

But I needed to see him. He didn't need to see me.

Remembering my own utter lack of vision when the blast hit, I wasn't sure if I would find him awake, though, even if he were alive.

The last time I saw him…trying to conjure him in my mind, where he was when the deck exploded beneath us, was impossible.

All I could see in my mind's eye was him telling me I was only alive because the guard would be too upset if he killed me. All I could see was the way he didn't see me anymore.

Wandering among the flurry of activity that always followed a battle, I turned a corner toward the front door of the castle and could finally take a full breath.

Clasping onto the sigil ring still hanging from the chain around my neck, I looked him over where he stood next to General Pace, checking and double checking for any sign that he was wounded.

I saw nothing.

He wasn't even wet like I was.

But then he looked at me.

Our eyes met, and I lost the ability to breathe.

Fighting beside him, standing at his back, and killing Corvids who got too damn close to my King was something I knew how to do. It was something I could focus on and not think about anything else. It was part of my bones and part of every single aspect of me.

But this?

Staring at a man I loved while he looked back at me wishing he could order my execution?

No. This I didn't know how to do.

I should go to Jacquetta and Gus. I should let them know I was okay.

Going to them was out of the question, though.

More than anyone else, they would see that I was alive, but I was far from okay.

And…I couldn't tell them.

How could I tell them that they wouldn't be Ladies when they got married? How could I tell them that *who* I was, who I turned myself into in the seven years since the last war, ruined the weddings we were all planning?

No King officiating the ceremony for them. No titles as part of the ceremony. Nothing that we had planned beside the dresses for them to wear was going to happen now.

And mine would never be.

The sigil ring on my necklace grew warm in my hand and tears collected at the backs of my eyes.

Rings.

Jacquetta's ring that Gus had made for her, the special sigil she created for them both…not even that would stand after my failure.

Sigils went along with titles and lands. And my friends, too good for someone like me, would never be titled.

I tried to watch where I was going and look for a chance to ask another guard how I could be helpful.

But every time I looked up from the floor, noticed anyone, it was Tristan.

Even now, when I knew what he thought of me, when I was in the position I actually deserved, I couldn't stop looking at him.

The pain in my chest worsened. The all-consuming darkness of this new reality deepened. And I grew colder.

CHAPTER 50

BURN

Tristan

She still walked around the castle as if she had yet to
wake up.

It was the last thing we had in common.

When I landed, her body sprawled on top of mine, shielding
me from the worst of the damage after that last attack. For a
moment I wanted to burn the world down because I thought
she was dead.

But then I remembered.

And all I had left was the rage and the pain from my invisible
wounds that had nothing to do with the war.

Her eyes were haunted, far away. Every time I caught sight
of them, I had to look anywhere but at her.

Every time I saw her at all, I needed to look anywhere else.

But it didn't matter what I needed. It never had.

Cinder was proof of that. She had been before, and she was
now more than ever.

I couldn't look at her, and I couldn't stop looking for her.

Now, though, seeing her didn't send the same kind of feeling flooding through my body.

Before, when I looked at her, warmth surged inside me. It was the kind that reminded me of a fireplace, a blanket, and a hot tea on a cold night. Like she was a balm to every ache in my soul.

That was then.

In my mind there would always be a demarcation line. A moment when the world looked one way, and a moment when it became something utterly different.

Once, I saw my chosen Queen, and my country, and a life laid out like a feast of all my favorite foods. Even if there were storm clouds on the horizon, it was impossible not to be buoyed with hope.

Now, I saw the storm blotting out everything else, my vision consumed by the vicious, unforgiving weather.

Just like now, when I looked at her wandering through the room, waiting for word from Bridgeton. The blood in my body was either ice or fire, and nothing in between. And when it was fire now, it was like white hot metal being pounded by the blacksmith's hammer.

Violent and fragile.

She did this. She made me this…

But that was a lie.

I allowed myself to become this. I fell in love with a woman who was plotting to kill me the entire time.

After so much time thinking all the women who wanted to be with me were only after my crown, the one who I thought wanted it least was the one who actually wanted me least.

Curling my hands into fists so tight my short fingernails cut into my palms and my knuckles popped, I tried to pay attention to the report one of the guards was giving me and General Pace.

No matter how much I needed time.

Away from her.

Away from myself.

Away from everyone and everything.

Time was something I would never get. Even during the good years. Now, with a war going on, there was no way.

"King Tristan," General Pace said, her face in that mask she wore when she didn't want me to know what she was thinking.

"Apologies, General, please continue," I said.

She nodded and started back into the report of the attack on Bridgeton in our absence.

But even as she gave me the first of the information trickling in, I saw it. The thing she was hiding from me.

I sucked in a breath, and she paused.

"General," I said, my voice not one I recognized, and yet what I heard more often since I found out the truth, low and full of bitter danger, "she was sent to kill me. She planned to kill me."

"True," she said, and waited, leaving me to wonder if she was going to fill the void in our conversation, if she was going to keep up with the report, or if she was going to continue and explain herself.

"Why, exactly, should I do anything other than what I am doing?" I asked, finally unable to just sit in the silence of her stare.

"Did I say you should do anything different?" she asked, unreadable again.

No. But I fucking saw it. I saw it in her face. The same judgment and disappointment of me she wore when I first told her about Cinder's betrayal.

Because that's what this was.

It didn't matter how many battles Cinder fought, how much she made herself known to the people as a hero. She betrayed me, and would have betrayed the kingdom. All she was waiting for was the crown I was going to stupidly place on her head before she was going to make mine roll off my shoulders.

There was only one reason she was still playing the same role.

Fighter Cinder still thought I was stupid enough to overlook who she really was, and marry her.

Swallowing, my gaze went to her again.

In some other world, where I wasn't a King, and I could do whatever I wanted, even if she was still going to kill me, I might have done it.

Even though I knew she wanted me dead, and didn't love me, just thinking she did was worth dying for.

But it didn't matter what I needed.

What I needed was her.

I had to settle for watching her as she stumbled over nothing and stared vacantly at the people rushing around her.

Her body even looked different, her body that always looked like a predator about to strike. The strength of her well-defined muscles was hidden now by the curl of her shoulders and the half-uncoordinated way she moved.

A guard ran in the front doors, breathless and road weary, their uniform in tatters on one side, that arm in a sling, and blood spattered on their face, dried into crusted brown.

They scanned the room. When we made eye contact, they ran right for me.

Cinder still wandered through the people. She didn't even register the guard running directly in front of her.

"King Tristan," the guard said, putting their hand over their heart and bowing in salute.

I nodded, tearing my gaze away from Cinder again.

"The report of the group headed for Bridgeton," the guard said, handing over a letter and turning right back around.

"Wait," I said, "you should get something to eat, and rest before you head back."

"No, King Tristan," the guard said, "I am sorry, I need to return for the search."

"Search?" I looked to General Pace, and she shook her head.

"Yes. My regimen is part of the search for the Shield House children, and I must get back to it."

"The Shield House children?" My voice was a croak, and my legs didn't seem to be attached to my body properly anymore.

"During the battle, a group of them somehow got separated from their security detail, and we are currently looking for them."

General Pace tapped my arm with the letter, and I grabbed it. Looking up to ask the guard another question about the kids, I found them already heading out the door.

"We need to get back to Shield House right now," I said, crumpling the letter in my fist.

"You need to read that first," General Pace said, her voice thick and her mouth trembling, nodding to the wad of paper she pulled from my hand and unfolded, holding it out to me.

"Nothing could be more important to me right—" But I couldn't finish the sentence. The words choked off by my closed-up throat.

My eyes found Cinder as she wandered through the chaos of the battle's aftermath.

It didn't matter that she betrayed me, my heart beat louder in my chest, pounding against my ribs on her behalf.

"Someone needs to inform Fighter Cinder and her Ladies." Jacquetta and Augustina…They were going to be married.

Cinder's history, who she was before I ever even thought to marry, and who she still was, destroyed our wedding.

The present, the war that surrounded us all in the people darting in and out of the castle in the aftermath of the battle was about to destroy Jacquetta and Augustina's wedding.

"If Lady Jacquetta wishes, Madam Valentin's funeral may be held at the palace."

CHAPTER 51

BROKEN

Cinder

"Lady Cinder," Prince Nevan said, appearing out of nowhere to stand in front of me, chewing on his lower lip, and working his hands together in front of himself.

"Prince." My voice was still a harsh scraping sound that marked me for what I was: barely human.

"Have you heard anything from Bridgeton?" He looked toward the door to the castle, those long slender fingers turning his many rings around and around.

"No." I wasn't able to say much more. I wasn't able to process much more.

Bridgeton. I needed to know, and yet the muscles in my body braced for the impact of when that news would come, my shoulders curling in further.

"Well, as soon as you hear something, please find me and tell me." He nodded and kept on his way, wherever that was.

I grabbed a passing guard, my grip on their arm little more than a touch, but they stopped as they went by me.

"Please tell Lady Jacquetta and Lady Augustina that I survived the battle." My voice cracked more than once, reduced to a hoarse whisper on some of the words, and I stuttered using the title Lady. But the guard nodded.

How I would ever explain the rest, tell them why they would not be returning to the palace, and would have to change all their plans for their lives, I didn't know and couldn't think about.

But, I could at least give them that. Give them the knowledge I lived. Because my friends, more parts of a world I never deserved, would worry if I didn't have someone tell them.

I went back to my wandering, waiting for what I didn't know.

What was left for me to do?

The only mission left to my life was to protect the same people I had on my list before. To do that, I needed to be here until I was sent away. And then…Maybe I would just stay at the edge of wherever they were.

On the day they went back to Bridgeton, I would follow and spend my time hovering between the barracks by the palace and Madam's house.

Now I had a plan. Such as it was.

My whole life was reduced to a version of what it had been for years anyway. I was going to be a strange mixture of Fighter and assassin, but only for the people I loved.

I took a deep, shuddering breath, but my chest ached. I had to stop with my eyes squeezed shut to keep from falling over.

Opening my eyes, Tristan stood before me, and I stepped back, almost tumbling onto my ass.

But General Pace was there to catch me, one shaking hand under my elbow.

Turning my gaze to where she stood at my side, I shook my head, not believing what I saw.

Her face crumpled, her lip quivered, and the corners of her mouth turned down. She sucked in a breath that hitched and caught in her throat as she tried to open her mouth. But nothing came out.

She squeezed her eyes shut and tears leaked down her cheeks as she hung her head.

"What happened?" I asked, knowing it was a stupid question, because what wasn't happening? But no matter what went on around us, General Pace never broke. Not like this.

It sent the shivers running through me into overdrive. Even as I turned back to Tristan, knowing the pain just looking at him caused, I prepared myself for whatever further blow he was about to deliver.

"Lady Cinder, I'm sorry to have to tell you this. But…" He swallowed, hard, looking at General Pace and not at me, even as he informed me of whatever she already knew. "At the battle in Bridgeton, Madam Valentin…"

He said the word. The last one I wanted to hear in relation to someone I loved, but it didn't make it through the cracking of one of the last pieces of my heart. The sound of it on his lips didn't make it past the rushing of the blood in my ears.

"No. No, no, no, no." My legs gave out, and I fell to the stone floor beneath me, pulling General Pace down with me. She wrapped me in her arms, but I wasn't there anymore, even as I clung to her.

I was in a scorched and empty field in Lehar—one that used to be so much more—ashes falling around me, making my lungs clog, and my throat cough as my world shattered.

Covered in ashes for the first time, I kneeled in the growing drift, staring into the field I kept searching. Looking for something. Anything. Any tiny fragment of something I thought was them, so I had something to bury.

Seven years ago, I lost my parents to the war, and nothing would ever be the same.

Now, I lost the closest thing I had to another parent, my friend's dear mother, and one of the people I swore I would protect to this war.

"Jacquetta?" I asked, not knowing where she was, if she knew, or how I would tell her.

"I will tell her," Tristan said from somewhere above me, his voice raw, "and Madam Valentin will have a palace funeral if Lady Jacquetta wishes."

"No," General Pace said, leaning away from me, and patting me on the shoulder as she levered herself up to standing, even though she wavered, and Tristan had to catch her. "I will tell her. She should hear it from me."

"Jacquetta." Maybe I said her whole name, I wasn't sure. What came out was more incoherent pain than a name.

"Stay here, Cinder." General Pace patted my shoulder again, nodding her head. "She knows. They both know."

Did Madam know?

Gus and Jacquetta might know I loved them without me being able to move and go to them, but did Madam know before her life was stolen?

The General walked away, one hand on her stomach as she took breaths that shook her shoulders, and all I could do was sit in a heap and cry. Useless to my friends when they needed me. Useless to Madam when she needed me, too.

"No. My fault. No." I buried my face in my hands, my entire body shaking and struggling for air. This was my fault. I went to save Tristan even though the entire guard and every ship nearby was here and going to help him.

I chose.

Madam Valentin died.

"Cin—" Tristan started to say my name and coughed halfway through.

I flinched.

He couldn't even stand to say my name. And why would I think he would act any differently? He was already more kind to me about Madam's death than I deserved.

Looking up at him, my face and hands soaked in my tears, it was his turn to flinch.

Of course he did. He could barely stand to be near me.

For the first time since he found out, he actually looked at me, saw me.

Staring into his eyes, I wanted to look away, sure he saw every way I betrayed him, every flaw, all the things he used to love and now hated.

But I couldn't force myself to continue to avoid his eyes and look anywhere but at him. I didn't have the strength not to stare into his mercurial eyes, and admit I didn't have the right anymore to see those changes.

With another cough, a flare of green in his ever-changing eyes, he nodded once and walked away, trailing my dreams and the shattered pieces of my heart.

CHAPTER 52
NEEDED

Tristan

I shook out my hands as I walked away from her, trying to shake off the heat that coursed through my veins, and made me want to hurt every Corvid for making her cry, and taking Madam Velentin from her.

Gods, but I wanted to hate her.

This fucking bullshit that remained in me made me ache not just for losing Madam Valentin, and not just for Jacquetta and Augustina, but for her…I wanted to have someone cut it out of me.

But I didn't get what I wanted.

"King Tristan," Prince Nevan called, looking back and forth between where I stood and where I knew Cinder still cried on the floor.

"Yes, Prince Nevan." My voice didn't sound like my own. It sounded rougher, more clipped.

And he blinked at me like he heard it, too.

"Do you have word from Bridgeton?" he asked, lifting one brow, eyes wide.

That's right. The Marquessa.

Somehow, I forgot he would want to get word of his cousin.

"Forgive me, yes, she is well." I shook my head, and refocused on him, shoving the fact that I could feel Cinder behind me no matter far I got from her, as I tried to be the King he expected. "Her carriage arrived at the Obsidian Palace, and she was safe inside before the attack began, as far as I understand."

He let out a long breath, bracing his hands on his hips, nodding his head.

There was more emotion there than I was expecting. I didn't think he liked Marquessa Ziya very much.

Maybe I was wrong.

It was becoming a terrible habit of mine.

But even as he gave me a small smile with a hand on his heart and walked away, there was only one person I wanted to see.

And I needed to do it before the General returned from Augustina and Jacquetta.

General Pace would have my ass for it eventually, but that didn't matter. I needed to do it.

Not for me. I didn't get what I wanted or what I needed.

I needed to do it for all of them.

The General would see that.

Eventually.

But he wasn't anywhere I could find.

Wandering through room after room of people, nodding at them as I passed, listening to well wishes and relieved exclamations from some, and even holding a hand and giving a kind word to the wounded, I still couldn't find him.

Making my way back into the main room, grinding my teeth because I was running out of time, I finally found him.

Standing next to Duchess Inara, golden and dark in her blue

gown while she held a white-faced Cinder in a tight embrace, Rath chewed on the side of his lip, holding out one of Cinder's spikes.

Already our friends, our worlds, were tangled together.

Rath always surprised me, but where he got her special weapon, I had no idea.

No, wait.

I stopped in the middle of the room on my way to them, because I did know where he would have found her spike.

Did he go down in the dungeon to retrieve it on his own?

How did he know to do that?

A second later, she pulled away from the hug with Inara, swiping at her eyes, and nodding her head to something one of them said.

Inara reached out a hand and brushed Cinder's tears off her face.

Shaking my head, I looked down at my feet while I took in a jagged breath.

"Pull yourself together. You're the fucking King," I mumbled to myself, rubbing the back on my neck.

The only way out of this was the way I was doing it.

No matter how much she betrayed me, how much of a traitorous liar she was, I couldn't kill her. The guard would never understand. And I couldn't send her away. The guard fought better when they had her as their hero.

But this wasn't going to work. Having her here, haunting me, wasn't going to work.

Somehow, someway, I needed to get past the memory of her.

Or she was still going to kill me.

Looking at them again, Rath handed Cinder her spike, gesturing over his shoulder.

Her smile shook, but she gave him one as she slipped the weapon back into the sheath on her thigh.

Rath needed to walk away.

I needed to talk to him.

But a moment later, he wrapped her in his arms, lifting her off the floor, and she squeezed him back.

My feet moved without me telling them to. I marched across the room toward them.

One of the guards I spoke to earlier popped up in front of me, a smile on his face as he held out a bow and two quivers.

"King Tristan," Guard Ji said, "here are the weapons you asked for. The rest of the supplies are ready to go on the sable horse out in the barn."

"Thank you," I said, taking a deep breath as I slung the quiver on and took the bow.

"And because I thought you would still need them." Guard Ji held out a rolled-up blanket with the handle of the short sword peeking out of one side.

"What's in here?" I asked, taking the whole thing from him.

"Short sword, throwing knives, and all the straps you need to secure it all to you. Also, that cloak should help. It has a large hood."

"Right." I took another look at the bundle in my hands. The cloak was made of a thick, woven fabric that didn't itch, but felt like it would be plenty warm. The hood was the important part, though.

"This is perfect. Thank you."

"Of course, my King." Guard Ji did the salute of the guard, and I put my hand on my heart in return, working around the pile of things in my arms before he smiled and walked away.

It wasn't the young Guard's fault that he said the words I never wanted to hear again.

Looking up toward the group, Cinder still stood with Rath and Inara, tears still fell from her eyes, and she still curled in on herself.

But there was a smile trying to form on her face. One she wasn't capable of when she was a crumpled mess on the floor.

Good. She needed her friends.

And while she struggled to even stand, maybe it would mean she wouldn't follow me.

It didn't matter.

My time was running out.

Whether they wanted me to interrupt, or not, and whether I was ready to be near her, or not, I needed to speak with Rath and then go before the General came back.

Prince Nevan joined their group, daring to touch one of his slender hands to Cinder's shoulder, his mouth in that narrow face turned down at the corners.

This wasn't the first time it seemed he genuinely did care about how she felt.

I stopped walking again, nodding to the guards that passed me, not inviting any conversation, but not ignoring them either.

What I should have done was stand to the side, not right in the middle of the traffic.

Fucking crown. Even when it wasn't on my head, everyone saw it, felt it, when I was somewhere like this.

I couldn't just be a man standing here with too much shit in his hands, and one too many weapons on after a battle in which he wasn't injured.

No. I was supposed to be doing something. Something important.

All I could manage though was staring at Cinder and the people around her, wondering if any of them had any idea what she actually was, or if she had them all as fooled as I was.

Maybe if she did, I wouldn't feel as stupid.

But I couldn't ask them that.

I didn't even want to tell everyone that there was no future queen.

All the other potentials were going to be sent home. Clearly, I should have just listened to the Chamberlain and married the Marquessa.

Thinking of her now, though, as I watched the woman I wanted to marry, a woman that was a figment of my imagination, I knew I couldn't just turn around and marry the Marquessa either.

Even after love tore through my heart, I couldn't imagine marrying without it now.

Part of me wondered if Prince Nevan's parents loved each other, or if, like my parents, they were just a good match politically at the time.

One more thing I would never bring up.

I sighed and managed to start walking toward them again.

They all loved her because she managed to make people think they could talk to her, that she was somehow bringing them into her confidence when she was lying to us all.

Meanwhile, they all knew there were a thousand things I could never say, a thousand confidences I had to keep with myself.

She found an easy target in me.

Cinder spotted me first as I neared them, a shine in her eyes, even as the tremor in her lip grew worse, and the tears pouring down her face increased.

With a swallow, she looked over Inara's shoulder, taller than the Duchess, and stared at me.

It made my heart ache all over again, and my legs feel like I was swimming instead of walking.

"Pardon my intrusion," I said to the group when I reached them.

"King," Rath said, his voice subdued and tinged with a heavy sadness I had not heard from him since two years prior when his father was swept overboard in a storm.

"Rath, may I speak with you?" I couldn't stop it, my eyes strayed to Cinder.

But she stared at the bundle in my hands, her gaze scanning

along my body, and snagging on the bow and quivers over my shoulder.

"Sure, King." Rath turned to her and gave her what could barely be called a smile before patting her shoulder and following me out into the night.

I had to do this, to find the Shield House kids, no matter how impossible it would be to explain it to Rath, and ask him to work for me while I was gone. Because he would never accept it if I told him the truth.

They were all I had left.

CHAPTER 53

MIDNIGHT STRIKES

Cinder

Tristan looked like he was going to be sick.

Most of the way over to us, as he was repeatedly stopped on his way across the room, he looked like he was growing more and more ill.

Now that he stood directly in front of me as he called Rath away, I realized why.

It wasn't because of me.

After everything that happened, I should have known that he didn't care about anything I did. He didn't care what was happening over here, or how broken I was now.

He was leaving.

The King was leaving and didn't want to let anyone know because he was planning on doing something on his own. Something stupid and dangerous, judging by the weapons he carried.

Unless…

My stomach roiled inside me, flipping from one side to the other.

"I need to get some fresh air," I said, interjecting myself into the conversation Inara and Prince Nevan were having around me, trying their best to be helpful.

"Cinder, I don't think that's safe," Inara said, looking toward the doors Tristan and Rath just exited through.

"We both know I'll be fine." I hugged her and stepped away. "Besides, I can just lean against the wall, and no crow would ever know I'm there."

She gave me a kind, soft smile. Nevan was beside her doing the same, and I left them behind.

Making my way to the other side of the little entry bridge, Tristan and Rath weren't around, and the shaking started up again in my hands and arms.

Did I miss them? Was he already gone?

A noise reached me, past the sound of the surf below the castle, the hum of the sea beyond, and creak of the bridge in the breeze, something came from down the lane.

I crept along the edge of the lane, away from the direction of the dock, and found a stable not far from the castle. One of the doors yawned wide open, the low glow of a stone light illuminating the inside and spilling out onto the gravel.

They had to be in there.

But to risk a light at night with the door open, when a crow could drop out of the sky at any moment, seemed too stupid for Tristan.

On silent feet, I darted to the open door, and leaned against the jam on the outside, listening to make out the words muffled by distance from the inside.

"You can't be serious," Rath said. Well, he yelled.

"I'm not asking your permission. This is what I need to do." Tristan's voice was hard and low, even with the distance and all the noise around me, I would hear him anywhere, be able to understand him no matter the situation.

But I still crouched down, and leaned further inside, trying to get a better idea of what was happening in there.

"No, what you need to do is stay safe, and have someone else go after them."

A horse whinnied and Tristan spoke to it as if it were a scared friend for a moment. The sound of Rath's heavy footfalls as he paced back and forth formed the backdrop to his kind words.

Rath was so angry. I didn't know he was capable of being this irate.

What was Tristan planning that set Rath off so badly?

Taking a chance, staying crouched low, I made my way inside the stable, moving along the stalls until I found the one they were in, and ducked into the one right next to it.

"I can't just stay safe and plan all day," Tristan said, his voice thick with some emotion I couldn't understand, but made me want to kill someone on his behalf. Something was really off with whatever he was planning on doing.

My stall mate, the horse in the corner of the stall I crouched in, came to my side and huffed hot breath along my cheek.

Running my hand along the soft hair of the horse's nose, I hoped it wouldn't do anything to give me away.

"King, listen, I know you think that this will never be better, but it will be. I promise. And someone else can go after the Shield House kids."

Shield House kids?

I paused in the petting of the horse, turning toward Tristan and Rath, trying to see him through the gaps between the boards of the stall.

All I could see were tiny slivers of what was happening on the other side.

"No one else can go get them." Tristan leaned his head

against the saddle on the horse in front of him. It already wore all the necessary tack for him to ride it out of the stable, and there seemed to be supplies already tied to it.

"Yes, they can. Why does it have to be you?" Rath yelled, throwing his arms in the air.

"Because they've already been through too much. They trust me. If anything happens to them between now and when I find them, they'll need me to be there. To help them through it." Tristan's voice was thick, and he ran a hand under his face.

I almost choked, my lungs seizing as if I were back in the Lehar ashes after spending too long away.

Turning back around, I scanned the horse next to me, but it wasn't wearing any tack at all.

With a look over my shoulder at the stall Tristan and Rath argued in, I made my way as quickly and as silently as possible to the end of the barn, looking for tack along the way, and only finding it in neat rows at the very end.

Gathering what I needed, I went back along the exact same track, placing my feet in the same places, and continuing to try and hide my approach.

There was no way Tristan would let me come with him if he knew that I was planning on it. My King didn't want me anywhere near him.

But the Shield House kids meant as much to me as they did to him, and I couldn't let him do this alone. No matter what he thought of me, he still had me and my blade at his back.

Part of me realized I was running from facing Gus and Jacquetta. But they didn't need to be faced with me in their grief.

It was my fault Madam was gone. They would never be able to forgive me for that.

The best thing I could do for them was stay out of their way.

Neither they, nor Madam, would ever have been at risk if it weren't for their ties to me.

Maybe I owed it to them to explain everything, but I wasn't sure if I would survive it. And I was fine if I was just another unknown and unmourned body on a battlefield. But falling apart in front of Gus and Jacquetta?

I couldn't make everything worse for them.

And I had to save my King from himself before anything else.

With the weapons on my back, a stolen horse, and not a damn thing else, I would be Tristan's shadow until he was safe.

The clock struck on my time pretending I was something other than a killer. Now, I needed to return to those roots to pay for planting them.

My payment for my betrayal was just beginning.

CHAPTER 54
LAST BELL

Tristan

"Please, Rath, just do this for me. You're the only one who can." Staring at my friend, I realized that wasn't entirely true.

He probably should have been going to do what I was, but he could pull off what I asked of him. Between him, General Pace, and the Chamberlain, they could do all the things the country needed without issue, and without the people knowing.

But what I needed more than anything right at that moment was strictly a job for Rathmoreland.

"Damn it, King." He put both hands on top of his head, and tilted it back toward the ceiling.

"I know. You are going to hate it, but you're the only one I trust not to let anything get fucked up so much that Prince Nevan finds out." Just thinking it sent a wave of nerves through me that made my hands want to shake. I stretched them out, and focused on what I was doing.

Maybe it wasn't the right thing, but it was the only thing I could think of that wouldn't leave me feeling like I was about to explode while I waited for news, pretending everything was normal.

"Some ally if you can't have him find out." Rath dropped his eyes to mine, his mouth a line.

"Even if I did trust him completely, I can't trust anyone else in that country. Not after what we know. I can be someone's ally, and know better than to trust them." I moved past Rath, leading the horse, and put my hand on my friend's shoulder.

"Then why can't you have your flame? It would be the same thing." He shook his head, and pulled me in for a rough hug. "Nevermind. I'll do what you need. I always do. I just wish I never gave you that lead."

"I know." They all did their part whenever I asked, but it wasn't for me. It was for the country. Still, I hugged him tighter.

Rath let me go, and let out a harsh sigh.

"Just get your stupid ass back as fast as possible."

"Done." I tried to laugh, but it was too forced. Instead, it was just a loud breath.

But I led the horse out of the stall and down the center lane of the barn to the larger door than the one I entered.

It didn't take long to open it, and even less time to find myself on the other side of it, hauling myself into the saddle.

With one last look toward the light shining through the door, giving me only a view of Rath's silhouette, I lifted a hand and kicked the horse into movement.

The horse moved beneath me, getting us up to speed.

Breakwater was a long and skinny duchy North to South. But I was going West. I would leave Duchess Inara's lands in no time.

Part of me wished I needed to go South, because the most direct route to where I was going was through Bridgeton. Going through the city would most likely get me noticed.

Once the horse was up to speed, I lifted the hood of my cloak, and hoped I could get through the city before the light of day. Night was the best time for me to travel.

Figuring out how to balance the delay involved with only traveling at night, and my need to get there faster, I feared would be an ongoing challenge.

I swallowed, tightened my grip on the reins, leaned forward, and drove the horse to speed up a touch.

"Hang on, kids," I whispered to the wind, hoping it would reach them, and I could save them from the same fate Angeline suffered.

Time wasn't on my side, or theirs.

All I could do was fight the ticking away of the clock. For the kids of Shield House, I wouldn't stop.

CHAPTER 55

LAST TOLL

Cinder

I waited to the count of twelve after Tristan rode away. Just when Rath started to close the large door, shaking his head, I swung open the stall door, leading out my horse.

His shadowed face probably showed more shock at seeing me than I could make out in the low light.

But I was able to spot when his mouth fell open.

"Flame, what are you doing?" His voice didn't even sound like him. There was a squeak to it that didn't belong.

"We both know I'm going after him, Rath. Someone has to protect him." I swung into the saddle, staring down at him as I brought the horse alongside him.

"I knew it. You really do love him." He grinned at me. The only light in the barn was from the stone in the stall he and Tristan were in, its filtered rays a weak illumination in the dark. Even with that, his smile was so large, so many white teeth showing, it was obvious.

"You know," I said, my throat tight, not believing that smile since he knew what I was.

"He tells me everything." Now his voice had a lullaby to it, a song of understanding and kindness I didn't deserve. "And I knew that the flame he described, the fighter who protected him so many times, whatever she started out as, she was his now."

Looking out the door, into the night, I knew that no matter what I was now, whatever I became, he was right. I was Tristan's.

Falling in love with him, my time with him at the palace and here, the chance to meet my friends and know Madam, had all remade me.

Now, whatever was left, I was his.

"Cover for me, please." I nodded to Rath as I led the horse past him to outside, calling back to him. "I'm going after him. No one is going to take the Dragon King from Onyx."

"From Onyx, or from you?" he yelled as I drove the horse on.

I didn't answer. I couldn't.

Because even if I didn't deserve to have him in my life, even if I was still every bit the killer Ash wanted me to be, I was his.

And he was mine.

AFTERWORD

Thank you for reading!
If you enjoyed this book, please leave a review at your favorite bookseller.
Don't forget to go to jdarleneeverly.com and sign up for the newsletter to be the first to know about all the updates on this series. The fourth book, After Midnight Strikes will be out in Summer of 2022.
As a special exclusive for those who sign up for the newsletter, the author is giving away and exclusive prequel in this series, as well as an exclusive free book in another story world, and more.

ACKNOWLEDGMENTS

A whole hearted thank you to Bean, the Rottens, and all of my friends and family. Again, huge thanks to Jupiter Alley and Krystal for their help in making this happen, Heather Cardona for all she does, Miblart for the gorgeous cover, Lucy at Jupiter Alley for the absolutely brilliant sigil covers for the interior of the hardcovers, as well as the team at Wishing Well.

In a special note, for my friends at Miblart, all my hopes for your safety, and may all your tomorrows be filled with sunflowers. Slava Ukraini!

One more thing, though, to all of the readers who have loved this series so far, especially those wonderful people who have gone out of their way and left me reviews, thank you.

I know it may seem as if the readers and the authors only connect in one direction, from the words in these books to you. But that isn't true. You, the readers, buying our books, reading our books, loving our books, and even those hating them, mean the world to us. Every single person who reads our words feels like a hug from a friend.

We write these stories, sending out these messages into the void, and every now and then one of the readers sends some light back to us.

You, dear reader, are that light.

Thank you.

ABOUT THE AUTHOR

J. Darlene Everly is an author of sci-fi and fantasy stories. Her serial, Crossroad Inn, is available on Vella, the entire first season will soon be out in book form. Her debut trilogy, The Grimm Star Saga: First Light is available everywhere, and two new series will begin soon. Keep an eye out for Major Arcana, and The Grimm Star Saga, and keep reading for all of Cinder's story.